GHOSTS
IN THE
RUINS

P.D. HOGAN

GHOSTS IN THE RUINS

STORIES AND SCRIPTS

Castlebound Press

Copyright © 2023 by P.D. Hogan

"A Single Death" © 2014
"Unraveled" © 2023
"To The Dead Sea" © 2015
"She Sells Sea Shells" © 2022
"Knock, Knock, Knock" © 2022
"Zombay, NL" © 2016
"Rainfall" © 1998, 2009, 2021

"Gadget" © 2022

First Castlebound Press paperback edition October 2023

Manufactured in the United States of America

Library and Archives Canada Data is available

ISBN 978-0-9869135-3-2 (hardcover)
ISBN 978-0-9869135-2-5 (paperback)
ISBN 978-0-9869135-4-9 (ebook)

For Casey

the greatest bad dog there ever was

CONTENTS

INTRODUCTION

The Purpose of All Written Things

It's no secret that writing is a very lonely exercise. For some, it is a job; for others, it is a hobby. And then there are those of us for which it is a compulsion bordering on obsession. All of these are valid. None of them are complete.

According to my grade 1 report card, I wrote my first story at a very young age. I don't recall what it was about, and I doubt it even had a title, but I know it existed because someone read it and recorded that fact. As an author, that is a wonderful, gratifying thing. And it continues to be so to this day.

I have always written for two reasons. The first is because stories come to me at all times of the day and in many forms, and I literally cannot rest until I have written something of them down, be it a title, opening line, or synopsis. Sometimes, on the rarest of occasions, it is all three. Most times, however, it is just a fragment of what will eventually be produced in the end. Those fragments often remain somewhere in the story, but not always. Like a tree that grows from a bud, what the world sees sometimes bears no resemblance to what it sprang from. That's life, and that's writing.

The second reason is less precious but equally important. It is the reason you hold this book in your hands. It is the true purpose of all written things: *to be read.* Just the knowledge that someone is sharing in your creation, whether they are enjoying it or not, is the ultimate satisfaction for a writer. I find reading my work to be a thankless exercise, fraught with self-doubt and constant revision. But releasing it out into the world to be experienced by others based on their imagination, interpretation, and personal experiences is priceless. The writer wishes they could be there for each of those first reads, but instead settles for the inspiration drawn from the simple knowledge that they created something that provided joy, sadness, fear, or laughter to a stranger they may never meet.

These tales will be a first read for each of you, kind readers. All of the stories and scripts in this collection are previously unpublished. That was by choice. They span a period in my life of almost twenty years when I was focused on writing spec screenplays and young adult fantasy novels. But *these* stories were just for me. In many ways, they reflect who and where I was as a writer at the time. I am proud of them all, and some I think are among the best writing I have ever done. Only one - an earlier version of the short script *To The Dead Sea* - has ever been read by people outside my trusted orbit. I sent it out to a handful of competitions a few years back, and it did quite well. That success gave me the confidence to keep going, and as any writer at almost any level will tell you, confidence is more elusive than diamonds and a million times more valuable.

The oldest story here, *Rainfall,* is also the one that has seen the most change. It began life as a segment of a feature screenplay while I was still in film school, then became a chapter in an unfinished novel based on that unproduced screenplay before finally finding life as a stand-alone story. Some may consider that a lot of failure to produce something so small.

I am not one of them. A sculpture is a block of stone until the sculptor chips away the parts that keep it bound inside, freeing it to be shared with the world. What remains is rarely comparable in size to the original stone.

The longest story here, the novella *Gadget*, was conceived almost as far back as *Rainfall*, but took far longer for me to finally put it down on paper. When I eventually did, it burst out of me over a two-week period, and when I was finished, I was exhausted both mentally and emotionally. Normally when that happens, I need a break from the keyboard for a few weeks. But in telling Gadget's story, I instead awoke something inside that I only realized much later had been waiting to be released for a long time but was being held captive behind that one story. The day after I finished *Gadget,* I wrote another story. Three days later, I started another. Both of those stories are included in this collection.

I won't say anything more about the stories in this book for now. I've included a little background at the beginning of each if, like me, you find such things to be of interest. Feel free to skip over them if you don't. And if you've stuck with me this far into the introduction, I commend you. The 80's pop rock band Roxette graced their greatest hits album with one of the best titles of all time – *Don't Bore Us, Get To The Chorus* - and if that sentiment has not crossed your mind up to this point, I consider myself lucky. No one wants you to get to the stories more than I do. But I do want to leave you with a few parting thoughts. Consider them to be the stars guiding you as you navigate the dark seas ahead.

I mentioned at the start that writing is a lonely exercise. And it is. Sometimes painfully, relentlessly so. But, as the balance of the universe would have it, reading is writing's solitary companion. The ying to its yang. There are times in life when others read to us, particularly when we are very young or very old, but in between, we tend to do it alone. And in the end, no matter how talented the writer, no matter how verbose their vocabulary or dynamic their phrasing, the image that forms in your imagination is uniquely yours. You and I, for all intents and purposes, are in this together. That relationship is some of the last true magic left in the world. I am eternally grateful you have taken the time to keep it alive.

Because of this symbiotic relationship, I am always eager to hear what readers think, whether it is positive or negative. Tastes vary wildly, and there is no real right or wrong. Few things are ever universally terrible, and even less are unanimously adored. For my part, I just want to entertain, to tell a good story, and hope that you have gotten from it what you needed to feel satisfied in that moment. If I have done so by the time you turn the final page, let me know. And if I haven't, let me know that as well. Whatever the case, reach out on social media or write a review.

Finally, while writing is a lonely exercise, it rarely sees the light of day without support from others. So if you know someone who writes, or feels that creative spark in any endeavor, fuel their passion in any way and as often as you can. You'll find it doesn't take much to make a positive impact, and the work they create is, in a way, paying it forward.

I hope you enjoy reading the stories that follow as much as I enjoyed writing them. They are each very special to me in their own way, and now they are finally let loose upon the world to fulfill their true purpose.

Until we meet again, there are always more stories to tell...

P.D. Hogan
May 1, 2023

Notes on A Single Death

The beauty of comic books isn't the art work. It is the economy of storytelling.

That isn't meant to take away from the efforts of the remarkably talented artists who visually bring to life on the page what we mere mortals can only envision in our heads. On the contrary, comic book artists (often in tandem with comic book writers) are able to achieve wonders in a handful of images and words. Sometimes in just a single panel. I envy their skill.

Like many in my generation, I grew up reading a lot of comic books. Superhero issues came and went for me, but I rarely stuck through a full story arc. If you haven't already gathered from the book in your hands, I fancied the supernatural more than superheroes. *House of Mystery, House of Secrets,* and my favorite – *Tomb of Dracula* – filled my collection. If Silver Surfer or Swamp Thing passed through the pages, I was perfectly happy to see them, but I wasn't chasing after them once they left.

So it was funny to me that, when an idea for a comic book wormed its way into my brain, it was much more aligned with traditional superhero storytelling than what I expected. But as I explored the idea further, I realized it wasn't the superhero I was interested in at all...

I wrote this story in one sitting. That never happens. But it kept the story economic, and that seems profoundly appropriate in retrospect. I think it'd make a terrific one-shot issue some day.

See if you agree.

A SINGLE DEATH

THE CAGE DOOR WAS OPEN, BUT THE NIGHTINGALE REFUSED TO FLY.

Kate stood leaning against the cell bars, looking in at the elderly woman framed by steel and the promise of freedom beyond. For the moment, everything else vanished. They were alone. Somewhere in the distance, a horn was raging.

"How many are dead?" the old woman asked.

"*What?*"

The old woman repeated her question, and Kate watched her lips, fascinated. Lavender and dry, as though the memory of beauty had faded with the color of youth. Something about the woman's face was oddly familiar.

Kate shook her head and said, "No idea. Maybe all of them."

The old woman arched an eyebrow. She sat cross-legged on her cot, facing the bars. Her beige one-piece standard issue jumper was two sizes too large, faded at the heels. That struck Kate as odd. The rest of the cell was immaculate and, now more than ever, stood in stark contrast to the rest of the prison crumbling down around it.

Kate anxiously shifted her weight back to both legs, folded her arms.

Her jumper was orange, bright and crisp – she had only been shackled with it for two days.

Two days into forever. Or so she had thought. Then the north wall of the prison had exploded out into the night, and nobody cared anymore that she'd run over a kid with her Bug. They were all gone. Or dead. Something terrible was happening to the world outside.

"You're not escaping with the others?" Kate asked, anxious to keep moving. She wondered if the old woman even had it in her. Kate pegged her at eighty-five, but there were enough lines in that old face for two lifetimes.

A loud *crack!* erupted on the level below, followed by a swell of darkness moving across the far side of the cell block as the lights dimmed one by one.

The old woman was unfazed. She smiled at Kate with those faded lips. "Escape implies that I have remained here against my will."

Kate might have found the old woman's statement intriguing were there not flaming toilet paper streamers sailing down from above like fading meteors or the incessant blare of the prison horn battering all of her senses at once. Instead, she was focused on the possibility of freedom a hundred paces away at the bottom of a cold metal staircase. She had stopped to help the woman. The window of that opportunity was now shutting rapidly.

"You think I'm crazy," the old woman said. It was more a statement than a question.

Kate sighed. "Look, I don't really care if you're crazy or not. I'm getting out of here. You can come with me, or you can stay."

The elderly woman's eyes probed through the tough veneer Kate had adopted in preparation for a long stay among the sinners. It did not take long to find the real Kate – childless alcoholic stretching twenty-nine as far as the lie would take her; former Miss Teen Arizona who'd had many lovers but never one that was true; only daughter of a renowned prosecutor who'd been unwilling to aid his little girl when she'd needed it most. *That* Kate would always be gliding just below the surface, and by the time you saw the fin crest the water, it was too late to get out of the way.

"What did you do?"

"I killed someone," Kate said tersely. "A little girl."

"Did you mean to?"

"*What?* No, of course not."

The old lady shrugged. "A single death is a tragedy."

This was hardly the time to quote monsters from the past. Behind Kate, the vast canyon of the prison was raining ash and breathing smoke. Bodies lay strewn about - some fallen, some flung like a child's discarded toys. Through the mammoth hollow in the north wall, she could see the desert stretching to the far horizon, where the city lay beneath a blanket of stars. It was on fire.

"Help me up," the old woman said. Her tiny legs uncoiled and stretched to the floor. The lights were still on in the cell block, but it was only a matter of time before they were snuffed-out like the rest. The bare bulb above the cot buzzed and flickered as though an angry wasp was trapped inside. The shadows it cast only made the elderly woman appear more gaunt and sickly.

Kate wrapped an arm around the woman's waist. She came off the cot, light and brittle as a scarecrow. "Careful now," the old woman muttered. Kate loosened her grip and stepped back. The horn ceased its screaming only to be replaced with the wail of sirens in the distance. Strangely, they were fading away.

3

"They've got bigger problems now, dear."

Kate did not know what could be more critical than a prison let loose, but the scattered infernos suddenly sprouting up among the urban landscape suggested the old woman had a point. Kate had been in a solitary containment cell in the south block when she heard the first explosion. The lights had sputtered a short time later, followed by the distinct sound of the bolt sliding back on the cell door. When she pushed it open and peered out, she assumed she was witnessing the tail end of an elaborate prison break. So she waited. Ten minutes later, the only sound she heard was the horn. No one came to check on her. No one locked her door. By then, there was no one left.

Assessing the damage, she felt lucky to be alive. The pieces of the wall that had not exploded into dust were scattered across the sand like giant concrete lollipops, lengths of snapped rebar protruding from the ends.

"What happened here?"

The old woman stepped to the small bookshelf at the foot of the bed. It was home to dog-eared paperbacks on meditation and various religions. She pulled the largest one down, fanned through the pages. Kate noted the title: **Hindu Literature, Or the Ancient Books of India**.

There isn't time for this, Kate thought. She already regretted asking the question. She was beginning to regret having stopped at the cell door. She did not want to leave this deteriorating old bird here to burn, but she would if necessary. Had the old woman not seen that when she looked through Kate with those piercing eyes?

The old woman dropped the book on the cot and placed a neatly folded newspaper clipping in Kate's hand.

"That's yesterday's headline," the old woman said. *"That's* what happened."

Kate unfolded the paper and stared at the two words splashed across the top in bold red ink. Her heart stopped. She read them again, then the byline. A sudden chill gripped her.

SOVEREIGN DEAD!!
World Mourns Loss of Greatest Protector

"That's... not possible." Her mouth was dry, pasty. "He was a... a *god.*"

The old woman scowled and shook her head. "I know nothing of gods or if he was one or not. But dead he is. And gone."

Kate skimmed the page, trying to glean some sort of sense from the impossible, but the ink ran together. It wasn't until she tasted the salt on her top lip that she realized she was crying.

"Everyone remembers the hero," the old woman said with a hint of disdain. She plucked the book back up and considered the cover. "But how quickly they forget the rest."

Kate looked up slowly. Her head felt heavy. "The rest?"

"The hero is just an instrument. Something wielded. Like a sword." The old woman placed her free hand on Kate's arm. Her long fingers were bone-thin, ashen and twisted. She guided Kate to the doorway of the cell. "Take me down there. I want to see." She paused, looking left and right along the cell block corridor. "Maybe it isn't too late."

They descended to the main floor. Five stairs from the bottom, the rest of the lights went out. It was more of a whimper than a bang, and a few seconds later the generator kicked in and brought on the remaining emergency backups. The intervening darkness ushered the night in through the blast hole, making the carnage easier to see beyond the wall. It also revealed a second gaping wound – this one on the floor. The earth around it was trawled and sunken, pulled under as someone – or some *thing* – had clawed its way out. More bodies lay in the radius. Beige and orange slaughtered without distinction or mercy for time served.

The pair made their way across the lower-level concourse. Mangled metal tables and chairs, once bolted into stone, were thrown about. Kate kicked something soft, and her foot slipped in the wet trail it left behind. She watched the object come to rest against a chunk of concrete. It was a hand, the letters H.A.T.E. tattooed across the fingers. Her stomach retched. The ground was littered with human remains. The massacre had happened so fast there had been no screams.

"The world was safe, now it is not," the old woman said, steering them away. "Everything that lives dies. This is not news. It is history."

They were now at the edge of the pit - forty feet in diameter and cavernous. A faint blue light emanated from fifty feet below. There was still some power down there. *Must have been on a different grid*, Kate thought.

"Sovereign was powerful." The old woman stared into the crater. "But still a man. Like the thing that did this, he was not from this world, but he was still a man. Somewhere along the way, we forgot that."

Kate looked from the hole in the floor to the one in the wall. "What did this? What was down there?"

"Thresher," the old woman said. Kate turned sharply. The old woman saw the fear in her eyes. "You know this name, yes?"

"Yes." Everyone knew that name. "But Thresher is dead."

The old woman uttered a quick laugh. She motioned to the trail of corpses lying in the desert like breadcrumbs. "They would beg to differ."

Kate knew what the world knew: Sovereign had defeated the alien behemoth known as Thresher twenty years earlier in what the press dubbed The Last Great Battle of the 21st Century. The fight raged across the continent, ending in the Rocky Mountains when Sovereign crushed the alien below an avalanche of rocks so immense it had reshaped the landscape. The wake of carnage had brought the President to the brink of a nuclear scenario that - once exposed by *The New York Times* a year later - cost the President re-election and undoubtedly would have cost millions of lives. In the end, according to the official UN report, eighty-thousand were dead or missing among the three trillion dollars of devastation. Two decades later, the country was still recovering.

Kate was only a child when it happened, but she remembered the televised images vividly. Crumbling buildings. The dark snow of ash and debris floating in the air. People running and screaming. Faces caked with blood. News stations had continued to replay the footage for weeks afterward, and the world obediently watched. She had been born into a world of prodigious heroes and villains, but little else had changed from the time before their arrival. Now it seemed the villains had won, and the world was not prepared. She looked at the newspaper clipping still clutched in her hand.

Everything that lives dies. That might be true of them all soon.

The sky roared like it was being ripped away, and a moment later, a pair of fighter jets tore across the horizon toward the city.

"A senseless creature. Without remorse. Savage." The old woman spat out the words like bile. "Not like the others."

Kate did not have to ask what she meant by that. Sovereign had faced many foes before Thresher, though none so destructive or deadly. But there was always a reason for their actions. A logic, a plan. Even Vega, the otherworldly woman who loved and betrayed Sovereign not long after his arrival on Earth, had a plan. Nothing more than lessons buried somewhere in history books now. Maybe the old woman was right: the rest *are* quickly forgotten.

The old woman continued: "After Thresher was defeated, it was buried beneath the desert. This desert. Beneath this prison in a prison all its own."

"Why? It was dead."

"Defeated. Not dead."

"How do you know this?" Kate asked. She could hear the concussive impact of explosives beyond the desert and fought the urge to look. People were dying. Nothing could stop it. She shut her eyes, the sense of urgency to leave fading.

Turn your back, and half the world disappears. That little nugget of wisdom was from her mother. Kate hated her for it. Her mother was long gone before Kate came of age, but the lesson remained. And she'd mastered it since the accident.

Except for the dead girl. Lying half on the sidewalk, half in the street, body contorted, frozen in time whenever Kate closed her eyes. There was no turning her back on that. It was tattooed on the darkness as permanent as the letters on that severed hand. And just as contemptible. But over time, it had become a beacon on the road to penance. The one thing she feared losing more than her freedom.

"Do you know what this place is? What it really is?" The old woman asked.

Kate opened her eyes and shook her head. The image faded slowly. "No," she whispered. It was true. This was just a temporary stop for her, a fateful sojourn on her way to permanent incarceration at *FCI Phoenix*. She'd never heard of *Helicon Prison* before passing through its gates and assumed it was a penitentiary like any other.

The old woman clutched Kate's arm more tightly and moved them both through the north wall. "Come, it's easier if I show you."

Kate resisted, her eyes finding the horizon once more. "There's just desert and sand... and death," she said. "We should go the other way."

The old woman's grip was remarkably strong and persistent. They were outside now, sand already working its way into their shoes. "And go where? Running won't help you anymore now than it did before."

Kate stopped. She *had* run. Twice. Once from the accident. And again before the trial. She had almost made it to the other side of the country – to the ocean – before the bounty hunter had caught up to her. Where she was going beyond that, she had no idea. Neither time nor distance mattered. They changed nothing. The image of the little girl with a twisted spine and blood-caked hair was always there.

"How—?"

The old woman let go. She leaned over, lifted a handful of sand from the desert. "Human nature. Everybody runs. But look around. It can only take you so far."

The bodies were already becoming submerged in drifting sand. By morning, they would be buried, forgotten. The old woman opened her fingers, letting the grains fall free. "It's not natural to trap things, to keep them prisoner, to contain their nature. So, given the chance, they escape." The old woman closed her hand around the remaining sand and squeezed. "But sometimes, under the right conditions - *the right circumstances* - that nature can change. And the transformation can be beautiful. Powerful."

The old woman placed her hand in Kate's. When she opened it, the sand was gone. A flawless orb of glass sat in Kate's palm. Startled, Kate dropped it, backed up, and tripped on her own feet. She fell in the sand.

"What the— *Who are you?*"

The old woman reached down and pulled Kate up in a single fluid motion. Kate could feel the old woman's pulse coursing through the warm flesh, matching the rhythm of her own. The sensation enveloped her.

"I'm the reason they built this place," the old woman said. She held her other hand out above the sand, and the glass sphere rose and found it. She held it between Kate and herself. The glass floated, flattened and stretched before her eyes. Kate could see through it now. On the other side, the old woman was youthful, her striking beauty restored. Kate realized why those lavender lips had fascinated her earlier – she recognized this woman. Not from her past. From *history*.

"Oh my God," Kate whispered. "You're Vega."

Vega touched a finger to the glass. It dissolved back into sand and rejoined the desert. The illusion disappeared with it. Only the old woman remained.

"I was," Vega said. "Now I am just…" She pursed her lips together and sighed. There was more than defeat in it. There was a sense of acceptance, of completion. "History."

"You were so powerful. The things you did were so—"

"Terrible," the old woman said.

The word was so exact - so all-encompassing - Kate forgot what she had been meaning to say. *How many faces did this old woman see when she closed her eyes at night?* There were not enough years in a lifetime to make them fade.

Vega took the headline from Kate's hand and let the breeze take it into the desert. She looked beyond Kate's shoulder to the burning city and said, "'*A single death is a tragedy. A million is a statistic*.'" She grimaced. "Do you think this is true?"

10

"No."

"Did you know this girl you killed?"

"No," Kate replied. Her voice was losing its resolve.

"And yet, you can't forget her."

"No..." Kate whispered.

"Sovereign gave his life for this world. It took half his power to protect it, and half to keep those that threatened it imprisoned here. Now that he's gone, that threat is free." Vega gazed skyward. "And more will come."

On the fiery horizon, a building collapsed from its wounds, sending bodies and debris thundering down. It was the beginning of the end. Cities would topple. The nuclear option would become a reality. Millions would die. The theoretical Rubicon was just another fading line in the sand.

Kate turned back. "You were Sovereign's equal. *You* can *stop* this."

Vega shook her head. "No," she said. She let go of Kate's hand. "But maybe..."

"What—?"

Vega placed her hands on Kate's chest and pushed. Kate felt the air leave her body in a violent rush. She fell back, weightless. The sand was rising all around her, the earth suddenly falling away from the sky. The sound of destruction became muffled, faint. She could sense the ground dropping further away. She gasped for breath, panicked, a fish thrown upon the shore. Life was leaving her.

Everything that lives dies.

She shut her eyes. The dead girl was waiting for her in the darkness.

I'm sorry. I won't leave you...

But already the image was fading. There was a burst of red, and a tremendous heat washed over her. When it passed, she opened her eyes and felt a searing pain in her lungs as they tasted oxygen as if for the first time. It spread throughout her body, heavy, immense.

The world was fighting to keep her.

She plummeted, landing in a crouch, the impact splitting the ground beneath the sand. The shock wave hit the crippled north wall. It broke free and crumbled at her feet. When the dust settled, she realized the old woman was gone.

Kate stood up. Alone. Beneath her feet, the sand had turned to glass. She could see herself in the reflection, floating among the stars. And rising. She felt extraordinary, fearless and… free. She could go anywhere. Do anything. Become *anyone*.

Behind her, in the city and beyond, half the world was disappearing. Desert and sand… and death.

She turned to face it.

And the Nightingale flew.

Notes on Unraveled

The 1980s were the golden years for horror. For anyone who grew up in that decade, the nostalgia for the era is powerful. You needn't look any further than the overwhelming success of *Stranger Things* for proof of that.

Horror movies in the '80s were only limited in execution, not imagination. There is a particular charm in the ingenious practical effects of the day, the over-the-top acting of scream queens, and the gonzo concepts of straight-to-video cheap flicks. There has never really been anything like it since.

My love of horror started when I was about five years old. The old Universal Monsters movies were staples on television, and you couldn't pry my eyes away. Then I saw *Jaws* on TV and became both terrified of the ocean and fascinated by film as art. As I got older, I watched and read everything I could. Directors like Spielberg and Carpenter, and authors like King and McCammon were my idols. I wanted to do what they did. In the time before the internet, the only way to gain that insight was from magazines. *Famous Monsters of Filmland*, *Starlog*, and *Fangoria* not only kept fans up to date on what was on the horizon but more importantly, pulled back the curtain on how things were made. Reading them was like devouring forbidden fruit. I may have wanted to be the next John Carpenter, but I *envied* the writers of those glossy pages. They were the Dr. Frankenstein to my stitched-together Monster.

This is my love letter to all of these things. They made me what I am.

UNRAVELED

THE GIANT MAN IN THE THEATER DOORWAY WAS A REAL PIECE OF WORK. His long, gaunt face loomed above my own with a look of displeasure I normally associated with having been interrupted doing something shameful. It was ten minutes to six on a Tuesday evening, so while I could imagine any number of carnal acts he might have been engaged in, I limited my options to the one or two least depraved. Even those were a stretch considering I was standing there with an invitation.

His narrow blue eyes peered at me suspiciously. I sighed. Like I said, I wasn't there by accident. I fished the piece of sepia paper from my coat pocket and held it up for him to see.

"My name is Jesse Thorne. I'm a reporter for *Strange Tides Magazine*. I was invited to cover the screening tonight." I watched those eyes for any sign of recognition of what I was saying, but they stared blankly at the invitation in my hand. "This is the Darklight Theater, right?"

I already knew it was. It was one of three open establishments on the entire stretch of road the town considered Main Street, the other two being a Chinese take-out and a gun shop. '80s America in a snapshot. The Darklight had a façade straight out of the 1920s and, unlike the others, was still well maintained. It wasn't hard to figure out I was in the right spot. Oh, and did I mention the giant red letters just overhead? Guess what *they* spelled out?

"Yes, this is the Darklight." The old man's voice was low and raspy, undoubtedly the result of smoking a chorus line of cigarettes every day for the last fifty years. If I sound unnecessarily judgmental, it's because I am. Four years of journalism school landed me in overwhelming debt, writing fluff pieces for horror geeks to read between jerk-off sessions over racy photos of scream queens. At least until the pages wound up brittle and stuck together. You know what I mean. Don't deny it.

"Excellent," I said with a smile. I'd say it was forced, but I'm sure that much is already clear. There was nothing about the tall old man or this awkward exchange that was going to genuinely make me happy. "And you have a screening tonight, yes? An anniversary showing of *The Mummy*?"

The old man blinked for the first time since he had opened the door. His eyes brightened slightly, though it may have just been the reflection of the pointless invitation I was waving in his face.

"Karloff," he said, the two syllables like tires on gravel. His breath followed, and my stomach dropped. I'm certain my left eye twitched, less certain he noticed. Small miracles.

"Yes, Karloff. *The Mummy*. It's a classic. Fifty years old." I could give a shit. I just wanted to get inside and be done with this encounter.

He confiscated the invitation from me with a giant gloved hand. He took several seconds to read through it - long enough for me to notice his hand was larger than my head, but not enough time to determine why it was clothed in tight black leather. Maybe that was for the best.

"Early," he said. I could see complete sentences were going to be a challenge. "Seven."

I sighed again and looked at my feet, grateful I had changed out of heels into Doc Martens at the last minute. I could do damage in either, but comfort was paramount. And besides, they went much better with my olive dress. I'm not a Philistine.

"I know it starts at seven, but I thought I'd come by early and get a look at the place. You know, for my article. Setting is integral to a good story. Know what I mean?"

He had no idea what I meant.

"Seven."

Jesus Christ. Realizing he hadn't offered his name when I provided mine, I took a chance. "Are you the manager, Mr....?"

Those dark blue eyes studied my face in a way it had never been before. As a reasonably attractive twenty-four-year-old California girl born and raised, I'd had my share of gazes, both lurid and welcome. Hell, I'd even reciprocated some of the latter on occasion - I'm a sucker for Clark Kent types who pick me out of a litter from across the room - what can I tell you? But that was not this. Not even close. The old man was looking *through* me, the way one would peer through a keyhole to the private room beyond. It cut through the late autumn warmth and my Joan Jett-inspired black leather jacket to sprout gooseflesh all along my arms.

"Hector," he said, blinking for just the second time. "I am not the manager. Just... Hector."

Right. I assumed he was the usher. I glanced over my shoulder to the parking lot. Just as empty as it had been when I pulled into it and sat smoking a joint fifteen minutes earlier. Sunlight reflected off the dusty windshield of my blue Gremlin as it dipped behind the theater.

I turned back to Hector. "I know I'm early, but would it be possible to just wait in the lobby? I won't get in the way or 'peak behind the curtain',

I promise. You won't even know I'm there."

The smell of freshly popped popcorn wafted through the doorway. The rich aroma of butter followed. Real butter. My stomach rumbled.

"It would be…" Hector paused, forgetting his words or searching for better ones, I could not tell. I was just glad to have his eyes looking elsewhere for a moment. "…unusual."

Word of the day. I put on my most charming smile. "Unusual is my specialty, Mr. Hector. You think *Strange Tides* would send a common girl all the way out here to write about your theater, your movie?"

"Many were invited," the giant intoned slowly. He nodded to the piece of paper in my hand. I tucked it away in my pocket. He looked past me to the parking lot. "Seven."

He slid back through the glass doorway, closing it before I could protest or stick my heavy boot in the way.

"Damn it."

I headed back to the Gremlin, the sweet scent of butter in my nostrils and the bitter taste of frustration on my tongue.

My watch said it was five after six. If you've ever sat waiting for something for more than five minutes, you know what the next fifty-five were going to be like for me. Nothing but the local gospel station (*K-BLV 99.9!*) on the radio to keep me company. An agitated old coot calling himself The Reverend Jacobs was ranting about the Risen Jesus like He was about to fly through town in a gunship chopper and mow down the unbelievers in a blaze of glory, like a scene out of *Apocalypse Now* if it had been directed by Jim Jones.

I shut off the radio and punched the lighter in. It took me a minute to fish the remainder of a tightly rolled joint out of the bottom of my purse, but worth the effort. Within thirty seconds of the first inhale, I was starting to relax. I rolled down the window and shared it with the world.

The neon lights of the Darklight sign sprang to life, casting the pavement in a scarlet hue. A wide set of stone steps in front led up to a pair of frosted glass doors. The box office window was to the right. Above everything, an enormous white backlit marquee filled the darkening sky with a soft glow. It had undoubtedly announced countless classics over the years, much as it did now. Giant black letters spelled out **THE MUMMY**, perfectly centered. Above it in a smaller font: 50th ANNIVERSARY. And below: ONE NIGHT ONLY.

"So fuckin' weird isn't it?"

I jumped at the voice, dropping the final nub of the joint into my lap. It was an instant from singeing a hole in my dress when I plucked it up and instinctively flicked it. It flew off into the twilight, just missing the plump face filling my driver's side window. At that moment, I was equally annoyed with what I had done and what had caused me to do it.

"Jesus Christ, Jasper - what the fuck, dude?"

Jasper Kincaid, feature writer for Forrest Ackerman's *Famous Monsters of Filmland* and wannabe screenwriter, just shrugged. He had plenty of little ticks and habits that you tried to overlook but worked their way under your skin until you itched like a maniac. Indifference was one of them.

"I would have knocked, but the window was down," he said. As if that would have somehow been better.

I pointed out the window. "Get the joint."

"What?"

I turned his plump face to the parking spaces behind. His cheek was scruffy with curly red hairs. Jasper was in his early thirties, but I'd never seen him grow anything more than a few random patches that looked more like water stains on a ceiling tile than a beard.

"The joint you made me throw away. I wasn't finished. Go get it."

Jasper glanced back at me. I know he saw my eyes blazing because he said nothing and immediately scurried over to pick it up. Just how angry I would be was entirely at the mercy of what he brought back.

He stooped down, pinched the white butt off the pavement, and hurried back, almost tripping over his own feet. Instead of passing it back to me, he walked around the front of my car, opened the passenger door, and slid his fat ass onto the vinyl seat. He stuck his hand out, joint pressed between his index finger and thumb. Both were stained yellow. Jasper was a heavy smoker. One of those many bad habits. The smell of *Hai Karate* cologne and Doritos filled the sacred space of my Gremlin.

"Anyway, as I was saying: so fucking weird isn't it?"

I took the nub carefully before he had a chance to drop it again. Not that it mattered. It was extinguished. I tucked it into the ashtray with a sigh. "What's weird?"

Jasper nodded to the theater. "This place, the movie, the whole fuckin' thing. Fuckin' weird, Jess. Doncha think?"

Jasper Kincaid liked to say "fuck" a lot, in all its variations. We weren't really friends, but we'd been to more than a handful of events together over the last year, and I'd had a chance to hear them all: *Fuck, fuckin', fucksakes, fucker, fuck you, fuck me,* and the old reliable - *mutherfucker.* A few months earlier, at a charity night screening of *E.T. The Extra-Terrestrial,* he stubbed his toe as he made his way to his seat, and I had the pleasure of hearing more than half of them in a single sentence. If cursing was a sin, he'd be in the first wave of victims when the Risen Jesus choppered in. Guaranteed.

I looked at the Darklight. He wasn't wrong, it was a bit weird. Up until the sepia-colored invitation landed on my desk a month ago looking like some ancient parchment, I'd never heard of the Darklight Theater or the town it sat in the middle of, like the monolith in Kubrick's *2001: A Space Odyssey*. My editor was intrigued, however, and decided to send me along. I figured the piece would wind up buried in the back end of the December issue if it saw the light of day at all, but I didn't care. Any chance to get out of L.A. was welcome.

"I guess."

"You guess?" Jasper loosened his tie. "You *are* high. Look at this place, Jess. It's straight out of a fuckin' Raymond Chandler novel. What's it doing in the middle of a little shit stain desert town halfway between Area 51 and the Nevada Proving Grounds?"

"You'd really think they'd market that nuclear angle more."

"Right?" Jasper said with a chuckle. He did a little drumbeat on his legs. One of his ticks. He had jimmy-leg too. *Legs*, actually. I was too stoned to be aggravated.

I looked at my watch. Thirty minutes to go. "Vance's gonna love this place, though. He's big into all this mummy shit, isn't he?"

Jasper shook his head. It seemed to take forever to go from one side to the other. "KT's not coming."

"He wasn't invited? Bullshit."

"No, he was invited. *Fangoria* wouldn't foot the bill. Said it wasn't worth it."

"Fucking *Fangoria*. Please."

"Right? Fucking *Fangoria*. *Vain-Glorious* more like it. Pompous mutherfuckers."

I giggled. *Fangoria* was the premier genre magazine of the day. They had the glossiest photos, the biggest scoops, and the most envied behind-the-scenes access in the business. And the readership to back it up. Their sci-fi sister mag, *Starlog*, was just as elevated and fancied themselves highbrow. It was all pretty silly. Horror and sci-fi were the twin ugly ducklings of fiction. But I guess if no one else takes you seriously, what choice do you have but to do it yourself? Story of my life.

"Thought you didn't like the guy anyway?"

I didn't really. Jasper had annoying ticks, but KT Vance had all the quirks I ran from in high school. I'm sure you know the type. He spoke so quietly that you constantly had to engage with him to get a replay of what he was saying. It seemed intentional, especially when he trapped you in conversation afterward like a verbal spider. Worse still, his eyes would linger on mine a little too long as I spoke, and he made a habit of running his hand along my lower back as he walked away.

"He's alright," I lied.

Jasper grunted. Without asking permission, he slid a cigarette out of a squat pack from his jean jacket pocket. The end was pinched tight like a butthole, but a few strands of wheat-colored tobacco dangled out the front. Jasper rolled his cigs, not because he preferred it but because he was cheap. I couldn't imagine what a date with him would be like. Actually, I could. Probably a lot like what was happening at the moment.

"He's got a thing for you, I think. Told me once you reminded him of his grandmother."

"Christ."

"Who's hot for their fuckin' grandma?" He pushed in the car lighter. "But yeah, this would have been his jam."

"Hey, where's the Mystery Machine?" I was eager to change the subject. I spotted his van about thirty yards away at the outer edge of the parking lot. It was hard to miss, with its black racing stripe splitting the green down the side. I dubbed it the Mystery Machine since it always stank of weed and was littered with more Scooby snacks than the Gang ever dreamed of. Before you ask, yes, my car had a name too. Girls have secrets, and cars have names. Sometimes they are one and the same. Stick around long enough, and I'll tell you. Now's not the time.

The lighter popped out, loud in the tiny space. He lit the cigarette and blew smoke to his right. It bounced off the closed window and was sucked across the front seat by the air outside mine.

"Sorry," Jasper said. He fumbled his window down and took another draw. "Didn't see a motel on my way into town. You stayin' somewhere tonight?"

If it were anyone but Jasper Kincaid, I'd have to put the breaks on the conversation there and then. Jasper didn't want to fuck me any more than I did him. I don't think he even considered me attractive for a girl, and that was A-OK.

"No," I said, taking the cigarette from his lips. I took a long drag and passed it back. It tasted vile. "This whole thing should be wrapped by ten. I'll take the highway back, hole up in a motel somewhere with a heartbeat after midnight."

"Smart." Jasper offered his smoke, but I declined. He extinguished it in the ashtray before tucking what was left back into the pack. Outside, the light had faded to blood orange. "Either everyone around here is as punctual as a Rolex, or we're gonna have no trouble snagging the best seats."

"I didn't tell you!"

"What?"

"I talked to the guy."

"The guy? What guy?"

"The usher. I think. Doesn't matter." I proceeded to tell him all about my encounter with Hector. By the time I finished, I was not entirely sure I had said anything at all. Maybe it was a good thing I had tossed the joint when I had.

"Guess they know the rules around here," Jasper said. "Joke's on us."

But, by five minutes to seven, the parking lot was still just a party of two. Jasper and I exchanged shrugs and climbed out of the car. The sky was full dark except for the soft glow of the marquee and the scarlet aura of the neon sign above it.

"Shit, one sec." I hurried back. My silver and black Pentax was sitting on the back seat, lens staring up at me like the cycloptic eye of an abandoned child. I swiped it by the strap and pulled it over my neck. It bounced across my chest as I rejoined Jasper on the steps.

"Remind me to get a shot on the way out."

"Take it now. We've got time."

I took a final pan across the barren parking lot. "It'll be better with cars in the foreground and people walking down the steps. Tuttle might pay extra if I have some shots."

"Might," Jasper winced. "He's such a cheap bastard."

I shrugged. "I didn't see you fly in on a jet."

"Touché, bitch."

The frosted glass door swung open just as we hit the top step. Hector stepped out and gently kicked down the door stopper with a lifted boot that would make Frankenstein's monster envious. He didn't acknowledge the two of us standing there until he stepped back into the doorway, gloved hand outstretched. His dark eyes moved quickly from my face to Jasper's, then back again. He smiled - a look so out of place on his face I hardly recognized it for what it was.

24

"Invitation?"

I heard the giggle escape me before I could react to contain it. Did he really not remember me?

"Yes, you've seen it already. I showed you like an hour ago."

Hector said nothing. His hand remained extended, waiting. I sighed and dug the paper out of my jacket pocket. He examined it up close, like a cop studying my driver's license. I looked at Jasper, who was straining to hold his smile in place while sniffing the air. The smell of popcorn was overwhelming this close.

Hector lowered the invitation and eyed the press badge poking out from behind my camera. I tugged it to the front, where he could see my credentials. He smiled again and passed the paper back. "Welcome, Ms. Thorne. Imhotep awaits."

Cryptic, but okay. Whatever. I didn't mind a little flourish and flavor. I was about to watch a fifty-year-old black-and-white flick in a dying movie theater in the middle of nowhere. And I was high as a kite. Bring it on.

Jasper pushed his invitation and badge into Hector's gloved hand before the giant had a chance to ask for it. Hector gave it far less consideration than he had mine and quickly returned it without a word. He stepped back into the lobby and ushered us in.

The floor was carpeted in a deep red low pile that might have never seen a footprint before that night. The paint was so perfectly applied, you'd have sworn to your god and whatever others were kicking about that the walls of the Darklight Theater were literally made of gold. An eight-foot tall sarcophagus stood beside the restroom alcove, surrounded by several large painted vases. The blue and gold sarcophagus was coffin-shaped, with various human features, including a sharply carved face surrounded by a gold Nemes headdress (reminiscent of the one popularized by Yul

Brynner in *The Ten Commandments*) and arms crossed at the chest. A story in hieroglyphics ran down the front and continued across the vases, its plot a mystery. The opposite wall contained a large poster of *The Mummy* ripped right out of the golden age of Hollywood, perfectly preserved behind a spotless glass frame. On each side of it stood a seven-foot-tall anthropomorphic jackal carved from marble. They also wore the traditional headdress, and carried threatening spears capped with large blue-winged scarab beetles. The detail was incredible. I raised my camera and snapped a quick shot.

"Pinch me, Jess," Jasper said. He turned my head.

A concession stand filled the wall opposite the front doors. It was tricked out with an endless variety of candy and chocolate, and behind it, two overflowing machines spilled out the puffiest golden popcorn I had ever seen. Each end of the black counter held a soda fountain, one for Coca-Cola products, the other for Pepsi. A perky blonde girl of no more than sixteen stood by the cash register waiting for us.

I turned to Jasper. He was already looking at me, eyes wide. We both laughed and hustled over, kneeling as one should at an altar.

"Oh my God, they have Big League Chew!" I grabbed two packs and continued to scan. "Reeses Pieces!"

"Fuck Reeses Pieces," Jasper spat. He was holding an Almond Joy and several packs of Skittles in front of his face. I stood up first and patted him on his curly-haired head. When he didn't rise, I tapped harder. "What, Jess?"

"Jasper."

"What? Fuck." He stood, his hands now overflowing with M&Ms as well. "The fuck?"

"Yeah." I was looking out into the parking lot through the open front doors. In the last five minutes, the first row had filled up around my car. The vehicles idled, then began shutting off.

Jasper cleared his throat. "So fuckin' weird."

The auditorium was less impressive than the lobby. The screen filled the far wall, bracketed by long brown curtains, and below it, a low stage with a centered podium and microphone. A section of seats, fifty across, descended toward the stage, about forty rows in total, with an aisle on each side. The walls were the color of arterial blood and decorated with hideous comedy and tragedy masks. If Universal Pictures had footed the bill for the lobby displays, the buck had stopped at the theater door.

We made our way to the third row from the front. I let Jasper choose the seats, and he settled into one in the middle. I sat beside him, very carefully laying my snacks out on the seat on the other side.

"Great interview with Carpenter, by the way," Jasper said, unwrapping his Almond Joy. "Not gonna lie, I was jealous. Nice scoop."

"Thanks." It *had* been a nice get, an exclusive one-on-one with the acclaimed director of *The Thing*. It should have led to more top-tier assignments, but the film was a commercial and critical disaster, and no one cared that Carpenter had poured his soul into it or that I had been the one he told that to. All anyone cared about that summer was—

"Fucking *E.T.*" Jasper snarled. "Fucking Spielberg. Little bug-eyed fucker."

I wasn't sure which one he was referring to.

"*The Thing* is a fucking masterpiece. The world is upside down, Jess. E-Fucking-T. You think if aliens came here they'd be gardeners? Fucking *gardeners*? No, they'd be disgusting shapeshifters trying to take over the planet. Not fucking gardeners. Lock up your flowers, lock up your weed,

E.T.'s comin'! Jesus Christ. Give me a break." He looked at me as I tried to stifle laughter. I was doing a terrible job of it.

"I liked it."

"What? No, Jess. No."

"It was cute."

"You're killing me. Give me your press pass, you don't deserve it."

"E.T. is on the cover of *Famous Monsters* as we speak!"

"Don't remind me. Forry's losing it upstairs." He swirled a finger by his ear to drive the point home. "At least it's still in theaters, though. What've you guys got? *Poltergeist*? *Cat People*?"

"*Amityville 2*," I muttered.

"Fuck off. Really?" Jasper laughed. "What a piece of shit. Jee-zus… Tuttle's a terrible editor, Jess. You're so much better than that rag. Or this gig." He craned his head around to look behind us. "Don't look now, but we're not alone anymore."

"Huh?" I turned to look. Four rows back, a thin man sat in the shadows. Or I thought it was a man. It was hard to focus without squinting, and squinting just made things darker. I was beginning to feel like I *should* turn in my pass. Being this stoned on the job was a hell of a coping mechanism for a lame assignment, but it was far from professional. Even Jasper, with his Mystery Machine and Scooby snacks, was sober.

Jasper raised his hand to wave to the thin man. "Hey."

I pushed his hand down and spun around. "What are you doing?"

"Being cordial."

"What if he decides to come sit with us now?"

"Why would he do that? Because I waved hello? If I had that kind of power, I'd be drowning in dick right now, Jess. Waving it in with one hand, fighting it off with the other." He swirled his hands in front of him like a chubby gay Chuck Norris. I laughed so hard my breath stopped. It only encouraged him. The movements got broader. "Stroke. Block. Stroke. Blo—"

"Stop!" I grabbed both his hands. "You're making a scene."

"So? Afraid they won't invite us back?" He giggled with me. As annoying as Jasper Kincaid could be, he was fun to have around at the movies. "Maybe next year they'll do one of these for *The Invisible Man*."

"Count me out."

"You think his dick is invisible?"

"What?"

"The Invisible Man. You think—"

"I heard what you said. I don't think about it."

"But if you did..."

"Sure. Why not? The rest of him is."

Jasper seemed to give it serious thought. "True. It would kind of defeat the whole purpose if everything else was invisible except a floating cock lurking in the corner like a cyclops watching you while you slept."

"If it's invisible, do you think he can even get it up?"

"What? Of course, he can. He's invisible, Jess, not a fucking ghost. He's all there, you just can't see it."

"Can he see it?"

"Yes, obvious—" Jasper paused, suddenly unsure. "Jeez, now that you mention it, I have no idea. Fuck, that's so fucked up."

It was my turn to glance around the theater. While we had been pondering the opacity of Claude Rains' penis, several more patrons had wandered in and settled into the seats toward the back. They were hard to make out clearly, but most appeared to be dressed in white sweaters and long hooded coats. I thought about K-BLV and their Risen Jesus cult.

"Speaking of fucked up," I said, squinting hard.

Jasper started to turn.

"Do. Not. Wave."

Jasper stared at me, wide-eyed, unblinking. It took all my effort to not laugh. "*Drowning* in dick, Jess. Drowning."

I pushed his face away. "Disgusting."

It was ten after seven. I looked at the podium and wondered when someone - Hector maybe - would step out from behind the curtain to introduce the film. The invitation bore no logos other than the Darklight, suggesting that this anniversary screening was not endorsed by the studio. The statues and sarcophagus *looked* like props from the movie on loan from the studio archives, but in my experience, those items were usually tagged to identify them as such and kept under the watchful eye of circling studio reps. And there had been no swag or studio paraphernalia for the guests. Most of the time, the marketing department provided some sort of memorabilia to take home, if only just a replica poster or lobby cards. Considering Universal was still riding the *E.T.* box office tsunami deep into autumn, it was unlikely they would have cheaped out on something like this, even if it was in the middle of nowhere.

I felt a tap on my shoulder and turned to see Jasper staring behind us. "Look at this guy. He went all out."

A mummy was shuffling in through the main doors. Had the studio sent a performance artist to walk among us before and after the feature? It moved stiffly, as though the joints were locked in position, and the left foot dragged behind at an awkward angle. Whoever it was, they were rake thin and wrapped horizontally head to toe in thick strands of aged cloth. I squinted to get a better look at the face, but the doors swung shut behind it and stole the light. In the darkness, the figure crossed behind the last row of seats and stopped dead center, facing the screen.

"So fucking weird," I muttered.

"Amen."

Both of us turned back to the screen.

"Did you see that?" Jasper whispered.

"Obviously."

"No, not the mummy guy. Everyone else."

"What about them?" I had only been vaguely aware of the rest of the bodies in the seats other than the fact there were more than before and definitely more than I had expected.

"They aren't moving. Not a bit. Just staring ahead."

"Bullshit," I said. I swatted him on the arm. "Stop trying to scare me, it ain't gonna work. I write about scary things for a living, remember?"

He stole a glance back again. "I can't see any faces either."

"It's dark."

"You know what I mean."

"No, Jasper, I don't. Stop being a dick."

"You're *scared.* Jesse Thorne is fuckin' scared." Jasper drummed on his legs before pretending to hit an invisible cymbal.

I wasn't scared, I was stoned. Which means I was paranoid. Like, Richard Nixon paranoid.

"Give me your camera." Jasper's hand was already reaching for it in my lap.

"What? Why?"

"Just for a sec. I want to see something." His fingers wrapped around the short lens. I grabbed the strap and held it firm.

"Jasper, let go. No pictures."

He chuckled. "We're the press, and they invited us. Pictures are expected."

I pulled hard, but his grip was too strong and determined. I felt the strap fall away. He snickered and turned the camera awkwardly in his hands. I was half-facing the audience when the flash went off, momentarily blinding him.

But not me. I saw them. My breath caught in my throat.

The two rows behind us were empty. Beyond those, the theater was half-full. The flash only lasted a second, but in that moment, I was able to make out two things: almost all of the patrons were dressed the same, and none of them had faces. Not in an Invisible Man kind of way, but not in a Jesse and Jasper kind of way either. I saw row after row of sunken, hardened flesh drawn tight across bone. Rotted teeth pushed forward without lips to hold them back. Dark, yellowed eyes sat unblinking in sallow sockets. Noses were reduced to a memory of flesh; hair all but lost to time. Some wore bandages across their scalps; others had clumps of matted material dangling loosely from one side or the other. All were bound from the neck down in soiled cloth strips that wound in rows from fingertips to torso.

None of them reacted to the flash. They just sat there staring up at the screen.

"Fucking piece of shit," Jasper said. It brought me back, and I let my held breath out quickly.

"Something weird is going on," I whispered to him. He rubbed his eyes with one hand while holding the camera out to me with the other.

"Yeah, your fucking camera sucks."

I took the Pentax and laid it safely out of Jasper's reach on the seat with all my food. "No, I mean here, now. Something really weird is happening. Everyone's a fucking mummy, Jasper."

"So? People do weird shit at the movies. I had the best handjob of my life last year at *Clash of the Titans* from a dude dressed like a fuckin' owl."

"But everyone else wasn't dressed like an owl and jerking people off, were they?"

"What? No." He finished wiping his eyes and glanced over his shoulder. "It's just weirdos being weird, Jess. I was just messing with you. People really get into these special screenings. *The Mummy* is a classic. It created an entirely new monster, you know. And it's Halloween next week, too. The Chinese place down the street is probably full of Draculas."

I tried not to picture what that would look like, but as a writer, my imagination is a well-oiled machine. The fear scattered, and I burst out laughing.

"Feel better?"

"Yeah." I closed my eyes, steadied my breathing. The afterimage from the flash burned there like a photo negative. Row after row of emaciated faces stared at me. I opened my eyes. The theater had gotten darker. When Jasper tore the rest of his Almond Joy wrapper, it was like little firecrackers going off in the silence.

A spotlight flickered on above the stage. A moment later, a squat little man in a bone-white suit emerged from behind the curtain. As he arrived at the podium, it was obvious that the microphone was too high, and he snapped his thick fingers in a flourish. On command, Hector appeared from the other side of the screen and adjusted the microphone down. He stood there awkwardly, a full three feet taller than the other man, until a second snap of fingers sent him back behind the screen once more.

I sipped my Pepsi, hoping the high would soon fade, and relieved that some semblance of normal had been restored to this experience. Surely this dark-haired man was from the studio or perhaps the theater manager about to introduce the film.

Jasper leaned into my ear, cheap chocolate mingled with his cheaper cologne. "I have to tell you something."

"What?" I asked, fixated on the little rotund man at the podium.

"A confession, actually. But you can't get mad at me. It's your own fault, really."

That did make me turn. Sharply. *"What?"*

Jasper swallowed the last of his Almond Joy too quickly and started coughing.

The man in the white suit adjusted his turquoise tie and cleared his throat. He leaned into the podium, his narrow eyes settling on mine. The corners of his mouth twitched upward and his gaze moved on.

"Ladies and gentlemen, thank you all for coming this evening. My name is Darius Beaumont, and I am the owner and operator of the Darklight Theater, Nevada's last truly independent cinema."

I punched Jasper on the thigh. He pulled his legs to the far side.

"Tonight is very special. Fifty years ago, my father, Leopold Beaumont, was a prop master on the film you're about to see. Originally from London, he and my mother actually met in Egypt while working as laborers on the excavation and unsealing of Tutankhamun's tomb in 1922. With the money and experience they earned on that adventure – and with more than a passing desire to escape King Tut's Curse - they moved to this country and started a new life in Hollywood. For my father, it was a chance to show the world the beauty of my mother's ancestors. He was very proud. And devoted. His hands crafted many of the ancient artifact replicas you will see on-screen tonight. Sadly, however, my mother passed in childbirth before the film was completed and never saw it." Beaumont paused, taking a moment to gather his breath and let his words settle over us. "When production wrapped, the studio planned to discard many of the film's sets and props. My father, not wanting to see the fruits of his labor destroyed, drove on to the backlot at night, loaded what he could into his truck and never returned, fearing they would know it was him. Those same props survive today in the basement of this very building. For tonight only, we have dusted some of them off just for you. You may have noticed one or two of his favorites in the lobby on your way in."

Well, that answered one of my questions, at least. And explained why no one from Universal was wandering about.

Mr. Beaumont cleared his throat again. "Now, return with me to the past. The year: 1932. The place: Cairo. The film: *The Mummy*. Enjoy the show."

The spotlight vanished with the loud bang of a heavy switch being thrown. The theater was momentarily pitch black. Several people clapped behind us. The projector whirred to life high above, its beam reaching through the darkness. Darius Beaumont was gone. From the corner of my eye, I saw Jasper pull his cigarettes out.

"Don't smoke those in here."

"I'm not." He held them up to me. "They're spiked."

"Spiked? With what?" Before he could answer, I felt a rush of heat move over me, not unlike the sensation of pissing down my own leg. "Oh fuck. You drugged me!"

"Technically, you drugged yourself, Jess."

"What the *fuck?*" I was trying to keep my voice low, but a good "fuck" is wasted in whispers. And I was pissed. "Why? With what?"

The Universal logo was finishing on screen. The old one with the biplane circling the spinning globe.

"LSD."

"You spiked your smokes with acid? Fucking acid, Jasper?"

"Just a little—"

"Just a little acid? There's no such thing!" I couldn't believe I was freaking out about being drugged with acid while the familiar strains of *Swan Lake* played over the opening titles in the background. It just made me angrier. "Jesus Christ. I have to drive in less than two hours. Wait, that means you're tripping too!"

Jasper's face scrunched together as he shrugged. "Sorry."

"You asshole. You idiot."

"You took my smoke from me. I didn't offer it to you."

And then I remembered how awful it had tasted. *Vile*, I believe was the word that struck me at the time. "You could have warned me. Or stopped me."

"You were already smoking a joint, I figured..."

I raised a fist, and he flinched, expecting another punch. The bag of popcorn in his lap bounced and toppled over his legs. In that moment, lit only by ambient cinema light, he looked pathetic and sad. I held off.

"You seemed to be having fun, at least until you thought everyone was a fucking for-real mummy, and then I knew you were trippin' the other way."

I glanced at the audience behind me. A few of them still looked like withered monsters, but most had removed their masks and were watching the screen intently. Just a bunch of nerdy teens and twenty-somethings at the movies.

"Masks," I muttered. I folded my arms, faced the screen. I should have felt relief, but whatever was in that cigarette was still pirouetting with the weed through my bloodstream, leaving me continually on edge.

"Yeah. Just masks. I'm really sorry, Jess. I should have stopped you."

"How long is this gonna last? Am I fucked for the night? Am I stuck in this desert town?"

"No. You only had one puff, it should wear off soon. But you smoked a lot of weed, so I can't say for—"

"Shut up. Watch the movie." I stared at the screen. Boris Karloff - in his one scene in full mummy make-up - was dragging his leg off-screen after terrifying his first victim. If Jasper Kincaid had met a similar fate then and there, I don't think I would have shed a tear.

We didn't speak for the next fifteen minutes. We munched popcorn in silence. After every few mouthfuls, Jasper slurped his Coke, then rattled his cup as though the ice were holding the last of his soda hostage. Finally, he leaned over and said: "I gotta take a piss. Be right back."

But he wasn't right back. After ten minutes, I figured he'd had to empty more than his bladder. When another ten minutes passed, I started to wonder if he'd left altogether. It wasn't like Jasper to not say goodbye. Even if he had shit his pants, he would have penguin-walked down the aisle to let me know. Had my anger really upset him that much?

I grabbed my purse and camera and hurried up the aisle, keeping my head down until I reached the door. I bumped it open with my butt. As the light spilled in, I noticed that the gimpy-legged mummy standing at the back was no longer there.

The sudden brightness of the lobby made my head pound. The sign for the washrooms was next to the sarcophagus display and I made my way over to wait outside.

"Ms. Thorne, isn't it?"

I stopped and turned. Darius Beaumont was waddling over to me from behind the concession counter. The dimness of the theater had previously obscured the fact he was wearing the most ill-fitting toupee I had ever seen. When he smiled, his forehead shrank, but the hair never moved. I struggled to not stare.

"Yes. Jesse Thorne—"

"*Strange Tides Magazine*. So glad you came all this way for our little event."

I forced a smile and nodded to the poster across the hall. "It's a classic. Hard to say no to those."

"What do you think of our *artifacts*?" Beaumont asked, moving around me to the sarcophagus.

"They're… beautiful." It was an odd word to use for a coffin, even one as fancy as this one. But it *was* beautiful. Ancient Egyptian royalty spared no expense, and the senior Mr. Beaumont had truly crafted a replica worthy of their hubris. "Your father is very talented."

"Indeed," he grinned.

"Is he around? I'd love to get a few words with him for my article." Given the recently revealed history of how these "artifacts" came to be in the possession of the Darklight Theater, it might have been better to leave Leopold Beaumont out of the article altogether. But I needed to remain professional in front of this man for fear of freaking out. A second high was inexplicably coursing through me when it should have been on the way out. My heart was racing. My ears felt clogged. Every time I turned my head, my vision appeared to have frames missing, like a chopped-up film reel.

"Unfortunately not, Ms. Thorne. My father passed some time ago. Only his work remains."

"I'm sorry for your loss," I said. I know what you're thinking: how the fuck is she keeping it together? Or maybe you're not. Maybe you're wondering where the hell is Jasper? Whatever he's gotten into has to be so much more interesting than listening to her prattle on with thrift store Danny DeVito. Trust me, I get it. All I wanted at that moment was to know what Jasper was up to as well. But I was trapped. "This is a lovely tribute."

He gave a slight nod. "Were you not enjoying the feature?"

"No. I mean, yes, of course. I've seen it before."

"But never like this." He held his arms out, did a slight turn. "Never in a theater."

"No. Just on TV."

"Hmm… Television." The word slid from his mouth like a worm.

I shifted on my feet, folded my arms. I glanced anxiously toward the washrooms. "I'm waiting for my friend, actually. We came together."

"He went in there?"

"Yeah. Too much Coke."

"I have been out here all evening. I saw no one come or go."

I frowned. "He must have slipped by. He's sneaky." Jasper couldn't sneak into a graveyard without raising the dead, but this diminutive man didn't know that.

"Perhaps I am mistaken. I will go check on your friend."

He walked away before I could reach out and stop him. I can't say I really tried that hard. I was more than a little curious to know what Mr. Beaumont would even say to a stranger in the bathroom, and Jasper, for his part, deserved the embarrassment.

Less than a minute later, Beaumont returned shaking his head. "He is not in there. Not anymore."

I sagged. Jasper *had* left. As hard as I wanted to remain mad at him, I felt a wave of guilt instead.

"Thank you." I walked to the front doors and pushed one open.

There were a lot more cars in the parking lot than before, all jammed into the first three rows. That made it easy to spot the Mystery Machine waiting patiently alone in the far corner. Right where it had always been.

"Please, Ms. Thorne. Come back in and enjoy the rest of the film. Perhaps your friend just needed some air. I am sure he isn't far."

I let the door close. Mr. Beaumont was smiling in the middle of the lobby. Hector had joined him, standing slightly behind. The giant's eyes locked on mine in that same unsettling way as before. I nodded to Mr. Beaumont and started back toward the theater.

"I hope your friend's behavior has no bearing on your article, Ms. Thorne."

"It won't. I promise." I pushed open the theater doors and slipped back into the darkness. The screen was briefly filled with the exotic beauty of Zita Johann in a close-up before cutting to a wide shot to include her stiff-as-a-post co-star David Manners and scene-stealing character actor Edward Van Sloan. A year before *The Mummy*, Van Sloan had become world famous for his portrayal of Abraham Van Helsing in Universal's smash hit *Dracula*. Here he had been tasked with essentially repeating the formula, to diminished returns. Still, standing next to Manners - who made an unassailable case for the death of high pants as a fashion - Van Sloan was an acting colossus.

Our seats were still empty. If Jasper hadn't left the theater, where the hell had he disappeared to?

I walked across the back of the last row. On the far side, there was a black door with a small sign that read: EMPLOYEES ONLY. That wouldn't have stopped Jasper Kincaid and it wasn't about to stop Jesse Thorne. I slipped through to the dim stairwell beyond.

I found myself in a small landing between staircases - one going up, the other down. The one going up was lit at the top, where the projection room lay behind a heavy door. The downward staircase was unlit and descended for nine steps before disappearing into total darkness. Seems like a no-brainer, right? Wrong. A crinkled Almond Joy wrapper sat on the second step down. Shaggy, high as a Six Flags rollercoaster, could have solved this one.

There were actually fifteen steps in total, the last six in darkness so complete it seemed like light was pulled up and away, like smoke from a fire. At the bottom, my cheek flattened against a solid surface. I leaned back and felt for a door handle, finding one. The door was heavy, but it swung inward enough for me to sneak through. A cough of musty air pushed out around me, smelling of sour earth and stale linens. I held my breath as it passed.

I stood at the threshold of a vast tomb. It was lit by a series of overhead pot lights. Several had burned out and were left unattended, leaving the remaining few to cast broad black shadows throughout the room. The floor was covered in sand or - more likely - composed of the Mojave desert itself. Multiple round posts embellished with hieroglyphs were spaced evenly throughout, bearing the load of the floors above. Several groupings of movie props were collected neatly in each corner. In the center of the room, where the light was the strongest, stood a stone sarcophagus identical to the one in the lobby above. It would have had my undivided attention except for the fact Jasper Kincaid was standing in front of it, his back to me. As the door thumped closed, he turned.

"Hey, Jess," he said casually, as if I hadn't been forced to sneak around looking for him in the bowels of the theater like the goddamn Phantom of the Opera.

"What the actual fuck, Jasper?"

"What?"

I stomped over to him, progress and aggression slowed by the drag of the sand. "What? Oh, I don't know. How about the fact you said you had to go pee a half hour ago, and instead I find you lurking down here like a fucking Morlock."

"Half an hour? What are you talking about? I've been gone like five minutes, tops."

His bewilderment sucked the wind from my sails.

"Are you messing with me again? I'm not in the mood. It's been thirty minutes. How much LSD did you do?"

He frowned. "Fuuuuck…"

"You're an asshole."

"That's fair," he said. He shrugged and brightened just as quickly. "But enough about me. Can you believe this fuckin' place, Jess?"

I punched him then. Not a knockout blow or even a bruiser, but my fist made solid contact with his upper arm, and he squealed. Satisfied, I lowered my hands.

"Let's just get out of here. It smells like a grandmother's vagina."

"I don't want to know how you know that," a voice said from behind the sarcophagus. I stumbled back. A mummy shuffled into the light, dragging its left leg. Only, it wasn't really a mummy: a mask rested on the top of its head. The exposed face below it was familiar but not one I was happy to see.

"What's he doing here?" I asked Jasper.

"Oh yeah, KT is--"

"Is there a problem?" KT Vance asked. He held his hands up as though I was holding him at gunpoint.

"I thought this was beneath your mag?"

42

"The editors weren't interested, but I couldn't miss this. *The Mummy* is my favorite film. You know that."

"Why would I know that?"

He was stung. I didn't care. I knew he was a fan, but if he'd told me it was his favorite movie, I hadn't filed it away. He rubbed his chin like he'd taken a punch. In the harsh overhead light, the pockmarks across his pale cheeks evoked the surface of the moon.

Jasper touched my arm. "Take some pictures or something. We'll leave in five minutes, I swear. A *real* five minutes."

I sighed, kicking sand with my boots. It sprayed out in a pretty peacock tail pattern. "Five minutes. And then I'm leaving you down here to rot."

I snapped a few photos of the posts and the walls, which the flash revealed were also covered in hieroglyphs. Leopold Beaumont may have never returned to the film work he so loved, but he clearly dedicated himself to constructing a shrine worthy of screening them here in the desert.

Jasper and KT busied themselves with trying to pry open the sarcophagus. For a movie prop, it was oddly real, to the point of being hermetically sealed.

"Give it up, guys. If they wanted it opened, it would have a button or switch. Or not be down here amongst the rubble, maybe. You think?"

"Where's the infamous Jesse Thorne curiosity?" Jasper asked, squatting at the base and running his chubby fingers along the seam. The crack of his ass grinned up at me.

I held back the urge to kick him. "It's hostage to an unplanned acid trip and a man-child who's about to get a prostate exam from Doc Marten."

"Don't tease."

"You two did acid?" KT asked. He faced me. "Got any left?"

"Not on purpose. And no. I dunno. Ask him."

Jasper stood up. He was about to answer, then frowned at the discomfort on my face. He turned to KT. "Uh, no. Wasn't that great anyway. Right, Jess?"

I nodded, pretended to adjust the lens on my camera.

"Shitty," KT said. He went back to trying to find a way to open the sarcophagus. I noticed he was still dragging his foot, something I had presumed to be part of the role-playing foolishness.

"What's wrong with your foot?"

"Sprained it last week. Skateboarding." His chest puffed out as he said the last part. He walked around the prop and smiled at me. "Nice of you to ask."

Gag me with a spoon.

"Let's head back, Jasper."

KT stepped forward. "I'll come with you guys. Just one last thing. I promise. Humor me."

"What now?"

He pointed at the Pentax. "Take a picture, nice and dramatic," He turned and faced the sarcophagus again. He held out his arms and spoke in a loud, booming voice. The words were gibberish, but I recognized them nonetheless. It was a recitation from the movie playing upstairs. The same one that had risen Imhotep from the dead.

"Such an idiot," I said, rolling my eyes. Even Jasper was shaking his head.

KT's voice grew louder, the foreign words echoing through the room. I kicked the sand again. It sprayed out in an arc. And then it did something very strange: it slid back into the divot my boot had created.

More followed. The floor was trembling.

44

KT's voice trailed off, quickly swallowed up by the rumble of earth moving beneath our feet, spreading outward from the base of the sarcophagus to the walls. A fissure snaked across the ceiling like an invisible hand drawing chalk across a blackboard.

"Earthquake!" I shouted. Unlike a man, logic is always the initial thought in a woman's mind and the first words from her lips. But logic had no place here. The drugs made that potently clear. They knew the truth.

KT knew it, too. It was written across his face. And then a withered hand fell across it and pulled him back. He screamed.

The sarcophagus split open down the center. The right side toppled into the sand with a deadened thud. The mummified hand pulled KT into the crevice, where another arm emerged and wrapped around his chest. The ground stopped shaking, but dust and sand continued to flutter down from above like ghostly starlight.

Jasper and I ran forward and grasped KT's outstretched hands. His eyes bulged white above the gray-black skin of the mummy's fingers. I tried to pry those dead digits away. It was like trying to snap a whole fistful of turkey wishbones at Thanksgiving dinner.

The mummy suddenly released KT's chest and pushed us back. I went down hard, my camera flying up and over my head in the type of slow motion that seems specifically reserved for life's most poorly timed moments. It landed in the sand near my head. The flash went off, blinding me.

"Piece of shit!"

"I told you!" Jasper yelled. He was on his back beside me, struggling like an overturned insect.

"SHUT UP, JASPER!" I was so done with his shit. I fumbled around

45

on all fours and found the strap. I yanked it up.

There were a million things I should have been thinking in that moment, not the least of which was simply: *Mummy!* But whether the strangeness of the night had prepared me for this culmination of events or whether the cocktail of drugs I had inhaled was suppressing my fear, I couldn't say. All I know is that in one moment, I was flailing in the sand, and in the next, I was firing the flash an inch away from the creature's eyes.

The reaction was instant. The mummy clawed at its face, bellowing out a startled cry that filled the chamber. KT fell into me, and we toppled to the floor next to Jasper.

KT leaped to his feet. He rushed for the door screaming, inadvertently kicking sand into my open mouth with his limp foot. I rolled, spit, grabbed Jasper's hand and pulled him over onto his side. Together, we watched as KT fled through the doorway. Hector appeared an instant later, Darius Beaumont scurrying in behind him. The theater owner's eyes fell on me, but the giant stared right past us at the broken sarcophagus and the creature writhing inside. I'd never seen the blood actually rush from someone's face until that precise moment. It is something you never forget.

"What have you done?" Beaumont uttered. He took several steps before halting again. By that time, I was dragging Jasper by the hand toward the door. I didn't have an answer anyway. Questions I had plenty of. But answers? Get out of the way, little man.

Beaumont gripped my arm hard. "This… This cannot be undone!"

I heard the distant, muffled sound of panicked screams from upstairs. The whole building had shaken, and undoubtedly, everyone was running for the exits. It struck me then that nothing about Beaumont's words conveyed shock at discovering a mummy down here. But his next words did shock me.

"Father... please!"

"The fuck?" Jasper and I both exclaimed. We backed up. Darius Beaumont had already forgotten we were there. He clearly had bigger issues to deal with. Daddy issues. My head was spinning.

Our backs hit the door a moment later, but neither of us turned. In the center of the room, the mummified remains of Leopold Beaumont emerged from the shattered sarcophagus and shuffled forward. Darius Beaumont held his hands out in front of his face like a mime. "Hector! Stop him, Hector!"

The giant, for his part, was uncommonly loyal. I did not get the sense that Beaumont had ever been particularly kind to the man, and the snapping of the fingers to usher him forward earlier had been keenly egregious. So when I watched Hector step between father and son, my heart sank at what I dreaded was about to happen.

Hector grabbed the mummy by the shoulders with his huge hands. The creature should have collapsed into a pile of dust and rags from the pressure. Instead, the mummy reached up and clasped the giant's head. Hector immediately let go and tried to pry the hands away. But it was too late. The giant's head imploded with a sickening soft crunch, chased by a gurgled scream that ended in a muted grunt. Hector's body slumped to the ground, blood and gray matter drooling out like spilled jam.

"Jesus Christ! Jesus Christ!" Jasper whispered. He turned and fumbled with the door handle. "Come on, Jess. We have to go!"

That was obvious. Our lives literally depended on it now. And yet, I couldn't look away. Part of me - maybe the journalist part, maybe the voyeur we all deny we have buried deep inside - had to stay a moment longer to witness the final farewell between father and son.

Jasper tugged my sleeve. I pulled away. "Wait."

"Jess, this isn't the drugs. This is really happening."

"I know."

Jasper let go and pried the door open. I felt the air blow softly past me. The sound of stomping and screaming from above grew louder, clearer.

"Father, I'm sorry! I... I... This was never supposed to—" But Darius Beaumont never finished that sentence. He may not have even finished the thought. His father's ossified right hand wrapped around his throat, cutting the oxygen from his brain. The left hand briefly caressed Darius's cheek before resting atop his head. For an instant, the mummy gazed past Beaumont to me. I cannot say there was a smile on what remained of that hideous face, but I would be lying if I said there wasn't.

"Jess!"

I let Jasper pull me through the door. The last thing I saw in that room was Darius Beaumont's pear-shaped body collapsing to its knees, bald and lifeless as the creature that had once been his father loomed above, a pulsating heart clenched in one rigid hand, the world's ugliest toupee in the other.

We raced up the stairs two at a time. Jasper gasped for air halfway, his legs hardening from hot lava to igneous rock. He either didn't count the steps originally on the way down or simply couldn't find the strength to go on because on the fourteenth step, just as the door below us smashed open, he flopped onto the landing. The auditorium door banged inward, and three makeshift mummies stumbled over him. I flattened my back against the wall as they fell past me down the stairs, their masks flying off.

Jasper heaved himself up and leaned out the doorway. He quickly retreated and shut it, pressing his considerable weight against it.

"We can't go that way!"

"Why?"

Jasper was pale. He offered no further explanation, but you'll recall, as I did, that the sarcophagus in the basement wasn't the only one in the building.

There was a piercing scream from the blackness of the bottom stairwell. Two of the fake mummies were scrambling back up the stairs on all fours. I didn't want to think about what had befallen the third.

I watched, frozen against the wall, as Leopold's mummy surfaced from shadows thick as swamp water a moment later. Blood dripped from his sodden hands. Splatters of scarlet were soaking into the gray bandages around his torso and neck. A few specks of Hector's brain matter clung like snot to the chin and forehead. The creature didn't seem to notice or care. His undead eyes were locked on the pair fleeing from him. I looked at Jasper. The door was beating steadily inward, in time with my racing heart.

One of the victims wailed, and I heard the sickening *thunk-thunk!* of their bandaged head smacking the stairs. I could smell the mummy now. Like wet leaves left to rot in the autumn sun. And just beneath it, the metallic scent of fresh blood and pungent meat. My stomach lurched as I sprinted up to the projection booth door. It was unlocked.

"Jasper!"

He bolted toward me. The door behind him crashed open. KT Vance was thrust through the doorway and across the landing into the opposite wall, impaled through the gut on a metal spear. A blue-winged scarab protruded just below his chest, preventing him from sliding off to the floor. A slender, linen-wrapped mummy followed, patches of long white hair poking out between bandages around the scalp. It gave a savage yank on the spear, freeing it in a single motion. KT collapsed in a heap, a splash of blood on concrete the last impression he made on the world.

We pushed into the projection room. Jasper shut the door, locked it. There was a rolling office chair and a long steel desk along one of the walls. I grabbed the chair and wedged it under the doorknob while Jasper wrestled with the table. It was bolted to the floor.

"Fuck, fuck, mutherfucker shit!" Jasper yelled.

The room was unpleasantly warm and bigger than I would have thought, with an enormous projector and a series of flat spinning platters filling the center. The film was still running, nearing the finale. Its ghostly frames passed through a small glass window to the screen at the end of the auditorium. In contrast to the stark black and white images flickering there, the aisles were a bloodbath, littered with a dozen or so bodies.

"There's two now," Jasper said between wheezing breaths. "How can there be two?"

"How can there be *any?*"

"I don't know. Vance was just goofing around. It was a joke!" Jasper plopped down into the chair. A heavy thump rocked the door behind him. He jumped up, turned to it. "He was joking!"

The banging halted. Under the persistent *chick-chick-chick* of the projector, I heard the tinny crackle of a radio inside the room. Somewhere out in the ether, the Reverend Jacobs was still pontificating about the Risen Jesus.

"*...winds of change, my brethren! Only God shall move the heaven and the earth! Those who try shall be cast down by those who rise! See for yourselves! Open your windows! Open your doors! Look to the sky, see the face of your—*"

The door suddenly crumpled inward, blowing the chair and Jasper across the room. He spilled heavily into a stack of large metal octagonal film canisters propped against the far wall. He lay motionless as several continued to fall, bouncing off his body. I ran over, knelt beside him. His scalp was busted open and blood leaked into his right eye. There was no reaction.

"Jasper…?"

A scream from the stairwell made me look up. At the end of the wall, there was a glowing red light encased in a wire frame above a door. I had no idea where it led, but it was away from certain death, and that was enough. I got up—

—or more accurately: I was *pulled* up by the hair. The pain was instant, sharp. A hand grabbed the collar of my jacket and tossed me across the room. My shoulder blades struck one of the platters, shooting a bright stab of pain along my spine to the base of my skull. The room dimmed, filled with speckles of light. The white-haired mummy lurched forward, reaching for my throat with a blackened hand. Some of the bandages had come loose across the chest. A lump of long-dead flesh peaked out, the crescent edge of a woman's nipple partially exposed. I had a hunch I was about to die at the hands of Leopold Beaumont's dead wife.

Screw that.

I thrust my left foot out, striking her in the shin with the heel of my boot. It was little more than a glancing blow. She clutched a handful of my dress to lift me again, so I planted both feet on the tiled floor and shoved my body back. I slid two feet under the platter, hearing the bottom of my dress rip. A swatch of olive fluttered to the floor. That pissed me off. I was never big on dresses, but this one I actually liked.

I dragged myself to the wall. The only path to the emergency exit was around the far side of the machine. But first, I had to get to my feet. The white-hot lens was above me. It gave me an idea.

I stood, raised my camera, and fired off three quick shots. The flash popped, machine gun bursts of light filling the room. The mummy threw a hand up to shield her eyes, the other slashing forward to grab the camera. I ran, even managed to get two whole steps before feeling a hot burn across my throat. My head snapped back with the force of the strap against my neck. And then my whole body spun, and I was enveloped in her outstretched arms. The pressure spit the air from my lungs, each breath like inhaling fire. I felt ribs snap and screamed. In desperation, I ripped her hair and pulled. Her head jerked back for a second, then came forward again. I felt it go slack and watched as part of her scalp peeled free of the skull. It dangled limp in my hand. Dark ash and sand trickled across the bone, sifted to the floor.

It was enough to distract her. She released me, reached a hand to her head, and patted the area I had torn away. Her sunken black eyes flared, pieces of coal in an oven. The skin around the mouth stretched parchment-thin as she wailed. I shoved her against the projector, a move that startled us both, and for an instant, everything froze in time. Her body was incredibly lightweight and frail. Despite the inhuman strength she summoned, there was little more beneath the bandages than dust and bone. And, suddenly, I was not afraid.

I thrust my entire weight forward. She buckled back, the spinning gears of the projector grinding against her. The film stuttered through the sprockets and almost stopped completely before she finally pushed me off. I fell hard and scrambled to the front wall again. She took a full step and part of another toward me, then suddenly staggered back and spun to face the door. A strip of bandage stretched from her lower back to the side of the projector. It threaded messily through a series of loops on top of the film and sputtered its way across the light. She grabbed frantically at the linen, but it was already too late. She was vanishing from the waist up before my eyes.

She did not go quiet into the night. Quite the opposite. A high-pitched shriek shattered the glass separating the projection booth from the auditorium. The last of the cloth sucked through the projector, jammed in the sprockets and held firm. Metal scraped metal, dark smoke burned. Holes scorched through film and linen, small at first, then spread rapidly into a strip of flame that flared out from the bulb. It took less than two seconds for the entire reel of nitrate to ignite.

A figure lurched through the open doorway. Leopold Beaumont watched as his wife's dead flesh softened to ash and sifted to the floor, leaving only a skeleton behind. The arc lamp exploded in a flash of bluish light, mercifully shielding me from the sight of her bones collapsing to the floor.

The fire spread across the ceiling. Smoke thickened the darkness. The red hue above the exit beckoned. It was now or never. I ran toward the light.

A pair of bloody, bandaged hands materialized through the haze. I attempted to duck, tripped over several film canisters, and smashed to the floor. My Pentax broke apart beneath me. There was no time to mourn its loss. There was only pain. I scrambled forward on my knees.

My head bumped into something soft. A pair of legs.

"Jasper?"

"Get behind me, Jess."

He didn't extend a hand to help me up, and as I rose to my feet, I saw why. He was holding a heavy canister by the handle in each hand. The Universal logo stood out like a blue eye. And just above it, in a font that made it appear to be burning through the sticker, the title: *John Carpenter's The Thing*.

I stepped behind him. A piece of the cracked ceiling had fallen and was burning on the floor, keeping the creature back. Jasper advanced two steps and swung one of the canisters in the air. It struck the mummy in the jaw, knocking it into the projector. The bloody torso hissed on the hot machine. The mummy pushed off. A black oval the size of a soccer ball was charred into the wrappings.

More fiery tiles fell. The mummy retreated. Jasper threw the second canister harder than the first. It caught the mummy across the brow, smashing it back to the wall. It didn't seem to feel pain, but it definitely got pissed off. It roared like a wounded animal.

Jasper snapped up another canister, wound his arm back like a pitcher, and yelled: "Yeah, fuck you too!" It hammered the mummy in the throat, dropping it to one knee. Jasper grabbed more canisters, flung them. I joined him, tossing two full reels of something called *The Atomic Cafe*. The first one missed, but the second hit dead center in the leg. Jasper's aim was remarkably more accurate, pummelling the creature in the head and neck. It fell, momentarily stunned before rising back up. I snatched another canister and was mid-arc when Jasper grabbed my arm.

"What are you doing?"

"What?" I followed his eyeline to the label: *Blade Runner*.

"Don't you dare." He took it from me, passed me another. It was *Grease 2*. Jesus Christ, did these people not send anything back? I put my whole weight behind it. No Travolta, no thank you. Fuck that trash.

Reel 1 of *Grease 2* clobbered the mummy square in the chest. The canister burst open, and the thick black spool of film dropped out, landing at the mummy's feet like a heavy flat turd. Jasper, still holding *Blade Runner* in one hand, launched the second half of *Grease 2* with the other. At the apex of his toss, it slipped from his fingers and flew into the ceiling tiles overhead, disappearing in the smoke.

"Oh fuck!" Jasper exclaimed. I heard *Blade Runner* fall to the floor.

The mummy stepped forward. It was still hesitant of the fire, but the flames on the floor were extinguishing. In the tomb below, I had been uncertain if Leopold Beaumont had smiled as he killed his son. Now, as he staggered toward us, I had no doubt. The skin on the left side had been torn free by one of the canisters, exposing rotted teeth and strings of sinew. Lopsided, maniacal, but it was undeniable.

I reached down to grab another canister and came away empty-handed. Jasper held the last two. Both bore the same famous image of a boy on his bicycle silhouetted against the moon.

"Run," Jasper said. I almost didn't hear him. His face was eerily calm. He turned to me and smiled. "Run!"

I did. I pulled open the exit door, turned to look. Jasper threw his arms back—

"Phone home, mutherfucker!"

—and swung them forward. The canisters spiraled up and crashed through the burning tiles.

There was an enormous creaking sound as the entire room rumbled. I pressed my back into the doorframe. The ceiling above the creature collapsed in a shower of flame and debris. The crack along the floor and up the wall snapped, splitting the room into two halves. Jasper tumbled back. In front of him, the entire section that hung over the rear of the auditorium tore away and crashed below. The projector dangled over the edge, held by a pair of bolts. The mummy clung to it with one arm. The other had torn away, leaving only a stub of bone protruding through the linen.

The first bolt fractured. The projector pitched violently forward, instantly snapping the other. The whole metal beast hung in mid-air for a moment, like Wile E. Coyote, before thundering down into the cheap seats, taking Leopold Beaumont with it.

And just like that, the mummy was no more.

Jasper stood on the precipice, catching his breath. I was willing to wait, but the fire was not. Most of the inferno had fallen to the floor below, but plenty remained, and it was circling the wagons.

"Jasper!"

He didn't move. The radio crackled back to life. Or maybe it had always been there, spitting volcanic religious fervor into the night, and I had been too preoccupied to notice. Can't imagine why.

"... failure of the wicked, depravity of the weak, and corruption of the soul! That is what has occurred on this night, my fellow brothers and sisters! In Christ, we pray! For He has risen, and He has brought forth those we left behind. In Christ's name, the evildoers shall be struck down. In the name of Jesus!..."

It was time to go. I let the door swing shut and hurried over to Jasper. He was staring into the dark auditorium, mumbling to himself. I saw movement among the seats. Shadows from the flames. Except—

"...the earth cracked open, its soul laid bare! I felt it, I know you felt it too! Man playing God in the desert! Did you think He would not see from the heavens? Did you think He would idly stand by? No, I tell you! No, He did not!"

—the shadows were alive. Smoke obscured the floor, but I could see that the strewn bodies were no longer scattered there. They shuffled toward the exit, already bound in cloth for burials they never had. Some wore masks, most did not.

"They came back, Jess," Jasper said, watching them. "They fuckin' came back."

I didn't know what to say. I took his arm, and we headed out the exit.

Sirens howled from the far side of town. It was only once we hit the parking lot that we saw the cap of the dissipating mushroom cloud fifty miles to the north. Terrifying and majestic all at once. The sky above it crackled with lightning, and higher still the very fabric of reality appeared ripped open. Clouds swirled, frothing red waves in an upside-down sea. The air was on fire, black smoke riding the jet streams of the upper atmosphere, searching for a way out. You could taste it even down on the ground, where the crack in the earth ran through the Darklight and across town as far as the eye could see. Beyond that, I imagine it continued in a straight line to ground zero.

Dark and terrible things had happened at the Proving Grounds.

The front of the theater was open to the world. The glass doors were scattered across the steps in a billion little pieces. In the lobby, the recently deceased were gathering. The living were long gone.

"Still want to take a picture?"

I held up my smashed camera. "People will have to take my word for it," I said. I laughed, not even wanting to. It went on far too long and hurt like hell, but I couldn't stop. When it finally subsided, I felt tears on my cheeks. I had never been so exhausted in all my life.

All the windows of the remaining cars were gone. We climbed into the Mystery Machine after brushing the glass to the floor. Jasper turned the key in the ignition and the van sputtered to life, then died almost immediately. He tried again. This time it made a rapid *click-click-click*, not unlike the film projector before it had expired. The clicking faded out, and on the third turn of the key, there was nothing at all.

"Fuck."

I nodded.

The risen started to shuffle out of the Darklight. Toward the back, one of them dragged their left foot. The sirens were moving west now, no longer toward us. I wondered what was happening in the local cemetery out that way. You've seen *Night of the Living Dead*, right? Of course you have.

Jasper pulled the key out, pocketed it. "Want to try the Virgin Mary?"

I gazed across the parking lot at my little Gremlin, windowless and violated by the atomic shockwave.

"In a minute." I opened my purse, pulled out my notepad and pencil, turned to a fresh page. "Got any of those cigarettes left?"

Jasper smirked, did a little drum roll on his leg, and hit an imaginary cymbal in the air. He held out the pack and punched the lighter.

I started to write:

The giant man in the theater doorway...

Notes on To the Dea Sea

Since the days of Ambrose Bierce and O. Henry, a common trope in horror and suspense has been a twist ending. Classic TV shows like *The Twilight Zone* and *The Outer Limits* were built around them, ensuring you stuck it out through the commercials to the very end. Decades later, M. Night Shyamalan became a household name for his often brilliant twists, until they became a yoke around his neck he struggled to free himself from. They are easy to do but hard to do right. They have to be earned. Like a magic trick, the clues have to be there for you to see all along or it loses its magic altogether.

Some of the best twists, though, are not at the end. They are the ones that can occur anywhere in the story, keeping you on your toes *and* on the edge of your seat all at the same time. The best example is probably *Psycho*, where the twist occurs around the halfway point. Quentin Tarantino used this to equal effect in his script for *From Dusk Till Dawn*... until the movie's trailers ruined it. Vampires – they ruin everything.

There are no vampires in the following script. Those come later.

Spoiler alert!

TO THE DEAD SEA

FADE IN:

EXT. MOUNTAIN FOREST - DAWN

A SERIES OF SHOTS: *the sun cresting the horizon; low mist in the trees; a still pond; a log CABIN in a clearing.*

INT. LOG CABIN - CONTINUOUS

CLOSE ON a typewriter. A pair of hands type: *"The years teach much which the days never know. -- Ralph Waldo Emerson"*

CLOSE ON a man's tired eyes, creasing in the corners.

A SERIES OF SHOTS: *a kettle boils on a wood stove; coffee poured into a mug; stirring.*

EXT. LOG CABIN - CONTINUOUS

The door opens and WASHINGTON CARVER, 45, walks onto the patio carrying a coffee, his greying beard a contrast to his thick, dark hair. He leans on the rail, stares out at the mist on the water. The forest is eerily quiet.

Carver sips his coffee. From behind him, a woman -
MARYANNE, 40's - speaks almost in a whisper:

>   MARYANNE (O.S.)
>   It's really good, Wash.

He lowers his head, eyes closed.

>   CARVER
>   Is it?

>   MARYANNE (O.S.)
>   Yes. You know it is.

>   CARVER
>   You always say that.

>   MARYANNE (O.S.)
>   This time it's true.

Carver grins, gives a subtle head shake.

>   CARVER
>   Thanks.

>   MARYANNE (O.S.)
>   Wash?

>   CARVER
>   I know.

>   MARYANNE (O.S.)
>   It's time to go.

He nods, straightens and eventually turns.

There is no one there.

INT. LOG CABIN - A LITTLE LATER

CLOSE ON the typewriter. The page rolls back, just
above the quote. A key inches forward, hesitates,
falls back. A second later - a series of strikes.

The page is rolled out and laid on a stack of
others, several hundred thick. Above the quote, it
now reads:

"For Maryanne..."

A SERIES OF SHOTS: *the manuscript is wrapped with
an elastic, placed in a shoebox; clothes are packed
in a duffel bag; water is poured on the fireplace;
a date is crossed off on a calendar - just like all
the previous.*

EXT. LOG CABIN - A LITTLE LATER

Carver opens the door to his pick-up truck, throws
the duffel in the back seat, gets in. He wipes dust
off the windshield. He turns the key. The vehicle dry
heaves, does not start. He gets out, pops the hood.

A moment later he re-enters the truck, starts it.

EXT. DIRT ROAD - MORNING - LATER

The truck moves through the forest, kicking up dust.

EXT. DIRT ROAD - LATER

The truck hits a bump, hiccups along, finally dies.

Carver gets out, pops the hood. Smoke billows up.
He waves it away. He fidgets with the engine.
He turns the key. Nothing. Back to the engine.
Fidgets. Turns key. Again - nothing. He stands
staring into the engine for a long time. He slams
the hood down.

EXT. DIRT ROAD - A LITTLE LATER

Carver walks, bag over his shoulder. He comes to an
overgrown car path off the main road. He takes it.

EXT. A RUNDOWN CABIN - MOMENTS LATER

Carver enters a clearing. An old cabin sits
surrounded by enough rusted parts to assemble a
complete ginger vehicle.

Carver peers inside a grimy window. He stands back.

                    CARVER
          Hello? Anyone home?

Silence. Carver takes a couple of steps back,
glances around. He walks back, knocks on the door.

                    CARVER (cont'd)
          Hello? Truck broke down
          about a mile back...
          Hello?

Silence. He turns the knob. Locked. He steps back,
considers his options, turns to the path again.

From inside the cabin, there is a very faint THUD.

Carver stops, listens. The THUD comes again. He
approaches, the THUDS echoing his footsteps,
growing more determined.

                    CARVER (cont'd)
          Hello?

He rattles the door. He presses an ear to it. The
banging increases. He goes to the window, peers
inside. Nothing.

Around back - another window. A shadow moves inside.

                    CARVER (cont'd)
          Hey! You okay in there?

The banging stops. He leans toward the glass--

A bloody hand HITS the window. He jumps. The hand
slides slowly away, leaving a trail.

Back at the door, he shoves his weight against it.
On the third try it bursts inward. Carver stumbles
to the floor.

INT. RUNDOWN CABIN - CONTINUOUS

He picks himself up. The interior is filthy, dark.
Ratty curtains hang in the windows, garbage and old
newspapers are strewn about the main room. The door
to a second room is ajar. From inside - a whimper
followed by a sob.

Carver stands at the bedroom door...

                    CARVER
          Hello?

... and pushes it in.

EMILY, 18 - a pale face hidden under a tangled mess
of black and purple hair - is slumped on the floor
by a bed. A torn, dirty tank top and a short black
skirt fail to conceal her many bruises. One foot is
bare, the other clad in a lace-up boot. Blood drips
down her left arm from an unseen wound. All of this
is lost on Carver. He only sees two things:

The HANDCUFF binding her to the steel bed frame.

The duct tape covering her mouth.

                    CARVER (cont'd)
          What the fuck?

He crouches. She recoils, scrambling on to the
mattress.

> CARVER (cont'd)
> Shh, it's OK. I'm not
> gonna hurt you.

Carver looks nervously around.

> CARVER (cont'd)
> Who did this to you?

Emily's eyes dart around. Carver peels the tape.

> EMILY
> Please... He's coming
> back...

> CARVER
> Who's coming back?

> EMILY
> Please...

She sobs, rattling the handcuff against the rail.

Carver looks for something to free her with.
He vaguely notices the myriad of newspapers
everywhere, pushes them aside in his search. He
starts to leave the room--

> EMILY (cont'd)
> No, no, no, no.

> CARVER
> It's okay. I'll be right
> back.

> EMILY
> He's coming back!

                    CARVER
         I'm going to get you out
         of here. I promise. What's
         your name?

She strains to peer out the window. She turns, scared.

                    EMILY
              Em... Emily.

He gives her a comforting smile.

                    CARVER
         Okay, Emily. I'm gonna get
         something to free you and
         then we're gone.

He enters the main room. Among the debris on the
counter, he finds a screwdriver. He hurries back,
gets to work.

                    EMILY
         Hurry. He's coming back.

                    CARVER
         I believe you. We're not
         gonna be here when he does.
         Okay?

He tries prying the links apart. They refuse.

                    CARVER (cont'd)
         There a phone around here?
         We need to get the cops
         out here.

                    EMILY
         There are none.

                    CARVER
              What?

                    EMILY
          He said they were all
          gone.

                    CARVER
          Gone? Gone where?

He tosses the screwdriver in the corner with a curse.

Back in the main room, he spots a wooden handle
sticking out among logs by the fireplace. He pulls
it free: An AXE.

In the bedroom, he shows her the axe. It elicits a
hopeful sob. Emily looks away as Carver raises the
axe to strike the chain--

--A large dirty HAND grasps his wrist.

Carver spins around. A fist PLOWS into his face. The
world goes dark as he falls to the floor, Emily's
scream fading him out like water down a drain.

IN THE BLACK:

                    MARYANNE (O.S.)
          Time to go...

Then, as WE FADE IN:

                    BOLGER (O.S.)
          I seen you.

INT. RUNDOWN CABIN - DAY

Carver's blurry eyes open, focus on the hulking
man standing over him. This is FRANK BOLGER: 30's,
fucked-up, filthy, a beast of a man. He's glaring
down, rubbing his scruffy chin the way men do when
contemplating dark deeds.

Carver slides back as far as the bedpost. He cranes
his head around to see Emily cowering in the corner
of the bed, mouth taped, a fresh bruise on one eye.

Bolger wipes a large drizzle of mucus from his
nose. The nostrils are red and raw, eyes bloodshot
and wet.

                    BOLGER
          I said: I seen you.

                    CARVER
          The fuck you talking
          about? You're in some
          pretty deep shit here--

Bolger PUNCHES him in the mouth. Carver winces,
spits blood. Bolger steps back, sits in a chair by
the bed.

                    BOLGER
          In the grocery store. You
          was on the back of a book.

Carver looks for the axe, struggles to sit up.

                    BOLGER (cont'd)
          Guess you wrote it.

                    CARVER
             (wincing)
          Brilliant.

Bolger pulls out a handkerchief, blows his nose.

                    BOLGER
          Never killed no one famous
          before. Figure you must be
          famous, your face bein' on
          the back of books an' all.

>   CARVER
>   Look, I don't know what's
>   goin' on here, but you can
>   still do right by it, okay.
>   Let us go and no one will
>   ever know we were here.
>   Swear to God.

Bolger leans, looks from Carver to Emily and back
again.

>   BOLGER
>   You think I'm stupid?

Carver wipes blood from his nose, says nothing.

>   BOLGER (cont'd)
>   Yeah... you do.

Bolger slowly grins. He stands and throws a PUNCH
into Carver's jaw. Carver slumps into the floor,
groaning. He turns his head, about to push back up
when he spots something beneath the bed: <u>the axe.</u>

Carver splays his arms out, reaches. An inch shy.

Bolger presses a boot to Carver's back. Carver
yells, but reaches the handle just as Bolger drags
him away.

Bolger flips Carver over and the axe SLAMS down
into Bolger's boot so hard it embeds all the way
to the floor. Bolger howls. Carver tackles him and
gets a single punch in before Bolger gets his arms
up and tosses Carver back.

Carver crashes into the bed, falls to the floor. He
lunges, grabs the axe, yanks it from the boot and
smashes it into Bolger's chest with a sickening thud.

Bolger spits blood, eyes bulge with rage. He pries
the axe free. Carver ducks as the big man swings.

Bolger advances, blood gushing down his chest.

Carver KICKS him in the knee, buckling it back. The force of Bolger's swing throws the big man forward, toppling toward the end of the bed. The axe flies out of his hand, embedding the wall inches from Emily's face. She screams.

Bolger impacts the bedpost with all his weight. The steel gores his throat, protrudes out the back of his neck. He slumps, the post holding him up like a dead man praying.

For a moment, Carver just stares at the body. Then he stands, grabs the axe out of the wall, holds Emily by the wrist, and strikes the chain. It breaks. She wraps herself around him tightly. He consoles her.

She suddenly sees Bolger and begins to kick at the corpse savagely. Carver pulls her out of the room.

                    CARVER
          Emily, listen to me: we
          have to get to town and
          tell them what happened--

                    EMILY
          You killed him.

                    CARVER
          Yeah. I did.

He lets her go, looks around the room. He sees blood on his hands, wipes it on newspaper from the floor.

                    EMILY
          No one's gonna miss him.

                    CARVER
          We still have to report
          it.

71

                    EMILY
          There's no one to tell--

                    CARVER
          You keep saying that.

She is quiet, staring at the blood-caked paper in
his hands. He looks at it, tosses it aside.

                    CARVER (cont'd)
          He can't hurt you anymore.
          People are probably
          looking for you. Your
          family, friends--

                    EMILY
          They're dead.

                    CARVER
          Did he tell you that? Or
          was it... before? Look at
          me. You're in shock, okay.
          It's nat--

                    EMILY
          Before. I remember. They
          got sick.

Carver looks in her eyes: bloodshot, haunted, scared.

                    CARVER
          Sick? All of them?

                    EMILY
          Yes.

                    CARVER
          With what?

She does not answer, just points to the crumpled
paper on the floor. He turns. The blood is drying
quickly to an ugly brown. He picks it up, opens it.

The headline is bold and large and partially hidden below the blood.

>   CARVER (cont'd)
>   The hell..?

He wipes blood away and just stares at the words for a moment: **CURE FAILS HUMAN TRIALS**. And below in smaller print: **DEATH TOLL SURPASSES ONE BILLION WORLDWIDE**.

Carver looks at Emily, awash in confusion. He eyes the date on the page: three months earlier. Then he sees headlines within the stacks of papers everywhere. He is horrified.

>   EMILY
>   You didn't know?

It is barely a question. Carver shakes his head.

>   CARVER
>   I've been here, on the
>   mountain. Writing... I...
>   I-- It's-- Jesus, how?

He leans on the table, overwhelmed.

>   CARVER (cont'd)
>   This can't be right.
>   How...? How bad did it
>   get?

>   EMILY
>   I don't know. I don't know
>   how long it's been.

She sits at the table.

>   EMILY (cont'd)
>   But it was fast. They
>   stopped burying the
>   bodies. Just burning them.

                    CARVER
          Christ.

                    EMILY
          Even the babies.

He looks up, anguished. He grabs a bunch of
newspapers. He sees Bolger's truck outside the door.

                    CARVER
          We need to get to town
          and... Jesus. This is
          crazy.

He takes her by the elbow, guides her to her feet.

                    CARVER (cont'd)
          We need to find others
          and--

He stops suddenly, staring toward the bedroom.
Bolger - or what used to be him - stands in the
doorway, looking down, blood oozing from a gaping
hole in his neck.

Emily screams. Bolger looks up, his grim face ashen
and stained with blood, his hollow eyes surprised
to see them.

The moment is brief. Bolger charges hungrily, teeth
gnashing, hands clawing the air.

Carver puts himself between the monster and the girl.
He grabs Bolger's wrists, momentum knocking him down
as Bolger's oozing mouth SNAPS at Carver's face.

Suddenly, Emily runs out of the bedroom wielding
the axe. She SLAMS it down into the top of Bolger's
head. He stiffens, falls forward on top of Carver,
motionless.

Emily helps Carver crawl out from under the body. He catches his breath, nudges the body with his boot.

> CARVER (cont'd)
> Thank you.

> EMILY
> (dazed)
> Sure.

He pulls the axe out of Bolger's head.

> CARVER
> Tell me everything you
> know.

INT. BOLGER'S PICKUP - MORNING - LATER

Emily flips through newspapers. Carver drives, fidgets with the radio. Static on static.

> CARVER
> No emergency signal,
> nothing.

> EMILY
> There was a radio in the
> cabin. He used to leave it
> on when he went out.

Carver lowers the volume. He looks at her.

> EMILY (cont'd)
> Then one day, it just
> stopped. For a while there
> was a message, on a loop.
> Just a recording. But it
> was something at least.
> Another voice in the air.

Carver faces the road. Then he shuts the radio off.

                    CARVER
          You said they were burning
          bodies. Why?

                    EMILY
          People were dying so fast.

                    CARVER
          You never got sick? Were
          you quarantined?

                    EMILY
          No.

                    CARVER
          But your family did. How
          did you not?

                    EMILY
          I don't know.

Carver considers it. Emily glances through an article.

                    EMILY (cont'd)
          Says here that it mutated.
          At first, it was only
          passed through fluids, but
          by the time they figured
          it out, it was already
          moving through the air.
          There was no way to
          contain it.
               (turns page)
          They estimated it had a
          98.4% mortality rate. Why
          not just say 100%?

                    CARVER
          No virus is ever 100%
          efficient. Some people are
          just genetically immune.
          Some develop resistance

CARVER (cont'd)
later. Every plague has
had survivors. Viruses are
resilient, always
adapting. But so are we.

EMILY
We?

CARVER
People. Human beings.

EMILY
You a doctor or something?

Carver checks his mirrors, gazes at his weary
reflection.

CARVER
In another life, yeah.

Emily puts the papers down for a moment, watching
the horizon roll by. In the distance, a <u>heavy fog</u>
threatens.

EMILY
He said he saw you on a
book. What did he mean?

CARVER
I wrote a novel a few
years ago. The right
people liked it. Then a
whole lot more. One book
led to another.

EMILY
And here you are.

CARVER
(quietly)
Here I am.

She turns away, rubbing her scarred wrists. The
broken cuffs clink against each other like cheap,
unwanted jewelry.

>   EMILY
>   I never thanked you.

>   CARVER
>   Don't worry about it.

>   EMILY
>   It's fucked up.

>   CARVER
>   What is?

>   EMILY
>   The world. Everything in
>   it.

>   CARVER
>   Yeah.

They are quiet for a moment.

>   EMILY
>   How long were you on the
>   mountain?

>   CARVER
>   Almost a year.

>   EMILY
>   No TV, no phone?

>   CARVER
>   No.

>   EMILY
>   Not even a radio?

                    CARVER
          No. It's the only way I
          can work.

                    EMILY
          You didn't find it scary,
          even at night, being all
          alone in the dark?

Carver considers her, frowns.

                    CARVER
          At first, maybe, yeah.
          But...

                    EMILY
          What?

                    CARVER
          It always felt scarier
          down here.

She sees blood in the creases of her knuckles, rubs
it.

                    EMILY
                 (quietly)
          Yeah. Maybe.

The truck screeches to a halt. Emily looks up at
Carver, then to the road ahead.

They are just outside of town. Several cars fill the
road, blocking it. There are no signs of life anywhere.

                    EMILY (cont'd)
          We can't go around?

                    CARVER
          No.
                 (looks back)
          You remember seeing an
          exit?

She shakes her head.

> CARVER (cont'd)
> Dammit.

He leans forward, peers out the window. The horn
BLARES, he jumps back. They stare at each other,
neither sure what to expect. Slowly, they turn and
look at the town ahead.

Nothing and no one seems to have noticed them.
Carver points to the glove box.

> CARVER (cont'd)
> Look in there. See if
> there's a gun.

She looks. It only contains napkins and scratched
lotto tickets. A lot of tickets. She shuts it.

> EMILY
> What now?

> CARVER
> (gets out)
> We walk. Load up on
> supplies. Try and find
> another vehicle out of
> here.

> EMILY
> Where to?

> CARVER
> East. Nearest city by the
> sea, I figure. There have
> to be people there. It
> can't be as bad as it
> seems.
> (beat)
> Can't be.

EXT. TOWN ROAD - MOMENTS LATER

They head into town, checking vehicles for weapons
and supplies, talking as they go:

>   EMILY
>   Did you have a family?

>   CARVER
>   My wife, Maryanne, she
>   died five years ago. Car
>   accident.

>   EMILY
>   Is that when you...
>   started coming up here?

>   CARVER
>   Yeah.

He rifles through the glove box, shuts it, leans out.

>   CARVER (cont'd)
>   Find anything useful?

He squints into the back seat. When Emily does not
answer, he looks across the top of the car.

Emily exits the passenger seat of another car.
She's holding a blood-stained doll, her eyes
fixated on it.

>   CARVER (cont'd)
>   You okay?

>   EMILY
>   My sister had one just
>   like it. I won it for her
>   at the fair. She called it
>   Charlie. I told her that
>   was a stupid name for a
>   girl. She didn't care.

Emily starts to cry. It overwhelms her. She wipes
tears angrily away.

> EMILY (cont'd)
> But it is, right?

> CARVER
> Sure, Em.

> EMILY
> Don't know why I told her
> that. I didn't even mean
> it. Just stupid sibling
> stuff, you know? She was
> always putting names on
> things that didn't belong.
> She tried to name our cat
> Einstein. I told her that
> was stupid too. She said
> it couldn't be stupid
> because he was so smart.
> Einstein, I mean. Not the
> cat. The cat was an idiot.

She giggles, then sobs.

> EMILY (cont'd)
> I should have told her it
> was brilliant. Just once
> before she was gone. I
> should have told her...

Carver walks around the car, puts a hand on her
shoulder.

> EMILY (cont'd)
> She never knew how
> brilliant she was. She
> never got to shine. And no
> one will ever know.

She breaks, cries into his chest. He holds her,
comforting. After a moment, he lets go, looks at her.

> CARVER
> Leave the doll. It'll just
> keep hurting if you don't.
> Understand?

She is confused, but his face continues to harden
and it sinks in: The world is moving on with or
without her.

She looks at the doll and nods. She drops it on the
ground, then kicks it under the car. She glances
around. Everything is quiet and still. The horizon
is gray with imminent fog.

> EMILY
> God, this really happened,
> didn't it?

Carver sighs, frowns at the dark horizon.

> CARVER
> Come on. We have a lot to
> do.

EXT. A MEDICAL CLINIC - DAY - LATER

Carver and Emily approach the front door. He
pulls on the handle and it opens. He lets it go,
surprised.

> EMILY
> Something wrong?

> CARVER
> No. Just expected it to be
> locked.

> EMILY
> Think anyone's inside?

Carver hesitates, glances back to the empty town
streets.

> CARVER
> This whole place feels...

> EMILY
> Dead.

Carver nods sourly. He pulls the door open. They enter.

INT. MEDICAL CLINIC

Blood stains the walls. Files and supplies are
scattered about. Empty pill bottles litter the
floor and desks. Carver picks one up, inspects it
and lets it drop.

> CARVER
> Shit.

> EMILY
> What are we looking for
> anyway?

> CARVER
> Antibiotics. Emergency
> supplies. Anything that
> might be useful.

> EMILY
> Weapons are useful. This
> is just shit.

> CARVER
> We'll look for those, too.
> I'm more concerned about
> what happens if you get
> hurt than hurting someone
> else.

                    EMILY
         First do no harm, right?

                    CARVER
         Something like that.

They split up, checking the examining rooms. They re-
emerge with little more than before: some gauze and
bandages, a scalpel, a handful of white medical masks.

                    CARVER (cont'd)
         Keep looking. We weren't
         the first to come through,
         but you never know.

They find a locked closet. Carver tries to force it.

                    CARVER (cont'd)
         Fuck.

                    EMILY
         Why would they lock just
         this?

                    CARVER
         Exactly. My guess is this
         is where the high-risk
         stuff is kept.

                    EMILY
         In a broom closet?

                    CARVER
         If you were a tweaker,
         where's the last place
         you'd look?

She gives him a "good point" shrug. Carver THRUSTS
his foot at the door. It cracks and opens. They
peer inside.

Pitch black. A figure suddenly lurches out at them. Carver barely has time to get his hands up to hold it back.

Carver falls against the hallway wall, a decaying CORPSE biting at him hungrily. Emily grabs a broom from the closet and smashes the corpse across the head. The creature falls away, gnashing at Carver's leg, missing by a hair. Carver scrambles up. He STOMPS his heavy boot on the corpse's head, crushing it with a sickening wet thud.

Emily looks away, disgusted. The closet is just that - a closet. Nothing but cleaning supplies.

> EMILY
> At least we know why it was
> locked.

Carver notices the corpse is wearing a lab coat. He reads the name tag to himself.

> EMILY (cont'd)
> Maybe she locked herself
> in. You know, when it was
> too late... First do no
> harm and stuff.

Carver straightens, rubs his head.

> CARVER
> Was this happening before
> you were taken?

> EMILY
> No. People were just
> dying... not coming back.

> CARVER
> You're sure?

> EMILY
> I think I'd remember
> something like that, don't
> you?

Carver frowns. He heads to the front of the clinic.

> CARVER
> Here.
> (passes a mask)
> This is bad. Seriously
> bad. I don't even know how
> a virus could mutate to
> this. But if it has, it
> might spread differently
> now and you might not be
> immune anymore. We have to
> be careful.

He puts his mask on. She slowly does the same.

> CARVER (cont'd)
> Assuming we aren't
> infected already. The next
> time we find a locked door
> be thankful... and keep
> moving.

EXT. TOWN STREET - LATER

Carver and Emily approach a small house. A truck is
in the driveway. She carries their supply knapsack.

> EMILY
> Shouldn't we have seen
> more like her?

> CARVER
> You said they burned the
> bodies.

                    EMILY
          They couldn't have burned
          them all. So where are
          they?

Carver looks inside the truck. He throws his duffel
bag in, takes her pack and does the same.

                    CARVER
          Sit. Let me check those
          wounds.

The handcuffs have chafed her wrists raw. She sits
on the front seat, facing him. He takes a few
supplies from his bag, opens a bottle of peroxide,
pours it on some cotton.

                    EMILY
          Is this gonna hurt?

Carver holds one wrist gently.

                    CARVER
          Look at me.

She does. He gives a gentle smile. As he presses the
swab to the wound, he never takes his eyes off hers.

                    CARVER (cont'd)
          Where would you go? If you
          were sick?

                    EMILY
              (hissing)
          That sick? Hospital.

                    CARVER
          This far gone? You know
          it's over. No. You go
          home.

He checks the wound, wraps gauze around it.

                    EMILY
        Home?

                    CARVER
        Yeah. You'd want to be
        with family.

She nods, looks at the bandage as he preps for the
next.

                    EMILY
        They all died in their
        beds.

He lifts her chin to face him.

                    CARVER
        Look at me.

He presses peroxide to flesh. She winces, stronger.

                    EMILY
        Jesus, it's like the
        fucking Old Testament.
        Wrath of God shit.

Carver grunts.

                    EMILY (cont'd)
        What?

                    CARVER
        Doubt He had anything to
        do with it.

                    EMILY
        A doctor _and_ an atheist?
        Never saw that coming.

Carver puts the peroxide away, begins to wrap her
wrist.

                    CARVER
         I'm not an atheist. But
         you're right - I used to
         be. You know what Doctors
         Without Borders is?

Emily nods.

                    CARVER (cont'd)
         My third time out was
         Darfur - this decimated
         region in the Sudan.
         Famine at first. Then
         genocide. The world's
         fucked up, and we fucked
         it, so if it bites back,
         well, we deal with it and
         move on. But one religion
         trying to wipe out
         another, there's no
         bandaging that up. We were
         just a tourniquet, but
         some bleeding can't be
         stopped. Hundreds of
         thousands of lives just
         seeping into the ground...

Carver frowns, chews his lip. Then he shrugs.

                    CARVER (cont'd)
         Four months in - I was
         done. Just empty inside,
         you know? And my lingering
         thought on the flight home
         was that God doesn't
         exist. We've been doing
         this to each other since
         we first saw our
         reflection in a puddle of
         mud and realized the
         person next to us looks
         different. And He's never

> CARVER (cont'd)
> intervened. Why is that?
> Gods don't sit on fences.
> You're either for
> something or against it,
> and if you're against it,
> you do something about
> it.
> (beat)
> Then one day about three
> years later, I'm seeing
> this patient - young girl,
> much younger than you -
> for a routine eye exam and
> I notice something in the
> iris, like a flaw, but not.
> So I order some tests.
> She had a brain tumor.
> And I knew: that's God's
> handiwork, His style. All
> that big, newsworthy shit -
> He doesn't have a hand in
> it at all. That's all us.
> He's just as shocked as we
> are.

Carver finishes the dressing, helps her down.

> EMILY
> If you think all that,
> then why do you think He
> wouldn't stop it?

Carver walks to the front door and opens it slowly.

> CARVER
> He probably thinks we
> deserve it.

INT. HOUSE - HALLWAY

A hallway runs the length of the main floor. They

pass the living room on one side and a kitchenette
on the other. The rest of the doors are closed.
They stop at the first.

>   EMILY
>   (quietly)
>   I think a part of you died
>   with that little girl.

>   CARVER
>   She didn't die.

>   EMILY
>   What?

>   CARVER
>   It went into remission.
>   She survived.

He turns the knob, stops. His face softens.

>   CARVER (cont'd)
>   Don't look for God in all
>   this, Em. It's in the
>   small stuff. In here.

He points to her heart.

>   CARVER (cont'd)
>   In the fact you're still
>   here.

Carver opens the bedroom door...

On the bed: the decaying, still bodies of an elderly
couple, one behind the other, holding tight. They
could almost be sleeping... except for a splatter of
blood on the headboard. And the gun on the floor.

A sharp, surprised sob escapes Emily. Carver closes
the door respectfully. Emily hurries out.

EXT. HOUSE

Carver finds her crying on the front step. He sits.

> CARVER
> You okay?

Carver eyes the road. Fog is weaving through town.

> CARVER (cont'd)
> I imagine we'll see a lot
> of that. And worse.

> EMILY
> I know.
> (looks at him)
> I'm not weak.

> CARVER
> I know that.

> EMILY
> I don't want you to think
> I'll slow you down or get
> you killed or...

Carver studies her for a moment.

> CARVER
> I'd think you were more
> dead than they were, Em,
> if you hadn't reacted.
> It's okay to feel bad for
> them.

> EMILY
> I don't even know them,
> it's just--

> CARVER
> They're at peace. Remember
> that when you think on it
> later. And you will.

He takes her hand in his and squeezes it.

>   CARVER (cont'd)
>   Just keep moving forward.
>   You won't slow me down. I
>   promise.

She looks at him, squeezes his hand back. She nods.

>   EMILY
>   I hope I go like that, in
>   my sleep.

>   CARVER
>   Don't think about that.
>   Come on. We need to find
>   food. It might be a while
>   before the next town.

EXT. STORE - LATER

Carver pulls the pickup into a store parking lot.
The fog has settled in now, concealing most of the
town beyond.

Carver gets out, grabs his duffel from the back.
He unzips it, pauses - the manuscript sits just
inside.

Emily comes around to his side, sees the shoe box.

>   EMILY
>   What's that?

>   CARVER
>   The mountain.

>   EMILY
>   Huh?

                    CARVER
         It's what I call it.
         My book. It's what they
         were all called at one
         point...

He reaches underneath the shoe box, removes a small
pocket knife. He zips up the duffel.

                    EMILY
         What will you call it for
         real?

Carver closes the truck door slowly.

                    CARVER
         I just realized it doesn't
         matter anymore.

Emily is unsure what to say. Carver heads to the
front glass door and pulls on it. It is locked.

Emily lowers her mask as he tugs the handle again.

                    EMILY
         So we move on, right?

                    CARVER
         We need food. Food trumps
         all.

                    EMILY
         Guess that makes sense.

She starts pulling on the door with him.

                    EMILY (cont'd)
         It's glass. Let's just
         break it.

She spots a large rock, picks it up. Carver stops her.

> CARVER
> I have a better idea.

EXT. STORE - BACK ENTRANCE - MOMENTS LATER

Carver checks the handle. Locked. He has a crowbar from the truck, wedges it in the frame. The door pops open.

INT. STORE

They emerge from the back into the main store: small with barren shelves. Emily gags, quickly raises her mask.

> CARVER
> I told you to keep that
> on.

> EMILY
> Sorry. What's that smell?

> CARVER
> Rotting meat. Vegetables
> maybe.

> EMILY
> So that's what the end of
> the world smells like:
> Like a shit took a shit.

Carver pulls a paperback from a spinning rack. He holds it up to her. His name is across the top.

> CARVER
> Maybe it's just this.

> EMILY
> Clever.

He drops it without another thought. He grabs a few

canned goods off a shelf and a large bottle of--

> EMILY (cont'd)
> Hey! I love these things!

At the front, she holds up a bag of Gobstoppers.

> CARVER
> You've never watched a kid
> choking on one.

Even behind the mask he can tell she's beaming like a child. He lets it go.

> EMILY
> Were you always such a
> Debbie Down--Holy shit, is
> that vodka?

He forgot he was holding the bottle. He holds it up.

> EMILY (cont'd)
> Guess we're set for--

A hand SLAPS the window behind her. Emily squeals and spins around, the open bag of candy SPILLING to the floor. Several over-sized balls dribble out and roll down the aisles.

Outside, one of the DEAD emerges from the thick fog and bangs on the glass, leaving bloody prints. Blood has caked around its eyes. Emily takes a step toward it, fascinated.

Carver rushes to Emily and pulls her back.

> EMILY (cont'd)
> Hey, what the fuck?

> CARVER
> Really?

Bothered, she reaches down and grabs the candy.

> EMILY
> It's not like I was
> opening the door.

Carver stares at the bloody handprints.

> CARVER
> I don't think doors matter
> to them anymore.

TWO MORE have gathered. Several OTHERS breach the fog. The three at the window begin to hit it more aggressively.

> CARVER (cont'd)
> We need to go. Grab what
> you can.

Carver reaches over the counter, grabs a bag and tosses his items in it. Emily continues to stare out the window.

> CARVER (cont'd)
> Em, come on!

> EMILY
> Just look at them...

Carver stops what he's doing and grabs her arm.

> CARVER
> No. No! Come on!

She pulls free, but follows him through the aisle, grabbing things as she goes, glancing back to the window.

At the rear door, Carver peers outside. It's clear as far as he can see... which isn't far.

                    CARVER (cont'd)
          We have to get to the
          truck before they overrun
          us.

He leans out to see around the side, turns back.

                    CARVER (cont'd)
          I can't see the truck, but
          I think I can make it.

                    EMILY
          Are you gonna leave me?

                    CARVER
          What? Jesus, no.

                    EMILY
          I'm sorry. I just...

He holds her head, leans in and kisses her forehead.

                    CARVER
          We're getting out of here.
          Together. I'm not leaving
          you, Em. Together.

                    EMILY
          Together.

                    CARVER
          Good.

He pulls the door open just as the sound of
SHATTERING GLASS reaches them from the front. Emily
screams. They rush to the corner and peer around.

                    CARVER (cont'd)
          Fuck.

Many shapes move in the heavy fog. The truck is
barely visible for a moment, then swallowed up.

                    EMILY
          What are we waiting for?

                    CARVER
          Getting there's not the
          issue. Being trapped
          inside the truck worries
          me.

She looks past his shoulder, straining to see.

                    EMILY
          Better there than out
          here.

Carver watches as several of the dead move in
and out of sight toward the front of the store,
followed by the sound of more GLASS BREAKING.

                    CARVER
          Did you shut the door on
          the way out?

                    EMILY
          There wasn't time...

                    CARVER
          Shit.

But it is too late. A bloody hand GRABS her hair,
snapping the mask free. Emily screams, falling back
into the fog. Carver tackles the CORPSE off of her.
More DEAD follow.

                    CARVER (cont'd)
          RUN!

Emily scrambles to her feet and races to the truck.
Carver stands. A DOZEN more of the dead have
reached him. They tear at his clothes, trying to
get to the flesh.

At the truck, Emily opens the door, climbs in. She looks back, expecting Carver to be there. He is not. Just fog swirling into her wake. On the other side of the truck, the dead push farther into the building. Several bump into the hood and bounce away. She reaches across to lock the driver's door. Her arm hits the horn. It ECHOES loudly.

Emily freezes, stares toward the building...

... where the dead have stopped. And then they turn.

EXT. ALLEY

Carver kicks one of the DEAD against the wall. Another clings, gnashes at his neck. Carver heaves back into the wall. CRUNCH! It falls. Carver stomps its head.

Many arrive. Hands claw out of the fog. Carver turns--

The way ahead is blocked.

INT./EXT. TRUCK

Emily watches in horror as the dead shuffle toward her with hungry, twitching mouths and limbs. She raises a shaking hand toward the door lock. Too far. She is forced to lean.

She fumbles the lock. And then it mercifully clicks in place. She raises her head.

The truck is surrounded.

EXT. ALLEY

Carver runs down the alley to the fence, pushing the dead out of the way. More scramble out the door. Carver climbs.

One of the dead grabs his leg and leans in to bite.

INT./EXT. TRUCK

Emily curls into the seat as the dead assault the truck. Suddenly, a rotting face hits violently against the driver's side window and falls, a pocket knife jutting out of the back. A familiar face appears: Carver.

Carver shoves one of the dead away, retrieves his knife, then grabs for the door. It does not open. He stares from Emily to the lock and back to her.

> CARVER
> Em! Open the door!

He ducks just in time to sidestep a lumbering corpse.

> CARVER (cont'd)
> Em!

She blinks, unlocks the door, swings it open.

The corpse lunges inside, gnashing at her. She scrambles across the seat, KICKING it in the face.

Carver grabs it by the neck and yanks it out of the truck. He jumps in and slams the door.

In moments, they are swarmed. Carver jams the key in the ignition. The truck jerks forward, then back, knocking bodies. There are too many. The truck grinds to a halt.

> EMILY
> What now?

Carver looks at the gears, throws it into 4-wheel drive.

                    CARVER
           Fuck this town.

He floors the gas. The truck SLAMS forward,
crunching bodies and THROWING others out of the
way. Once clear, he turns the truck toward the
road. As they speed away through the fog, Emily
leans out her window, gives the town the finger.

INT./EXT. TRUCK -- LATER

Racing along the highway. The fog has thinned.

Carver wipes blood from his face, trying to see the
road. Emily watches him. He avoids looking at her.

                    EMILY
           You mad?

Carver sighs, looks out the side window.

                    EMILY (cont'd)
           You're mad.

                    CARVER
           No.

                    EMILY
           You told me to run.

                    CARVER
           I know.

She looks at her hands fidgeting in her lap.

                    EMILY
           I thought they were going
           to get in.

He starts to respond, changes his mind. He stares
back out the window. A moment later, he looks at
her, up and down.

> CARVER
> Are you hurt? Did any of
> them bite or scratch you?

His concern brings a small smile to her face.

> EMILY
> First do no harm, right?

> CARVER
> Try locking me out again.

Her smile fades. He slowly grins. She sticks her hands in her coat pocket. She notices something, brings it out:

The bag of candy.

She grunts and plops a Gobstopper in her mouth.

> EMILY
> Want one?

Carver looks over, gives a disgusted head shake.

> CARVER
> Did we manage to get any
> real food?

Emily pulls a few cans from a bag. Carver eyes them.

> CARVER (cont'd)
> What's that? Olives?
> Jesus.

She mumbles something about "marbles". Carver frowns. She apologetically plucks the Gobstopper out.

> EMILY
> Sorry... We can make
> martinis...

> CARVER
> I dropped the vodka. What
> else?

> EMILY
> Tuna, more olives, couple
> of bars - you like Twix?

> CARVER
> Sure.

She opens it, passes him a piece. He takes it. She
puts the Gobstopper back in her mouth. He turns
back to the road --

--and slams on the brakes, swerving the truck.
Something impacts the hood and falls away - a BODY.
The truck spins and skids into the ditch before
coming to a stop. Carver hits his head on the
wheel, setting off the horn.

Carver leans back, dazed, bleeding from the head.
Emily's hand reaches out and jerkily clutches his
shoulder.

He looks at her hand - reaching, grasping. Then he
sees why:

She is choking. Badly.

> CARVER (cont'd)
> Em?

He unsnaps his seatbelt, leans across. Her
eyes bulge. She clasps at her throat, her skin
darkening. No air!

Carver tries to keep her calm. He holds her head
back, but she resists. He pushes harder, pulling
her jaw down.

> CARVER (cont'd)
> I can't see it! I can't
> see it. Em...

She thrashes, terrified. He reaches a finger into
her mouth to pry the candy free. It's too far in.
In her terror, she tries to fight him off. He
presses on.

> CARVER (cont'd)
> Emily, listen to me! I
> have to get it out. You're
> going to pass out in a
> moment.

She shakes her head, tearing at her own
throat. Carver kicks open his door to get more
maneuverability. He undoes Emily's seatbelt, grabs
her around the waste, turns her around. He pulls
forcefully into her abdomen. Her body heaves
forward, but to no avail. Again and again. Nothing.
He can feel her going limp, sees her turning blue.

> CARVER (cont'd)
> Fuck, fuck, fuck...

Carver lays her on the seat, reaches into the back,
spills the medical supplies on the floor. He grabs
the scalpel.

A decaying HAND grips his ankle from outside.
Carver spins.

A CORPSE snaps at his calve, its face half torn away.

Carver kicks it in the face. It holds on. Snap,
snap, snap! Its one eye twitches in the socket.
Carver suddenly finds himself on his back being
pulled out of the truck.

He grabs the steering wheel with one hand and
slashes the scalpel. It cuts through the corpse's

106

flesh. A second swipe embeds the blade through the eye to the brain. It falls.

Carver scrambles back in. Emily is barely holding on. Carver grabs his pocket knife out of his pocket.

She sees the blade. She thrashes. He pushes her arms back.

> CARVER (cont'd)
> It's okay. It's okay.

He shuts his eyes, takes a deep breath. As she passes out, he presses on her throat, finds the blockage. He spreads the skin, flattening it. He brings the knife down.

The incision is quick, messy. He presses his fingers in the wound, frees the candy. He drops it. His hands are crimson.

There is too much blood. He checks the wound.

> CARVER (cont'd)
> Fuck.

He has nicked the artery. She's bleeding out. Fast. He reaches back and grabs as much gauze as he can, presses it to the wound. In an instant it is thick with blood.

> CARVER (cont'd)
> Don't do this. Don't do
> this to me. Come on, Em!

The color is draining from her face, spilling into the gauze. He presses all he has to the wound with both hands.

Some bleeding cannot be stopped.

Emily lies still. Carver lets go. His bloody hands shake.

After a moment, he punches the seat. Again. And again.

                                        DISSOLVE TO:

A SERIES OF SHOTS: *the sun setting on the horizon; low fog retreating in the trees; smoke billowing from a fire.*

EXT. HIGHWAY -- LATER

Carver is sitting in front of the truck. A fire burns before him. He gazes at the flame, broken.

He pulls his novel out of his bag. His hands smear blood across the pages. He does not care. He stares at it, firelight flickering in his eyes.

                    MARYANNE (O.S.)
            It won't help.

He tilts his head at the sound of her voice, continues to stare at the manuscript in his hands.

                    MARYANNE (O.S.) (cont'd)
            It won't change anything.

                    CARVER
            No.

                    MARYANNE (O.S.)
            It's good.

He shuts his eyes. Tears slide through the blood.

                    CARVER
            Is it?

                    MARYANNE (O.S.)
            Yes.

                    CARVER
            You always say that.

>   MARYANNE (O.S.)
>   This time it's true.

Behind him, a bloody hand hits the front windshield.

Carver opens his eyes... but does not turn around.

Another hit to the windshield. Stronger this time.

Carver rips the title page off and, after a moment of hesitation, tosses it on the fire. It burns quickly.

More bloody hand prints. Carver stares at the dedication page: *"The years teach much which the days never know."*

He rips it away, tosses it in the fire. More follow.

Emily drags her face to the window, eyes like a doll's - black and dead. She strikes the glass, savage and hungry.

Carver throws the rest on the fire.

>   MARYANNE (O.S.)
>   Wash...?

>   CARVER
>   I know.

>   MARYANNE (O.S.)
>   It's time to go.

Carver wipes his face and stands up. He pulls his duffel over his shoulder and looks at the highway ahead. Behind him, Emily thrashes in the truck, silently screaming.

>   CUT TO BLACK

>   ***THE END***

Notes on She Sels Sea Shells

I've spent most of my life by the sea and visited many shops like the one in the following story. The proprietors are always kind, salt-of-the-earth folk who are never in a hurry to sell you something you don't want, but are more than happy to take your money when you decide to buy something you don't *need*. Hey, they have to make a living, too. It's not personal. It's just business.

We never had much growing up, and my dad made sure I understood the cost of things. I learned very early on to appreciate the small stuff. I also learned that there was always a price to pay for being wasteful or wanting too much. Everything had a price, it seemed. And every price came with a tough lesson. Looking back, it can be said that my dad taught me *a lot*. I never understood what made him that way, and perhaps I never will. In the end, though, I think it kept me grounded. But being grounded can never keep you from reaching for the stars.

Or that forgotten shelf at the back of the store...

SHE SELLS SEA SHELLS

JULIE TEACHES A LESSON

IT WAS THE SECOND LAST DAY OF THEIR TRIP WHEN THEY VISITED THE tiny shop overlooking the cliff.

The previous three days had brought heavy rain, unusual for August along the coast and terrible for the tourist traps and restaurants. Now that the sun had emerged, the streets were beginning to fill with shoppers, and the stores eagerly welcomed them. As Julie Cameron and her daughter stopped in front of the small teal and pink building with the oval sign, she doubled down on her feelings about what was in store for them.

"Five dollars, tops."

"*Five?* Are you crazy, Mom?" Zooey asked. She was nine, twenty-six years younger than her mother. Even without the matching blonde hair, rounded nose and pouty lips, a stranger would instantly deduce they were related just by catching a glimpse of their eyes. The shape of Zooey's matched her delinquent father Eoin's – small, with heavy lids – but the color was all Julie: timber wolf gray. Up close and in the right light, they were startling.

"Five. This isn't a negotiation." Julie opened her purse, slid her wallet out. "What do you say?"

"I thought we weren't negotiating?" Zooey also had her father's bad habit of pushing the envelope as far as it would go. Eoin had learned far too late that envelopes are made of paper, and paper burns. Zooey seemed destined to walk in her father's footsteps.

"I'm not. I'm giving you a chance to agree."

"Or?"

Julie locked eyes with her daughter, hand dangling the wallet over the open purse. "What do you think?"

Zooey slumped in her pink denim overalls. The white T-shirt underneath still bore the stain of chocolate ice cream inhaled two hours earlier. No amount of scrubbing with the paper napkin at the parlor had erased it. It remained as much a souvenir as anything they would find inside this store.

"Fine. Five bucks." She stuck out her hand. Remnants of the chocolate cone lingered there, too. Julie unzipped the wallet and pulled a five-dollar bill free. Zooey crumpled it into the front pocket of her overalls. Her hand came out holding a yellow scrunchie. She tied her pair of pigtails together behind her neck. "Probably nothing that cheap even in there."

"Then you'll be up five bucks when we leave and carrying one less piece of junk."

"It's not junk, Mom. It's culture."

Julie snorted a laugh. She was also wearing overalls, though hers were green, and the straps dangled from her waist. Her pale blue blouse had escaped the ice cream parlor unscathed.

"It wasn't *that* funny," Zooey muttered, grabbing her mother's hand and pulling her forward. At the foot of the steps, Julie tugged her daughter to a full stop, knelt and wiped a few curls back across Zooey's head. The curl was pure Eoin. His hair had been impossible to tame unless neutered with a buzz cut. That pretty much summed Eoin up in a nutshell. *Bastard.*

"How do we address every person?"

Zooey sighed.

"Zooey?"

"Sir or Ma'am."

"Correct. And how do we end every conversation?"

"Please."

"Or thank you. Right?"

"Right."

Julie glanced at her watch. It was almost 10 a.m. Ice cream wasn't much of a breakfast. If past was prologue, Zooey would grow bored with this store within minutes, complain about her hunger, and leave empty-handed. That was hunky-dory with Julie Cameron, whose father had been exhaustingly rigid and a world-class frugalist. The curly-haired guitarist she had fallen for three weeks into her second semester at college was the polar opposite: an aloof hipster more interested in playing weekend shows than attending weekday classes. It was rebellious and attractive until college had ended and the real world took over, at which point she realized far too late that Eoin was as free with his love as he was with his spirit, burning through groupies and cash with equal abandon.

Zooey tugged her mother's hand. "Mom, come on!"

"Okay, okay." Julie mounted the four short steps, catching one last glimpse of the painted sign above as she passed under the overhang: **SHE SELLS SEA SHELLS**. The color of the building was gaudy, but the sign was the chef's kiss. A sun-bleached piece of paper was taped to the glass of the door. The word MISSING was barely visible above a heavily faded photo of a young woman with dark hair. Julie hardly noticed. Her eyes were focused on the sign below it: *'Cash Only, No Refunds'*. Julie grunted quietly. Of course it was cash only. Cash under the table was cash in hand. Summer dollars had to last all winter long, and the less reported to the IRS, the better. No refunds, though? That was a risky proposition. The five-dollar spending cap was a wise decision.

Julie reached for the knob, but Zooey turned it and pushed the door inward first. A tiny gold bell at the top announced their entrance. It chimed again as the door swung shut behind them.

The interior was dim and remarkably quiet. No low hum of a local artist's cheaply recorded CD, no endless loop of ocean white noise straining to invoke authenticity. Just silence. The three burnt-orange walls opposite the door were lined with shelves, each cluttered with an assortment of objects. Three long tables were set out in the middle of the room, draped in dark red cloth, the frayed ends dangling just out of reach above a well-tread charcoal carpet. A row of upright glass canisters of varying height and girth sat upon each table. None were empty, but the soft overhead lamp and lazily hung string lights along the crown molding provided insufficient illumination to make out the contents. Julie recognized the murky ambiance as a staple of last-in-line gift shops, consummated by a smoky haze that diffused the light, hiding the cheapness of the merchandise in shadow. The air was heavy with simulated sea breeze, but like most dollar store incense, it smelled more like desperation. If hunger didn't speed Zooey along, Julie had little doubt such redolence would do the trick. Until that happened, Julie had to endure, and it gave her a sudden sense of unease. In her experience, tenebrous, quiet rooms were the unsettling hallmarks of funeral parlors and tombs.

"It's like a museum," Zooey said, voice just above a whisper.

Julie glanced around, slowly nodding. Museum was more appropriate, less dreadful. And yet, it had never crossed her mind.

Zooey approached the middle table, leaning forward to peer into the nearest glass canister. "Does that mean I can't touch anything?"

"Heaven's no!" a voice said from above. Zooey straightened and backed up until she pressed against her mother's legs. In the far left corner, a previously unnoticed doorway revealed a dark stairwell. A loud creak from the steps preceded the appearance of a *very* old woman. She glided into the room, the tail of her flowing mauve gown just crossing the threshold. "How can you know if something belongs to you until you hold it in your hands?" The old woman looked from mother to daughter. "Touch *everything.*"

"Mom says I'll break it. And if I break it, she'll have to buy it."

"Zooey!"

"Nonsense, child," the old woman said, stepping into the light. Julie estimated the woman had to be in her nineties but moved with the grace and speed of a ballerina. Wherever the dress did not conceal, tanned skin spread tight over withered muscle, knotty bone. A thick silver necklace hung against her chest, ending in a large onyx pendant shaped like an eye. When the old woman casually reached up to touch it, Julie noticed an unusual ring on the index finger made of unpolished silver. It took a moment to recognize what it was – or rather, what it had once been: a teaspoon. Just the sort of artisan crap Eoin would have lapped up. And he would have overpaid for it, too, without batting an eye.

"Sometimes things need a little breaking if only to remind us how important they are." The old shopkeeper leaned down eye to eye with Zooey. "Especially rules."

Zooey slowly matched the old woman's smile. The pendulum of

influence had swung quickly inside the store, increasing the unpleasant sensation in Julie's stomach.

Just like with Eoin. Accept it: you'll never be her favorite.

She forced the thought away. The sooner they were back outside, the better. She did not want this place to be the lingering impression of what they had experienced on the first meaningful trip together since Zooey's father had exited the picture.

A long overdue exit, Julie reminded herself. Caught fucking the model from his band's last video shoot, Eoin had the gall to say it meant nothing, then moved in with the bitch after Julie cremated his favorite guitar in the backyard fire pit. She had regretted letting him off so easily in the seven months since.

"You listen to your mom now. Touch, but be careful. Be careful, but unafraid." The old woman straightened, extended her hand to Julie. "Name's Maren. Pleasure to meet you both."

Julie forced a smile and shook hands. The old lady's skin was oily, the fingers long and segmented by thick knuckles. Julie pulled away and pressed her hand to the small of her back, subtly wiping it dry. Maren's eyes narrowed ever so slightly.

Zooey returned to the center table.

"Zooey, what do you say?"

"Thank you, ma'am," Zooey said absently. She was already on her knees, peering into the first canister. Maren stepped away to the far right corner, where a small counter faced the room. An ancient analog cash register dominated the space, surrounded by a series of small bowls overflowing with assorted knick-knacks like pin-on buttons and colored string bracelets. *Impulse buys*, Julie's dad would have called them. *Pocket trash for pack rats.*

As the old woman slipped behind the counter, Julie busied herself with the shelves on the far wall. The lower three were bestrewed with driftwood carved into shapes of various sea creatures. Anatomical accuracy was vague. A hint of a whale here, a modicum of a crab there. Seals seemed to be particularly popular, or rather *unpopular*, depending on how you viewed their abundance this late in the summer. Julie plucked one up, noting its outline left in thick dust. She rotated it in her hand. It wasn't a seal at all. It had a tail and a lengthy torso, but instead of flippers, there were arms, only one of which ended in a hand. A short neck topped with an oval head sat above the shoulders. Dried seaweed had been fastened to the crown and cascaded down the back like dead vines. The face was a featureless void.

"Mermaid," Maren said from across the room. "Our top seller."

Julie turned the lightweight wooden ornament over. A tiny round sticker was attached to the bottom with a hand-drawn '$20' scrawled in black ink. She laid the piece back on the shelf.

"Not today."

Zooey rushed over to take a look. "A mermaid? Mommy, can I have a mermaid? Like Ariel!"

Julie pulled her daughter's hand away as it was about to grab the driftwood. "I said no, Zooey."

"But Ariel!"

"It's not Ariel. It's junk. Just a piece of wood even the sea spit back." It came out quick, vanguard to her coiled anger. Her father's anger, hot in her veins, sharp on her tongue. *Of course* the mermaid was the top seller. At twenty bucks a pop, placed right at the level of a child's eyes, every second parent passing through must have surrendered an Andrew Jackson to ebb the flow of tears that tighter purse strings ushered forth.

"Well, can I touch it? I can't break it if it's wood."

Julie relented and let go of her daughter's arm. Zooey scooped up the ugly-tree Ariel and pressed it against her chest.

"You're not junk," Zooey whispered to it. "You're an underwater princess trapped by an evil witch and kept prisoner against your will."

As Zooey uttered the word "witch", Julie snuck a glance at the shopkeeper, but the old woman didn't seem to hear. She was sitting on a stool behind the counter, arranging a handful of pebbles on a clear glass plate.

"Why can't I keep her, Mommy?"

"Because she costs twenty dollars and you only have five."

"But you could buy her for me."

"What did I tell you outside?"

Zooey pouted and stomped her foot, holding the driftwood tighter.

"Excuse you, young lady?" Julie grabbed the tail of the mermaid and tugged it free. Zooey cued up a wail, and Julie held up her open palm. "You want to see how fast five dollars can become zero? Try me." She lowered her fingers one after the other until only the index and thumb remained. They came together to form a circle, then Julie waved her hand away.

"So not funny," Zooey said and shuffled back to the tables with the curious glass canisters.

Julie checked her watch. "Five more minutes, Zooey. Not a minute more."

She tossed the carving back on the shelf. The eclectic state of the store was grating on her now. Junk was everywhere. Handcrafted bookmarks, fishtail keychains and hollowed-out sea urchins were on brand. But plenty was jarringly out of place. Tarot decks, cell phone chargers, and ceramic outhouse figurines. Items so incongruous that her conjoined feelings of anger and unease began to mutate into sadness. The sight of the elderly woman behind the counter coalesced that sadness into guilt. *She Sells Sea Shells* – propped up here overlooking the ocean one hundred feet below, isolated from the rest of the town's tourist traps lining Main Street – was a potpourri of random junk, cheaply made and outlandishly marked up for a single purpose: survival. Barely accessible by a narrow lane on one side and a footpath on the other, the only alternative reason to make the trek was the view, and even that was far from ideal. The cliff faced north, robbed of the romantic appeal of early sunrises and late sunsets that many ocean vistas offered. More often than not, the horizon was encumbered with a dense rolling fog that lingered throughout the day. Why this eccentric shopkeeper had staked her claim on the outskirts of common sense was baffling.

"Mom, come see! There's a waterfall! It's crazy!"

Julie blinked, unsure exactly how long she had been standing there holding her breath, staring. She let it out in a long, slow exhale. The cloying scent of incense made her stomach roll.

"Mom!"

Julie crouched. "What, Zooey? There's no need to yell. We're the only ones here." That double-edged stab of guilt and sadness again. No one had been behind them on the hill, and you could see for miles. Getting out down only five bucks was becoming increasingly unlikely.

It was at that moment that the front door opened. A tall, thin man in his early sixties moseyed in, letting the door close slowly behind him. He wore a large-brimmed hat, a beige dress shirt with a tie, and neatly pressed slacks. The hat, tie, and pants were all the same shade of brown. A yellow seam ran up the outside of each leg to a heavy black belt sagging to one side under the weight of a holstered revolver.

"Mornin', Sheriff Dan," Maren said, attention still squarely on the arrangement of pebbles. If she had glanced at the lawman at all, Julie had missed it.

Sheriff Dan lowered his hat and wiped a thick coat of bead sweat from his brow. An unwieldy comb-over flopped back to its natural side. The sheriff swiftly brushed it across the barren dome of the scalp, using the moisture to pat it into place. There it stayed, looking like someone had laid a glove there and walked away.

"Same to you, Maren. Same to you." Sheriff Dan waved the hat in front of his face to generate a breeze. He leaned on the register, eyeing the plate of pebbles. A rolled-up piece of paper jutted from his back pocket, sliding out an inch further when he bent forward. "What you workin' on?"

"Don't recognize it?" the old woman asked. "You sure you're from around here?"

"Just some stones right now, Maren. I'm a good cop, but not that good." He chuckled. "I'm sure this time tomorrow it'll be plain as day. And just as pretty as that waterfall over the—"

Sheriff Dan's words ended abruptly. He had turned to point at the tables in the middle of the room and found himself staring at a pretty young blond woman and a little girl kneeling together on the floor. He popped his hat back in place and stood upright.

"Ma'am. Little miss."

Julie stood up. "Sheriff is it?"

"That's right. Sheriff Langford. Most folks 'round here call me Sheriff Dan, though. And you would be…?"

"Julie Cameron. This is Zooey."

Sheriff Dan offered Zooey a smile. His teeth were stained yellow from a career of coffee and cigarettes. Zooey smiled back.

"Your daughter?"

"Yes." Men often asked that question, only to follow it up with a tired quip of surprise at the discovery that the girls were not sisters. Never charming, and in some cases downright creepy, it amazed her that men thought lines like that beguiled women.

No such comment emerged from Sheriff Dan. "Up here on holiday?"

Zooey wrapped an arm around Julie's legs. Julie ran her hand across her daughter's hair. "Yes. Almost over now, sadly. Lots of pictures, though." The chuckle that followed was a little too forced, but Sheriff Dan did not seem to notice. He was a good cop, but not that good after all.

"Never taken one myself," Sheriff Dan glanced back at Maren and shrugged.

Julie blinked in surprise. "Pictures?"

It was the sheriff's turn to laugh. "Vacation," he said. "Never really had time or anywhere else to be."

"Oh." Julie looked down at Zooey, who was more perplexed than amused. "Isn't that the point of a vacation, though: to make time to be somewhere else, anywhere else?"

The sheriff smiled politely, then frowned just as quickly as he remembered the rolled-up paper in his back pocket. He reached for it, saying, "Always something 'round here to keep me busy."

Sheriff Dan unrolled the paper. The side facing him was dark with enough color to be visible through the other side. When he turned to face the counter again, Julie managed to catch a glimpse of what it was: a photograph.

"Damn near almost forgot why I came in here, Maren."

"Wouldn't be the first time."

"Mommy, look, look!" Zooey tugged at the straps on her mother's overalls until Julie looked down. "Come see it."

"See what, baby?" She let herself be guided down to the floor, still trying to hear what was being said at the counter.

"This." Zooey extended her tiny hand toward the table with all the bluster of a circus showman.

Julie peered at the glass container for a solid ten seconds. It stood about a foot high and was rounded at the top, like a large drinking glass turned upside down. A small section of the front was opaque with receding condensation, but the rest allowed for a very clear – and startling – view of what was inside. A green hillside ran up to the top of the glass and was split down the middle by a black rocky façade. A waterfall flowed down the front, where it formed a sapphire pool over a sandy bottom. Fully developed tiny pine trees dotted the hillside, interspersed with no less than four different types of flowers.

"Isn't it amazing, Mommy? Can we—"

"No," Julie said quickly. She continued to stare, leaning closer. "I mean, yes, it's amazing. No, we can't buy it."

"Why not?"

"Zooey." Julie shuffled forward on her knees so she could press her nose to the glass. The detail up close was even more stunning, like putting on a pair of reading glasses for the first time. The waterfall was generating foam as it hit the pool, and the leaves and grass swayed in an unseen breeze.

"You're no fun," Zooey groaned. "I bet it's not even that expensive."

A short, sharp laugh escaped Julie before she could contain it. "Want to bet?"

"No."

Julie reached out with both hands to lift the glass container.

"I thought we couldn't touch?"

"Don't be a smart-ass, Zooey. Your dad was a smart-ass, look where it got him."

"Is," Zooey said softly. "'Is' a smart-ass."

Julie sighed. 'Was' implied Eoin was no longer around, permanently gone, ergo: dead. Even a nine-year-old could infer that. Wishful thinking aside, the cheating bastard was still very much alive. Still very much a smart-ass. And, still very much into his fashion model whore.

Despite her instruction to her daughter about touching things in the shop, Julie Cameron cupped the glass container in both hands. It was warm – significantly warmer than the room. The heat slid along her arms just under the skin, slow like a snake in the grass. Julie pondered where the heat source originated from. The base was fused to the main glass, creating a single sealed canister. Turning it slowly revealed it was sitting on a wooden plate made from a cross-section of pine about an inch thick. She pressed a finger to the edge. Cold to the touch, not even retaining warmth from the glass. Julie searched for an electrical cable or battery slot. None were found.

"I want to hold it!" Zooey exclaimed. Julie held her hand out, an instinctual act of protection from the unknown. She saw the rest of the canisters lined along the low table. The dim light when they first entered had obscured the contents from the doorway, but down here, at *their* level, she could see them for what they were in all their splendor. As they wanted to be seen.

They.

125

That sense of unease rolled in her belly again. She pulled her other hand free of the glass.

"Mommy."

"In a minute, baby," Julie said. She was frustrated with the riddle of it all. She was good with numbers, able to quickly identify patterns and equations, to find the shortest route through a maze. She had a knack for it, something her father had encouraged early on. By adulthood, that knack helped her to rise quickly above the testosterone haze of the second-largest accounting firm in the city. There was math and logic in everything. You just had to know how and where to look.

But she wasn't seeing it here. And it was maddening.

She grabbed the canister again, lifted it straight up. Like the driftwood, it was remarkably light. Another puzzle. It was constructed of glass, contained rocks, earth *and* water. And yet she could have held it aloft with one hand rather than two. Right now, though, she just wanted to see—

"How much is it?"

Exactly. But Julie didn't have an answer for her daughter because the bottom of the glass had no price. Not even a faded sticker or gummy residue from one that might have fallen off. She lowered it to the table and turned over the wooden plate. It was blank.

"Those aren't for sale, ma'am." It was Sheriff Dan. Julie had momentarily forgotten he was even in the store. She placed the glass back on the plate and stood up.

"Not for sale?" Julie looked past the lawman to the elderly shopkeeper. Maren stepped around the counter, wiping sand from her hands into her dress.

"No, ma'am," Sheriff Dan said. "Ain't that right, Maren?"

"Not for sale, that's right." The old lady finished wringing her hands clean and placed them on her tiny hips. "Not yet, anyway. Terrariums take time. To get just right."

Julie observed the three tables taking up the best real estate in the shop. Each displayed a dozen of the so-called *terrariums*, all different, all remarkably detailed as though a god-like hand had scooped up the best parts of the world and poured them inside. And none of it was for sale! Zooey had been right: it did feel like a museum. This old woman was hawking dried-up beach trash and dollar store phone chargers to stay afloat when she was clearly a master artist sitting on a goldmine just waiting to be fawned over and sold to the walking wallets currently throwing their money away on trinkets all along Main Street. Nothing about this place made sense. And it all made her uneasy.

Zooey had already lost interest and wandered off to the back wall of shelves, looking for something that *was* for sale.

Sheriff Dan cleared his throat. "Don't forget to put that picture up now, Maren. All the shops and offices are doin' the same."

"Sure thing. Anything I can do to help the family out."

The sheriff walked to the door, saying: "I don't expect much to come of it if I'm being honest. But we do what we can. Staties figure he panicked and took off for the border, and I'm prone to agree. Wouldn't be the first man to run out on a lady."

"Or the last," Maren said. She walked back around the counter and picked up the photo. "Crimson Cove's a long way up the coast, though."

"Our county, our problem, Maren. Just like always." Sheriff Dan opened the door. The sunlight spilled in like it had been listening right outside. He turned back. "Until he dries out on a beach somewhere and comes to his senses. In the meantime, if anyone mentions they've seen him passing through, you send 'em my way. Got a pretty young thing down to the station about eight months pregnant won't stop crying. G'day, ladies."

With a tip of his hat, he was gone, taking the sunshine with him. Dim shadows crept back to fill the corners. The sounds of the outside world retreated through the cracks in the walls.

Julie wrapped her arms around her body to push back goosebumps. "Zooey, baby, come on now. Hurry and pick something out."

The old shopkeeper removed the sun-bleached MISSING sign from the front door glass and taped the new picture in its place. Even through the paper, Julie could see the face on the other side. Young male, maybe twenty-five, clean cut, smiling. Not exactly the poster boy for wayward fathers-to-be. *Except now he was*, Julie thought. *Quite literally.*

Is, she corrected herself. *Was* implied something else altogether. She watched as the old lady crumpled the faded paper and dropped it absently in the waste bucket by the counter.

Zooey rushed up the aisle between two of the tables, her pink rubber boots scuffing the carpet every step of the way. She stopped and held her selection above her head with both hands. Julie sighed.

"Really, Zooey? A shell?"

"Well, it is what the sign says, Mom."

She couldn't argue with her about that. Julie took the shell and turned it over several times. It was a conch, cream in color, shot through with splashes of light orange and caramel. Inside the siphonal canal aperture, where a large sea snail would have once made its home, the color darkened increasingly to blood red. Tip to tip, it was the size of a trade paperback, with smoothed spikes along the edges of the spire. For an object that felt ceramic in texture, it weighed surprisingly more than it had any right to.

"I don't see a price, baby. Maybe it isn't for sale either."

"No, it is! It is for sale! It's the last one, too."

Even from this distance, Julie could see that the shelves at the back were littered with large, round beach rocks and small, flat clam shells. Nothing as unique or naturally beautiful as a conch remained. And she saw something else, too: a sign, handwritten like all the rest, on the front end of a folded piece of cardboard in the middle of the second shelf from the top.

'PAY WHAT YOU CAN'.

Considering what the old woman was charging for wood carvings, this was a bit of a shock. Pay what you can could be plenty or almost nothing at all. Like her father before her, Julie Cameron was nobody's fool. And her daughter wouldn't be either.

"You see that sign, know what it says?"

"Pay what you can."

"Exactly."

"I can pay five bucks."

"Sure, yeah." Julie crouched down once more, still holding the conch. Not intentionally keeping it from her daughter, but not *not* keeping it from her either. She'd read *Lord of the Flies* in junior high with its conceit that holding the conch meant it was her time to speak. Very little good had come from the power of the conch in Golding's novel. But she had her own lesson to teach. "You know why it says that? Because this - this shell - all those shells down there and those rocks too, they all came from the ocean. They weren't carved or painted or even polished by any human hand. They just *are*. There's probably plenty more just like this one down on the beach right now, just waiting to be found. Just waiting to be taken. Why would you pay for something like that?"

Zooey watched her mother's eyes. Gray on gray. Finally, she looked away to the conch in her mother's hand. "Because I heard them singing."

"What?"

Zooey took the conch in both hands and held it to her ear. "I heard them. I heard them all."

"Heard who, baby?"

They.

"The mermaids."

"Mermaids don't live in shells, Zooey." Moment of truth. Julie had never wanted to tell her nine-year-old daughter the truth about something make-believe more in her life, but a rogue wave of guilt washed over her. She would only be doing so for herself, to drive home a point about money. Of all things, money. Her father would be proud. Her mother would be mortified. Neither of them were there to guide her. "They live in the ocean."

"Listen!" Zooey said, thrusting the conch to her mother's ear. Before Julie had a chance to capitulate to her daughter's wishes, Maren appeared behind the girl. She wore an empathetic smile that did not fit properly among the creases and crow's feet of her face.

"Come now, don't trouble your mother. That song you hear is for you alone and no one else. She couldn't hear it if she tried. And neither could I."

Julie stood up. Zooey lowered the conch and turned around.

"Why not?"

"Zooey—"

"Why not, *ma'am?*"

"That's not what I..." Julie flashed an apologetic smile of her own at the old lady. "Sorry, she's nine. We're hoping the questions run out by ten."

Maren's smile drew tight as though reined in by her rising brow. "'We're'? Your husband must be the wandering type."

"I'm *sorry?*"

"Off sightseeing on his own? Maybe on a sport fishing trip?"

Julie let out a breath. The tension in her shoulders remained. The sooner she got out of this place, the better. "No. He didn't come with us this time. Work." She hated herself for making excuses for the son of a bitch. It wasn't work that kept Eoin away. It was pussy half his age. But she would no sooner admit that to this stranger than she would her daughter.

"There's always next year. Now, young lady, let's get you squared away so you and your mother can enjoy the rest of your day outside. After all the rain, you don't want to be cooped up staring at the world through a glass window." Maren extended her gnarled hand and led Zooey to the counter.

"Sorry if I was rude earlier," Julie said, following them. Maren walked around to the other side. "Guess we *were* cooped up, as you say. Makes you a little stir crazy."

Maren moved her plate of pebbles out of the way. "Nothing to be sorry for. I'm glad you stopped by."

"She's just, you know, very impressionable. I try to keep her grounded, teach her things. About money and value."

"Everything has a cost these days," the old lady said. She tapped the top of the counter where the plate had been. "Okay, young lady, let's see what you've got and what it's worth."

Everything has a cost. It had sounded like an offhanded remark, yet Julie felt silenced at a time when she was feeling vulnerable. It was something Eoin had done to her for years. Manipulated her, spun her words around, used her silence as a weapon against herself until she felt to blame for every argument, no matter the cause. She wanted to keep explaining to this old woman the valuable lessons her father had provided her, wanted her daughter to hear and understand that only things of value have a cost and that some things, many things, just *are*. She wanted to tell them both that this lady had it backward, that she was selling random wood and rocks for an undeserved fortune while the things of real value were sitting in glass cages like animals in a zoo.

Or artifacts in a museum.

Julie watched Zooey excitedly place the conch on the counter. Her nine-year-old daughter had figured it out right away, while Julie, with all her logic and paternal life lessons, was too blind to see: you can't buy the art and artifacts in a museum. You admire them, ponder them, become bewitched by them. And on the way out, you buy overpriced souvenirs to mark the experience as tangible and take a little piece of it with you.

Maren held the conch up, peering inside. "Said you heard the mermaids singing, huh?" She pressed it to her ear and, after a moment, removed it with a shrug.

"You really don't hear them? Not even a little?" Zooey frowned.

"I told you I wouldn't. If they were singing for you, it was meant just for you, and you alone." She leaned in close over the counter, lowering her voice. "That's how it works, you know."

"How what works?"

Maren flashed a quick look in Julie's direction before continuing. "Magic."

"The shell is magic?" Zooey's eyes were like saucers. "Really?"

"Of course! And I can prove it."

Julie stifled a chuckle. All children believed in magic. Trying to prove that it was real was often what convinced them it was not and made them question what other lies adults had been feeding them. Her father had never been so foolish. From the time she could count, he had explained that the only magic in the world was the fact that people believed the lies they continued to tell themselves as they grew older.

How long did you lie to yourself about Eoin?

Shut up!

"When you get back to where you're staying today, take a walk on the beach and see if you can find any more shells like this one. When you do, put them to your ear and listen real close. If you don't hear the mermaids sing, well…"

"Well, what?"

Maren leaned even closer. "You'll know this one's magic." She straightened quickly. "And if I'm wrong, tell you what, you bring those shells to me, and I'll pay you double whatever you put down for this one today."

Julie wondered if this was how the old shopkeeper came by most of the beach junk lining the shelves. She certainly didn't seem like she could scour and drag it all up the hill on her own.

Zooey was already hunting in her front pocket for the five-dollar bill. She plucked it out and laid it on the counter. She started to pull her hand free, then stopped and locked eyes with the old lady.

"Do you swear?"

Maren laughed. In the quiet of the dim shop, it sounded uniquely genuine. "I do, like the sailor's daughter that I am, but I don't think you or your mother want to hear it."

Zooey cocked an eyebrow. "Not that kind of swear. I mean: do you swear on it?"

Maren extended her hand, knobby and twisted like a vulture claw. Julie

133

wondered how such ugliness could have created the beauty on display inside the terrariums. "I swear it's as true as the sea is blue."

Zooey giggled and released the five dollars to shake the old lady's hand.

The exchange was quick. The shopkeeper pushed the conch forward to the edge of the counter, and when Zooey lifted it free, the five was nowhere to be seen. Despite herself, a pang of guilt slid along the lining of Julie's stomach. Five bucks wasn't much, even if it was just a stupid sea shell. It might have been the only sale the old lady had all week. She slid back the zipper on her purse.

"Zooey, baby, wait for mommy outside."

Zooey lowered the conch from her ear, tucked it safely under her arm and walked to the door. Her hand was on the doorknob when she turned and said: "Thank you, ma'am!"

"You're very welcome, child. See you again soon."

When the door chime ended, Julie removed her wallet.

"She already paid what she could," Maren said, waving a hand.

"But I can pay more. I should pay more."

"That's not how it works, Mrs. Cameron."

"Not how what works?" Through the window in the doorway, Julie spotted Zooey pacing back and forth outside, the conch to her left ear. Her lips were moving.

"The lesson." The old shopkeeper turned and placed the glass plate with the pebbles back on the counter next to the register. She spread a handful of wheat-colored sand over the top. Somehow, none of it spilled over the edge.

Julie's hand was tingling from squeezing her wallet so hard. She loosened her grip but kept the wallet out. She opened her mouth to speak.

"Go and enjoy your day with your daughter, Mrs. Cameron." Maren wiped her hand on her dress. "You have nothing to feel guilty about. She paid a fair price."

The bell chimed, and a young couple in matching *Legend of Zelda* T-shirts walked in holding hands. They let go long enough to remove their sunglasses before linking back together as they approached the counter. The old shopkeeper put on her brightest smile.

Julie stepped back, let the wallet sink into her purse. By the time she joined her daughter outside, the tingling in her hand had stopped, but the sense of unease remained.

What business was it of the old lady if Julie wanted to teach her daughter life lessons? Better than learning the hard way.

Like you did?

Inside, the young couple had found the shelves of driftwood animals, and the old lady was gliding up behind them. Julie lost sight of their exchange behind the paper notices taped to the glass.

She studied the smiling face of the missing man. In the lower right corner of the picture there was a smaller photo of the man in full, presumably to show what he had last been seen wearing: black T-shirt, khaki shorts and orange Converse sneakers. There was nothing distinct about his features, the kind of face that would have little trouble blending into any crowd. She knew the type well and wondered if maybe the mother-to-be was better off.

Zooey's exaggerated sigh pulled her away. "Can we get some food now? Real food, I mean."

"Absolutely, baby."

ZOOEY WALKS THE BEACH.

Zooey held her mother's hand down the grassy hill while her other hand held the conch over her ear. The mermaids were silent, but the roar of the waves was loud and clear. The waves battering the shore on the other side of the cliff were less pronounced. Hearing both at once messed up her balance and made her uncovered ear feel flooded with liquid. She stumbled and almost fell before her mother held her up. They stopped moving.

"Do I need to take that from you already, Zooey?"

"No."

Her mother knelt in front of her. She had been doing that a lot lately, constantly correcting Zooey on something she had said or enforcing a rule or restriction before they went anywhere. *Some vacation!* Her dad *never* did that. Zooey wished he was with them now instead of a thousand miles away. Her mother had lied to the old lady in the shop about him. He wasn't working. He was with *her*.

"No? Well, you can't keep it on your ear if you can't walk right while doing it. Especially not in these boots." Her mother brushed away a thorny branch that had caught in the strap of Zooey's overalls, then reached for the conch. Zooey held it behind her back.

"Okay, okay, I won't. Just don't take it."

"I'm serious, Zooey. No more until we get to the B&B."

"But that's like a hundred miles!"

Her mother's eyes narrowed, the *grump* lines scrunching across her brow. "Don't be so dramatic. It's twenty minutes walk, tops."

"Twenty minutes!"

"Zooey."

"Ugh. Fine."

"Fine, what?"

"Fine, I won't use it until we get back." This last part she stretched and mumbled like the words had to climb through a mouthful of marbles. Her mother sighed and stood up, taking Zooey's hand once more.

At the bottom of the hill, her mother's mood finally shifted. "What were they saying anyway? The mermaids."

Zooey gave her a distrusting glance. "They weren't saying anything. They were singing."

"Singing. Right. Well, what were they singing about?"

"Why are you asking all of a sudden?"

Her mother laughed. She hadn't heard her mother laugh genuinely for much of the trip. In fact, she hadn't heard her mother laugh much at all since—

"You are your father's daughter, Zooey. Through and through."

It sounded like a bad thing, but Zooey knew her mom didn't mean it that way. She knew her mother still loved her father, just as Zooey still did. She heard her mother crying in her room some nights, heard her whisper Zooey's father's name to the shadows, almost like prayers. She didn't understand a lot of things adults did, but she understood enough to know that they didn't pray for things they didn't want. They prayed for things they lost and wanted back.

"Do you know what they call mermaid songs?"

Zooey did not. Her mother must have known that because she continued without waiting for an answer.

"Siren song."

"Siren? Like police cars and fire trucks?"

"No, silly goose." Her mother twisted her fingers like claws and lurched toward her. "Mermaids would sing to lure sailors to... their... *DOOM!*"

Zooey's fear quickly exploded into laughter. "That's not true. Mermaids aren't ev—"

Her mother reached into the sides of Zooey's overalls and tickled her until she could barely breathe. She fell into the grass, clutching the conch to her chest with both hands. Her mother sat beside her, also catching her breath.

"Mommy?"

"Yeah, baby?"

"Maybe *she's* a mermaid?"

"She who?"

"Daddy's friend."

Zooey could only see the side of her mom's face, but it was enough to see the joy ease out of it like air from a tire. What remained was pale and blank.

"No, baby. I wish she was."

"Why?"

"Because then it wouldn't have been his fault that he left us."

Her mom was silent and didn't look at her the rest of the way to the bed and breakfast. Every so often, they would pass someone on the street, and her mother would look down at the pavement rather than say hello, and the sunlight would reflect off her wet cheek.

On a couple of occasions, Zooey furtively lifted the conch to her ear. With each attempt, the sound of the ocean was farther away, growing faint with every step. After three listens, she stopped altogether, fearing her covert disobedience was causing the magic to fade.

They split a clubhouse sandwich and fries on the patio of the B&B

overlooking the beach. The late August sky was cloudless and full of dandelion fluff. Far up the rocky shore, the waves crashed heavily against the base of the cliff, and small rainbows came and went in the lingering spray.

After lunch, her mother let her search the beach for more shells on the condition that she stay clear of the water and stay within sight of the B&B. Zooey kissed her on the cheek, put the conch in her Pinkie Pie backpack, and set off along the shore.

Peak tourist season had wound down a week earlier, and now there were only a few other people on the beach. Zooey passed an elderly couple trying to take a selfie with the water behind them and the sun in their faces. Her grandmother couldn't operate the television remote, let alone a smartphone, and so she imagined they'd still be trying by the time she got back. A few yards further along, a middle-aged man with a remarkably hairy back almost bumped into her with his metal detector. She hopped to the right at the last second, and he bustled by her without ever looking up.

It proved a fortuitous moment in her search, as she was now standing directly in front of a small conch shell partially buried below a patch of sand. She squatted down and tugged it free. After brushing lingering sand away, she held it to her ear, plugging the other ear with a finger for good measure.

Silence. Not even the splash of waves.

She carefully swapped the new conch for the larger one in her backpack. She placed the big conch to her ear. Before she could even put a finger to her free ear, she heard the water crashing ashore inside, followed immediately by the gentle notes of a song. She pressed it tighter. The waves receded, the voices rose. The language was foreign, unlike anything she had heard.

Zooey giggled and pressed the conch to her heart. It *was* magic! She opened the secondary pocket of the backpack and dropped it in, careful to keep it separate from the new one. She looked back along the beach. She had come further than expected. The B&B was still fully visible, but the details were faint, out of focus.

She thought about heading back. If her mother looked out the window and couldn't see Zooey, there'd be trouble. There always was. The longer her dad was gone, the shorter Zooey's leash stretched.

But the small conch wasn't as big or pretty as the one she'd bought. If she found a nicer one, the old lady in the shop would pay even more! Her mom couldn't argue with that.

She continued. The cliff wall stood a few hundred yards ahead and ran for at least a mile along the shore before curving out into the sea for another mile. *She Sells Sea Shells* was just at the top of the nearest peak, though it could not be seen from this close to the cliff face. The rock wall rose almost 100 feet from the sea below. It had the refined smoothness of marble, as though the rest of the earth had been cleaved away in a single blow by the sword of an ancient titan.

Zooey walked another ten feet, her head craned up toward the top of the cliff. Her right foot caught under a large beach rock, and she spilled forward, twisting around. She landed hard on her side, the air kicking from her lungs in a single thrust. She lay there for a moment, gasping, biting back tears. When her breath returned, she got to her knees. She refused to cry out. Crying was for babies, and she was almost ten.

After a few deep breaths, Zooey glanced around to see if anyone had witnessed her fall. She was relieved to see that this part of the beach was clear. She was about to swing her backpack around to check on the shells when she spotted something orange and white jutting from a cluster of rocks about twenty feet ahead.

She scrambled to her feet and brushed kelp and sand from her knees. Damp stains remained, but her overalls weren't torn. The last thing she wanted was to have to explain that to her mother. Each remaining step to the shell was carefully considered and slowly taken, yet they only brought her to disappointment.

It was not a conch. It was a Converse.

Everything except the toe of the sneaker was buried beneath rocks and sand, as if years of give and take by the ocean had conspired to cover it up. Zooey attempted to pull it free. It rose about three inches before a small crab scrambled out from under the tongue. Zooey screamed, staggered back two steps, and fell on her backside. She kicked at the crab, but it had already changed course and was halfway to the sea.

The second tumble was certain to leave a bruise, and the pain from the previous fall still lingered. Not wanting to press her luck or risk further injury, Zooey hastily checked on the two shells in her bag, then took a cue from the crab and headed home.

ZOOEY AT NIGHT

Her mother was arguing on the phone in the master bedroom when Zooey returned to the B&B. Stretches of silence were interspersed with short angry bursts, many of which cut off mid-sentence. Every so often, Zooey heard the bang of the bedside table being struck with a hand. She didn't need to hear the voice on the other end to know it was her dad. The only time she'd ever seen or heard her mother strike anything was when she was talking to him.

Zooey kicked off her boots and stretched out on the fancy-looking chaise in the main room. She held a conch in each hand, alternating them between her ears. The soft lapping of waves could be heard faintly in the one she had purchased. The one she had found was deathly silent. She lay it on the seat.

"Any luck, baby girl?"

Her mom was standing in the open doorway of the bedroom, arms folded tight across her chest, eyes puffy and red. The call had taken a toll.

"A little," Zooey said. "I found one shell. And a sneaker. I left it on the beach."

"A sneaker?" Julie made her way to the chaise and sat down. Zooey pulled her legs up to her chest. "What kind of sneaker?"

"I dunno. Like dad wears."

Julie was still gripping her cell phone tight. She tossed it on the coffee table in front of her. "Sea trash, I guess. Did you wash your hands when you got back?"

Zooey glanced at her fingers, thought about saying yes, then shook her head.

"Do it now, okay? Who knows what could be crawling around out there."

"A crab," Zooey said as she uncurled from the chaise and stood up. "Came right out of it."

Julie gave an exaggerated shiver. "Wash 'em twice in that case."

"Okay. If you say so."

"I do say so." Julie held out her hand. "Leave that."

Zooey handed the conch to her and hurried to the bathroom. She gave her hands a quick wash. The soap smelled like honey. When she returned to the main room, her mom was holding the conch to her left

142

ear and frowning.

"I don't hear anything. Maybe I broke it."

Zooey put her hands on her hips. "You didn't break it. Only I can hear it."

"Right." Julie passed the shell back, pointed to the smaller one on the seat. "What about that one?"

"Nothing."

"Let me try."

Zooey gave her mom the other shell. Julie pressed it to her right ear and listened. A moment passed. Her eyes grew wide.

"What?" Zooey asked, shuffling her feet. "What is it?"

"I hear it."

"Hear what?"

"Shhh."

"Mom!"

Julie grinned and lowered the conch. "False alarm. Was just my stomach rumbling. You hungry?"

Zooey was not impressed. She took the conch and laid it on the table. "Not funny."

"It was a little funny."

"Nope."

"Tough crowd." Julie stood up. "Where should we go for supper?"

They decided on *Pappy's*, a 1950s-style diner at the end of the boardwalk that ran along the other side of the cove. Zooey had onion rings and a chocolate milkshake that quickly contributed to the stains on her shirt. Her mom was in the middle of wiping it clean when the cell phone vibrated on the table. It was Zooey's dad. Julie let it go to voicemail.

After supper, they made their way back to the B&B. Her mom said she was feeling tired and wanted to go to bed early. Zooey settled into the recliner opposite the TV and watched re-runs of *The Big Bang Theory*. She didn't get a lot of the jokes, but she liked the lady in the glasses a lot. She dozed.

She awoke sometime later to the sound of heavy waves striking the shore. The room was dark except for the glow of the television. She shut it off. The sound of the swells increased. Zooey and her mom had been at the B&B for six days, and she had not heard the ocean while inside before now. She walked to the window and looked outside. The moon was full, reflecting brightly off still water.

The sound of crashing waves persisted. Zooey plucked her conch off the chaise and turned it so the aperture was facing her. The waves eased. A faint melody came and went. Zooey pressed the shell to her ear.

They were calling to her. But they were distant, far offshore and fading.

"No, no, no. Come back!" Zooey whispered. She stepped back.

The lights were off behind the door to the master bedroom. The soft rhythmic snoring within was the telltale sign her mom had taken the special pills she kept at the bottom of her purse.

Zooey returned to the window. The water was a black mirror from the shoreline to the breakwater - a thousand yards of pure darkness. She scanned the beach as far as the cliff. Night enveloped the entire town. The roads were empty, dark. She looked back at the beach.

Her breathing stalled.

A man was standing at the edge of the water directly across from the B&B. His back was to her, but in the moonlight, she could clearly see that he was wearing a brown leather jacket, black jeans and black sneakers. His curly hair fell over his collar in a familiar way.

He turned and faced the window.

"Dad?"

Her voice was barely audible in the room. She swallowed and felt the scratchy, dry air slide down her throat. She pressed her face to the glass. What was her dad doing here? She had to be mistaken. He was a thousand miles away with his band and lady friend.

The window steamed over, and he vanished behind it. She frantically wiped it clear. There he was, standing as still as the water behind him. His eyes found hers. Hollow and dark.

Zooey waved. Her dad turned and began walking in the direction of the cliff.

Follow...

The word was clear in the room. She spun around, not wanting to look away, but afraid that there was someone there with her. Someone unknown.

But the room was empty. The sound of waves weakened. The siren song vibrated like frequencies passing between distant speakers. And then it came again—

Follow

—rising from the conch in her hand. She dropped it. The aperture grinned from the floor. More words flowed out in overlapping enraptured voices:

Follow him. He is with us. Be with him. Be with us!

Zooey's hands were shaking. She should tell her mom. Tell her what she heard. Tell her what she *saw*.

Tell her *what* exactly? Her mom had let her dad's calls go to voicemail and argued with him later to the point of tears - to the point where she needed her special pills to sleep. No, she could not tell her mom. Her

145

mom wanted nothing to do with her dad. Not now, at least. Not here, on vacation. Her mom needed to sleep. If her dad was here, it was to see Zooey. And if he'd been calling all night and got no response, he must have come all this way to make sure she was okay!

She had to tell him. She had to let him know she was fine, that she still loved him, no matter what. She had to—

Follow.

She stared out the window. Her dad was gone.

"No!" she whimpered. Desperate, she grabbed her backpack off the floor and dropped the conch in beside the other one. She slung it over her shoulders, stepped into her rubber boots, and left the room without looking back.

The street was empty, as was the boardwalk running along the berm of the beach. She could hear her own breathing between the *scuff-scuff* of her boots on the pavement. She headed for the sand.

Clouds moved in, smothering the moon. Lights along the boardwalk enabled her to see until the walkway ended, and only rocks and sand remained ahead. She kept to the water's edge, trusting memory to keep her on the path forward. The water stirred, gently lapping ashore, but gaining power the further she ventured. By the time the cliff face filled the horizon, white-capped waves were splashing eagerly across her ankles.

The clouds thinned. Her father was on the path up the hill, awash in the glow of the moon. His progress was slow, shortening the gap between them without stopping to wait.

Why wasn't he waiting for her? Why had he walked away at all? They were far enough away from the B&B to talk without her mom seeing them, weren't they?

Too many questions. She pushed them away, doubled her speed. She just wanted to see her dad, to hug him, to tell him she loved and missed him. She cut toward the base of the hill and the beaten path that waited there. Her dad reached the crest, his pace unchanged. His curly hair blew in the breeze the same way she had seen it move a thousand times before. It gave her comfort.

Follow him. Be with us.

She hesitated. The voices were louder. The tone had changed. Pleasant melody replaced with raspy urgency. She pulled the backpack around and lifted the conch out. It fell strangely silent, pensive. Dead air on the radio.

Her dad paused at the summit. His left hand ushered her forward. She climbed.

She Sells Sea Shells stood waiting just over the shoulder, fifty feet ahead. By daylight, the store's pastel palette had been warmly inviting. But at night, the structure embraced the inherent malevolence of darkness. Even the moon shied from it, reserving its pale glow for the cliff beyond.

Stop it! It's just a store! Her dad was behind the building, walking slowly away.

"Dad!" Zooey yelled. "Wait for me!"

He did not stop. She ran after him. Tall grass and brambles nicked and pierced her shins as she ran, but she was too afraid to slow down.

At the back of the building, she *did* stop. Her dad stood thirty feet ahead, facing her across the grassy brow. The ground vanished into shadow beyond the halfway mark. Her dad held out his left hand, pointing.

"Do you hear them, Zooey?" There was a strange warble to his voice, like water in his mouth. Before she could reply, he stabbed his finger toward her. "I want to hear them too."

She took several hesitant steps forward, sliding her backpack off and pulling the conch free. Many voices called out as one.

Go to him.

Join him.

JOIN US!

"Daddy?"

"I heard them. Bring it here so I can hear better."

She hurried her steps, then stopped. How had her dad heard the mermaids? The lady in the store had said no one else could hear them. Her mom had not even heard them.

The conch was glowing in her hand. A white aura had formed around it.

Zooey looked up at her dad. "What did they say?"

His pleasant expression faltered. She saw it happen in his eyes first and then the corners of his mouth.

"They said to come here," her dad said. "Come *here*, Zooey."

Still, she hesitated. "The lady said only I could hear them."

He stared, then cocked his head slightly to the side. His mouth formed a new smile, and his head straightened again. "That's right, Zooey. Only you can hear *that* shell. But what about the other one?"

"It sang to you?"

"Yes. It's why I came. You found it. For me."

Zooey glanced at her backpack. The second conch had revealed nothing to her or her mom. Maybe it was meant just for her dad.

"Zooey."

She reached toward the open pocket, paused.

"Zooey, come here."

"I didn't tell Mom I was leaving. We should go back."

"Your mom is sleeping. You don't want to disturb her. You know how upset she gets when you wake her."

The glow expanded and contracted, pulsating like a heartbeat.

"I just need to let her know. You can come with me."

"I don't have much time, Zooey. I have to get back." Her dad ushered her forward. "Bring it here, let me listen. *They'll* tell us what to do. We can listen to them together."

She peered across the remaining darkness. She had wanted him here. She loved her mom, but the trip wasn't the same without her dad. And now here he was, as if her heart and mind had been read in tandem and her wish granted. What other wishes could be granted? More than anything, she wanted her mom and dad to be together. Perhaps if her dad wished for that too—

"That's good," her dad said. She had been slowly inching forward. Just a few steps separated them now. He held out both arms. "Almost there."

Her conch was a white torch in her hand, the glow so powerful she could no longer see around it. She felt the ground beneath her, but it was lost in the haze. The wind whipped her hair. It caught in her mouth and eyes. She swiped at it.

Her dad was a mere arm's length away.

"Together," he said.

Together.

The word echoed, euphorically filling the air. Zooey reached out, taking the final step.

The ground disappeared. She tried to scream, thinking her dad would surely grab her, but he was gone. The wind stole the breath from her lungs, the backpack from her hand. She clutched the conch tight, but it grew massive and slipped from her fingers. As she fell, the ground dropped farther away. Her stomach lurched. The aperture thrust open below like a pale, toothless mouth. The inner light was blinding and cold. So cold. It swallowed her. She saw movement, shapes in the distance, shadows in the light. They were guiding her forward, calling her name, their voices so beautiful. She forgot about the cold. She forgot about breathing. Eventually, *they* came into focus, and she forgot about her mom and her dad, too. There was only the beauty of light and song.

The mouth closed.

JULIE IN THE MORNING

Julie Cameron awoke to the sound of screaming, vulgar in volume and pitch. It pulled her from a pleasant dream that vanished in the light. The room was bright, even with the curtains drawn. She rolled over and picked her cell phone off the bedside table. It continued to scream at her until she focused, shut it off, and tossed it to the far side of the bed.

Julie sat up swiftly, checked the phone again. It was almost noon.

"Shit."

She dressed quickly in yesterday's clothes. There would be time for a shower and change once she got her bearings.

"Zooey?"

She paused, waiting for a response. None came. "Zooey? Baby?"

Nothing. Not even the TV from the other room. She opened the door. The main room was empty. She went to Zooey's bedroom door.

"Zooey? You still sleeping?" Julie did not wait for an answer and opened the door. The curtains were wide apart, the bed fully made. Zooey was not in the habit of making her bed. It had been untouched since the day before.

Something was off. Everything about this was wrong.

She tried to control the oncoming panic with rational thoughts: Zooey probably fell asleep watching TV, got up early, saw that Julie was still asleep, and went to get a bite to eat on the boardwalk. It was the logical thing. The smart thing. And Zooey was sharp as a tack.

Julie grabbed her purse.

Zooey was not at either of the restaurants along the beach. She wasn't at the ice cream parlor either. In fact, she wasn't anywhere along the boardwalk or the beachfront.

That sinking feeling dug deeper inside. Cold sweat settled on Julie's skin. She fumbled with her phone, wondering if she should call someone. But who? Sheriff Dan? And what would she say? That she took one too many sedatives and overslept while her nine-year-old wandered off?

One too many? Let's be honest, Mrs. Cameron, it was a lot more than one, wasn't it?

So what if it was? It's not the point. Zooey is missing.

But it is the point. This isn't the first time this has happened, is it Mrs. Cameron?

Shut up.

Should we call your husband? He'll know what to do. He wouldn't have taken a bunch of pills, and he's a rock star.

Shut up, shut up!

She pressed her fists into her eyes, tried to think. She was being irrational. There was a very simple explanation. Out of sight or not, Zooey wouldn't have gone far. She was here *somewhere*.

Julie opened her phone again and shuffled through the pictures. She found one of Zooey and left it open on the screen.

That's good. That'll look great on the poster, Mrs. Cameron. We'll get those up all over town right away.

SHUT UP!

She went back to each location with the photo in hand. They all recognized Zooey, but none of them had seen her today. With each passing moment, with each dead end, it became more and more difficult to maintain her calm.

Outside, the overcast sky meant fewer tourists were walking the streets than usual. Zooey was not among them. On her second glance up the road, Julie noticed a heavy cloud of fog easing back from the top of the cliff, revealing the little pink and teal building sitting there.

Of course! Zooey would have gone there to sell her conch. She should have waited for her mother, but that was a conversation for later. Julie headed for the slope at a fast trot.

She was out of breath as she reached the summit. The small parking lot in front was unexpectedly full, with one vehicle parked half in the parking zone and half on the lane leading up from the other side of the hill. It looked like a presidential motorcade, with all but one of the vehicles being a black SUV.

The front door of the shop opened, and a large elderly woman followed the sound of the bell out into the fresh air. She wore a large-brimmed hat and carried a tall object wrapped in brown butcher paper pressed tight to her chest. Her plump fingers were pinched with gold rings adorned with large jewels. She was clearly from out of town, her disdain for the sea air written in the harsh lines around her tight lips and pursed nostrils. She never gave Julie so much as a glance before climbing inside the SUV furthest from the door.

Julie entered the shop. Unlike the day before, it was buzzing with people. The door shut behind her, and everyone turned to look, their mumbled conversations falling silent. Julie considered how she must have appeared to them – dressed in clothes still wrinkled from a night on the floor, hair untouched since rising off the pillow, skin drenched in sweat from the climb. The onlookers, on the other hand, were all dressed in black and standing around the tables in the center of the shop. Armani suits for the men, Vera Wang and Chanel for the women. One lady clutched a shivering Pomeranian to her bosom and leered at Julie over her low-perched bifocals. The Pomeranian bared its fangs like a rabid teddy bear.

At the front register, Maren was in the middle of a transaction with a stout middle-aged man. She turned and made eye contact with Julie.

"Have you seen my daughter? Her name is Zooey, we were—"

"I remember, Mrs. Cameron. I have not seen her." Maren flashed an apologetic smile to the man. His hand was outstretched over the register, holding several hundred dollar bills. Maren took the money, and her hand disappeared under the counter. There was no receipt exchanged.

Julie stepped further inside, words spilling out of her: "She would have come here, probably this morning. She had a shell she found that she wanted to sell you like you told her."

The man hefted his purchase off the counter and held it close, almost protectively. He turned for the door, and Julie was momentarily distracted by what she saw in his arms.

A terrarium.

"You sure I can't wrap that for you?" Maren asked.

"All good. Thank you."

The man hurried by, his feet scuffing the carpet as Zooey had done the day before. As he passed, Julie recognized the terrarium as the one she had held herself. The waterfall sprayed the glass with a tiny mist. For a split second, she thought she saw a figure sitting next to the pool below. And then the man and his purchase were gone.

A rake-thin woman with a gaudy-looking broach pinned to her chest stepped to the register. Julie forced her way to the front.

"Excuse me?" the lady said disgustedly. Julie ignored her. Maren frowned at them both.

"My daughter. Did you hear what I said?"

"Yes," Maren said. "But she has not been by. Not since yesterday."

"Are you sure? I've looked everywhere else and—"

"I am certain, Mrs. Cameron. Now, if you'd be so kind as to let me continue to serve these people..."

Julie's heart pounded in her chest, her temples pulsed. Everyone was staring at her. Not like she was crazy, but like she did not belong among them. Who did they think they were? And why were they all there at once anyway?

Julie backed up. The room spun. The broach lady laid a fishbowl-shaped terrarium on the counter and reached inside her purse, saying: "At least you won't have to deal with the riff-raff anymore after today."

What was happening after today?

Julie realized the question was only in her head. She blurted it out. "What's after today?"

Maren did not look at her. "Closed for the season."

"Closed?" Julie looked around. Each of the patrons was holding a terrarium. The tables were bare. "I... I thought you said they weren't for sale. The terrariums. You said they weren't for—"

"I said they take time, Mrs. Cameron. To get right. And now they are."

The broach lady counted more than a dozen hundreds and slid them across the counter. Maren slipped them under the register the way one would sneak food to a dog at the dinner table. "Wrapped?"

"If you wouldn't mind."

"My pleasure."

Maren moved the terrarium to the middle of the counter and turned to a vertical roll of brown paper mounted on the back wall. Julie watched it unfold, replaying the old shopkeeper's words in her head: *Time to get right. Time to get...*

Something orange caught her eye from inside the fishbowl. It stood out against the lush green foliage surrounding a low field of blue flowers. She approached the counter. Near the top of the inside of the glass, a small cloud hovered. Below the cloud lay the figure of a young man, arms behind his head, eyes staring lifelessly up at the sky. The level of detail was extraordinary. He wore khaki shorts and a black T-shirt. One knee was bent, bare foot pressed into the grass. The other foot dangled across the knee, clad in a bright orange Converse sneaker.

"Ma'am? Are you okay?" the broach lady asked. Instead of being concerned, she was backing away. "I think she's going to be sick."

Julie barely heard her. The pulse in her head was thundering. Her vision spiraled, swirls of darkness tugging at the light. She stumbled forward and bumped into a man old enough to be her grandfather. He brushed her off like a piece of lint. As she spun around, she saw inside the terrarium he held in his arms. A beautiful young brunette in a red summer dress was frozen in time, swinging from a tree branch, her hair blown back in the breeze. Julie blinked, tried to gain her balance. She spun again, and the patrons shuffled out of her way, clutching their items tightly. She found herself facing the back wall. The PAY WHAT YOU CAN sign was no longer there. The shelf was empty except for a single large shell.

A conch.

Hot vomit rose in her throat. She forced it back. All eyes were on her. Staring. Judging. The room closed in. Her strength gave way. She gripped the nearest table, stumbled back toward the front of the store. She reached out and caught herself on the door. Then it opened.

The bell chimed, and a man said, "On second thought, I think I will get it wrapped."

Julie turned. The stout man paused, waiting for her to move. But she never did. She stood there, staring at the glass terrarium in his arms. And when she saw the little gray-eyed girl in pink rubber boots staring up at her from below the waterfall, she started to scream.

Notes on Knock, Knock, Knock

Love is hard. Relationships are harder. Happiness is the hardest of all. And nothing lasts forever. Everyone knows this.

I'm always fascinated by people who have every reason to *not* be together, but decide to do so anyway. We've all seen them – the couples sitting silently together at a restaurant scrolling through their phones, never speaking until they ask for the bill; or the couples who argue their way through the grocery store, out into the parking lot, and all the way home. Their pain and suffering make our day-to-day worries all the easier to manage. Give me a chair and a bag of popcorn, and I could watch them for hours.

What? Like you wouldn't join me.

Despite my fascination, I still don't know what the glue is that keeps those people together. Love? Sex? Desperation? Maybe all three? Or none of the above.

The following story is about just such a couple. And a few other things, to keep it interesting. I still don't have the answer. But I'm getting closer.

KNOCK, KNOCK, KNOCK

By THE TIME THEY HEARD THE SIREN, STACEY HAD FRAYED SCOTT'S LAST fucking nerve, and he was ready to smash her pretty face through the windshield. He loved her, though, and that was proving to be a problem. A big fucking problem. She had a vice around his heart and a penchant to tighten it at will. *Bitch.*

Scott flicked the signal light on and started to ease the '91 Cadillac over to the shoulder. Stacey stared at him from the passenger seat, a soft pulse of red and blue alternating across her pale skin and satin-black hair. She was about to say something. It was one of her two states of being: about to say something or in the middle of saying it already. Both drove him over the edge, but the former gave him a chance to cut her off. Once the words started to spill out, all he could do was sit and take it. And he was pretty much done with taking it. He'd been taking it for five hundred miles across two state lines.

"Don't," he said.

"Don't what?" she asked. Her blue eyes flared wide, her chin flinched up. "The fuck I won't."

The car rolled to a stop on the gravel. Traffic flew by on the highway, everyone but them heading somewhere worthwhile. They were stuck - had been stuck for some time now. Scott couldn't remember the last time they'd shared a pleasant meal or sincere laugh. He was starting to forget what her laugh even sounded like. It had once reminded him of cotton candy, it was so sweet. Now it was lost in the darkness of the miles behind them, hitching a ride in the opposite direction.

He put the car in park and turned sharply to her. "Don't fucking say anything about—"

"About what?"

Scott glanced toward the back, tilted his head subtly. Through the rear windshield, he could see the Arizona State Trooper's heavy cruiser stop twenty feet behind. The siren had ceased, but the lights continued to spin lazily. Sunset was still an hour ahead to the west. The trooper was looking down to his right, where a computer monitor had most likely been mounted. Scott whistled a breath through gritted teeth. He couldn't recall if the plates were expired or not. He couldn't recall a lot of things. That had started in Texas. Fucking Texas.

"You think I'm an idiot?"

Scott looked at her squarely before responding. The second of silence was enough. He heard the slap before he felt the sting. His pudgy cheek offered little resistance, and her hand only stopped when it came up solid against the headrest behind him. He winced and grabbed her wrist, twisting it back so hard she bent toward the dashboard. His mouth tasted like iron.

The trooper was still studying his computer screen. Scott dug his nails into the soft flesh of her forearm. She hissed.

"Ouch, you fucking asshole!" She squirmed, tugging her arm back. Scott tightened his grip. The inside of his left cheek was numb. She'd clocked him good. It was going to leave a mark. That was going to raise an eyebrow from the trooper, if not a whole series of questions. Jesus Christ, she was going to pay for it. Unlike her, his hand would be closed when it connected with her face. *Guaran-fucking-teed.*

Scott shifted his attention from the back window. He pulled her close to him. She sucked in a breath. His free hand shot up and slid around her thin neck. His thumb hooked under the black lace choker she wore. At one time, seeing her lying on her back, milky white skin naked except for that choker, had made him painfully hard. Some nights, he thought his cock would tear a hole in the world trying to get to her. Now it sat flaccid with disgust against his thigh as the lace tightened on her throat.

"You're not an idiot, Stace. But sometimes I swear to Christ you're the stupidest cunt alive." His thick fingers pressed harder. Her mouth opened as if on command. It reminded him of those little toy garbage can candy dispensers they sold at the corner store that would pop their top when you squeezed tight. The sound of her gasping was sickening in the stale air of the Cadillac. "I don't need to tell you how fucking precarious a situation we are in. I know that you know that. Nod if you know that."

Stacey's head bobbed once. Scott could feel her throat pulse as she tried to swallow. He figured he had about ten seconds before she puked all over the front seat.

"Right now, you need to get your head out of your ass and just sit there and keep quiet. I'll do the talking, and you'll sit there and not say a goddamn word and with any luck, we'll be back on the road to Vegas faster than you can say: 'fuck you, Scotty'. Got it? Nod if you got it, Stace. I need to see that pretty head go up and down before I let go."

Another bob. Her eyes were fixed on the overhead light, her tongue dancing in and out in short stabs. Scott turned to view the trooper and let her go. She twisted in her seat and retched, but nothing came up. They hadn't eaten in over two days. She sucked in air and wiped her eyes, streaking purple eye shadow at odd angles. As Scott watched the state trooper slide out of his cruiser, he heard Stacey's reedy voice whisper, "That's the last time you touch me, mutherfucker. Ever. We are done."

The trooper paused and leaned back in through the open window of his vehicle. Scott rotated his head and watched him in the side mirror. He inhaled a deep breath, let it out slowly. He needed to be on his A-game, not carrying a weaker player. And with Stacey lately, it was like carrying the whole fucking team.

"When this pig is gone, you can get out. How's that for 'done'?"

A short, brittle laugh escaped her. It was anything but sweet. *"He* needs us both to be there, dumbfuck."

"I can manage." Scott continued to eye the trooper. The officer finished whatever he had been doing and was walking toward the Cadillac at a deliberate pace. Scott spun on her. "Not another—"

Three soft knocks sounded from the back end of the car, unhurried, evenly spaced. Scott's words choked off in his mouth. A drop of sweat emerged over his left eyebrow. Stacey slowly turned her head toward the back.

"Evening, folks."

Scott swiveled back around in his seat at the sound of the trooper's southern drawl. The lawman was standing a few feet away from the open driver-side window, right hand hitched on his belt just in front of his sidearm. The other was shielding his eyes as he glanced to the horizon at the front of the car, then the back. The traffic had thinned out across the long flat stretch of dry land. He leaned forward.

"Where you two headed?"

Scott forced a smile. His eyes desperately tried to see past the mirrors of the trooper's aviator glasses, hoping the bead of sweat stayed put and went unnoticed. His fat face was distorted and round in the reflection. "Something wrong, officer?"

The trooper's smile twitched but held on. Scott noticed how attractive and tanned he was and then wondered if Stacey did too. *Of course she did. She's probably soaking the seat as we speak.* The droplet slid into his eye and stung.

"How about I ask the questions, and you provide me with your license and registration?" The trooper turned his gaze on Stacey, who was sitting at an unnatural ninety-degree angle, staring forward.

Scott pulled his wallet out of his back pocket, then turned to her. "Stace, can you pass me the registration out of the... thing?" He wiped his eye and pointed to the glovebox, the word escaping him. Stacey did not move.

"Ma'am, are you okay?"

The trooper's voice seemed to pull her back from whatever mental ledge she was leaning out on. She smiled at him. "Oh, yeah. Peachy-keen." That was one of her pet phrases Scott had always hated. She hadn't dragged it out in a while, and doing so now was like a needle jabbed under his fingernail. He made a fist, then flexed it out and pointed again.

"Hon, the registration? In there."

She smiled a moment longer at the trooper, sticking the needle in a little deeper, then popped open the glove compartment. A bushel of Wendy's napkins spilled out on her lap. A couple made it as far as the floor. She reached down to grab them, hearing the soft *ping!* of her engagement ring strike the tire iron wedged along the runner. Like everything in the car, it was not where it belonged. She straightened and pushed the napkins between her legs before finally plucking the registration out of the dashboard. Scott took it from her immediately.

"Here you go." Scott offered the paper to the trooper along with his license. The trooper continued to watch Stacey a moment longer, then scooped the items from Scott's hand.

"This your vehicle, Mr...?"

"Stark," Scott said quickly. His smile strained. "Like Iron Man."

"Or naked," the trooper deadpanned. Stacey spit out a laugh, a single spiteful 'ha'. Scott tilted his head. His hand squeezed into a fist by his side. Riding the rest of the way in the backseat of the cruiser might just be worth splitting her face wide open. He bit down on his lower lip, and the rage refocused.

"Right," Scott said. The trooper flipped the registration over. Scott watched the man's eyebrows rise above the top of his sunglasses.

"You didn't answer the question."

Scott swallowed hard. *What was the question?* He couldn't recall in the slightest. *Fuck!* And he couldn't ask either. The trooper had been very clear about who got to ask what. *Cocksucker.* How many seconds had passed? More sweat perched above his stinging eye. He glanced out the windshield, wracking his brain. The sun ahead of them was unmoving.

"It's my father's," Stacey said suddenly. "We borrowed it. Well, he insisted we take it, really. He didn't trust us taking Scott's cross country. Said it was 'a piece of shit a fly wouldn't give a second glance to'. Which is mean - I know it sounds mean - but my dad, he just wants me to be safe, you know?"

"Are you?" the trooper asked, cutting her off. Despite the loaded question, Scott was actually relieved. The sun would have set before she finished. And that would have been bad for them all. Very bad.

Stacey was startled by the question, her big eyes blinking slowly. She ran her heavily gnawed fingertips along her choker and cleared her throat. "Of... of course."

The trooper's face gave no sign he believed her one way or the other. He held the registration up for her to see. "What's your father's name?"

"Steve. Or Big Steve. That's what everyone calls him. Even me." She laughed awkwardly. "I know that's weird, right? I should call him dad or pop or something, but no, he's always been Big Steve—"

"Stacey." Scott felt crippled with the fear of what he might do to her if she didn't shut up.

"What? It's true. And interesting." She grinned at the trooper. "It's interesting, right?"

The trooper took off his glasses and slid them into his shirt pocket. He turned his dark green eyes to her. He was even more attractive unmasked. Scott closed his eyes so no one would see them roll.

"Sure," the trooper said. "But let's try and stick to the facts."

"But it is a fact. Everyone calls him Big Steve. Tell him, Scotty."

The trooper sighed, glancing past her to the backseat. He arched an eyebrow that would make Dwayne Johnson proud. A blue suitcase sat on one side, a larger pink and black one on the other. A spare tire was wedged between the back of the front seats and the suitcases. Black stains stretched along the lower edge of the seat from where the tire had rolled back and forth across it.

"Something wrong with your trunk?"

"No," Scott answered, so fast he practically cut a full syllable from a two-letter word. Stacey echoed him a second later.

"Doesn't seem fair to Big Steve, making a mess of his car like that," the trooper stated.

Scott opened and clenched his fist again. Red grooves had formed on his palm. His unkempt nails settled back into them as he wondered what the fuck business it was of this asshole what they did to the inside of Big Steve's car. Big Steve was a piece of shit whose one worthwhile contribution to the world had been depositing sufficient sperm in Mrs. Big Steve to create a real-life Chatty Cathy doll. And the pros and cons of that achievement were currently under review.

Stacey continued to ignore everything Scott had said when his hand had been around her throat. "We've bought a lot of stuff along the way. Gifts and stuff. Clothes. I guess it's mostly clothes, and mostly for me. Guilty, haha. As charged. Trunk filled up pretty quickly." She was waving her hands around as she spoke and stopped suddenly, staring out the front window. The late-day sunlight was deep orange on her pale skin. A smile formed at the corners of her mouth. When she spoke, her eyes were still on the horizon. "Wanna see?"

Scott sucked in a breath as he slowly turned to look at her. It whistled through the gap in his front teeth. His eyes bulged, but hers were smiling, devious.

"Wait here, please," the trooper said. "Stay in the vehicle."

The trooper started back toward his cruiser. He tapped the license and registration against the roof and trunk as he went. When he was halfway, Scott punched the steering wheel.

"What the fuck are you doing? You trying to get us killed?"

Stacey pointed out the front window. She leaned close to him, her lips an inch from his right ear. He could smell a hint of her perfume - lilac and vanilla. That also had power over him once. Now it was buried in an aura of fear and slight decay. Slight only because they had somehow managed to keep themselves alive this far by not royally fucking things up. But the road ahead would come to an end before long. Stacey seemed intent on speeding toward it.

"This is our chance," she whispered. Her voice was so quiet it took him a moment to piece together those four words. It took him another moment to consider if she had really been stupid enough to utter them.

He pressed his mouth next to her ear. "Are you fucking crazy?"

She shook her head. "Think about it."

Maybe he had choked her too hard, too long, and cut off the oxygen to her brain. How long could the brain go without oxygen before irreparable damage occurred? In her case, apparently mere moments. "I don't need to think about it, Stace. I don't think you're thinking at all. Jesus H. Fucking Christ."

"You're a vulgar asshole, you know that?" She pulled her head away and locked eyes with him. "And you're stupid. Stupid and vulgar and full of shit. What are those insects that live in shit and eat shit all day?"

"Most," he said flatly. Part of him, the part that still loved her despite all that was logical in the world, wanted to laugh. Three days ago, he would have. He *was* vulgar and more than a little mean, it was true. She put up with a lot of shit and had always had a playful way of putting him in his place. That had been one of her best qualities. Now when he tried to remember what that was like, it felt just out of reach, distorted, like trying to see a prize inside a half-inflated balloon. The last three days had changed everything, including who they were. They looked the same, but inside... inside they were... *his*.

"Dung beetle. That's it, that's you. Dung beetle."

Scott sighed and glanced in the rearview mirror. The trooper was studying his computer screen. Scott could see the license and registration still in the trooper's hand as it gripped the top of the steering wheel. They hadn't done anything wrong by borrowing the car and it wouldn't show up as stolen. Unless there was damage to the rear end that they weren't aware of, or some excessive traffic violations Big Steve had failed to pay, this should all be over soon enough. So long as Stacey refrained from unspooling her tongue again like a party kazoo. The odds on that were low.

Scott gazed at the sun, then motioned her head forward again. Stacey reluctantly obliged, fearing a slap or a second go-round at *choke-your-gal*. Scott pressed his lips against her ear. "We don't even know if that would work. And if it didn't, we're..." He ran a stiff finger across his throat, ear to ear.

"It'll— Jesus, just forget it." She shook her head and leaned back into her seat. The tire in the back rolled into the space behind his. "Dumbfuck."

Scott opened his mouth to say something entirely regrettable but shut it instantly as three short knocks emanated from behind the backseat. He ground his jaws and held up his index finger to her before folding it into the rest of his fist and biting down on it.

Stacey scratched at her neck, tugging the choker side to side. It slid up slightly, and Scott could see pink, mottled skin just below. He stole a glance out the rear window, then reached out to tug the choker down. As he touched it, Stacey's head suddenly snapped back against the headrest. Her eyes rolled back, showing only the bloodshot whites. Her jaw hung open, slack. A string of drool spilled slowly out the corner of her mouth.

"Stace...?" Scott said sickly. His voice was low and thin. He turned sharply to the backseat. "She— she didn't mean it. I swear she didn't. She just runs her mouth, saying shit all the time. She can't help it. She didn't mean it. Please!"

Stacey continued to claw at her choker. Scott forced her hands down into her lap, held them there. He heard a door close in the distance. He stared out the rear window and watched the improbably handsome state trooper exit his vehicle.

*   *   *

They had decided to remain in West Texas for an extra day. That was a mistake.

Their engagement was only a year old, but the cracks were starting to show. In fact, the cracks had been there for a while, they had just been putting cheap glue in them week after week. It had been Stacey's idea to hit the road, see some of the country, and maybe discover if their desire for love was greater than their desire to kill one another. Before El Paso, those balls had still been juggling in the air.

The trip had started slowly out of Georgia and through most of Alabama, but they made up time with minimal stops in Mississippi and Louisiana. Stacey had a great-aunt she insisted they visit in Austin, and they stayed the night. Aunt Gerta was a short, plump woman of eighty-nine who was up at the crack of dawn cooking them a three-course breakfast before they hit the road. The night before, she had regaled them with stories of her youth, including standing roadside in Dealey Plaza the day Kennedy took a bullet to the head and another to his throat, a moment that scarred her and the rest of her generation for life. Listening to her, it wasn't hard to see which side of the family Stacey got her gift of gab from. And according to Stacey, Aunt Gerta wasn't much of a fan of Big Steve either, a point Scott filed with pleasure in his memory bank.

Full of eggs, three kinds of meat, toast and pancakes, they set out across the state just before eleven and, after several sightseeing stops along the way, pulled into a Super 8 motel just outside El Paso around nine in the evening. Their room was nothing to write home about, but the bed was firm, the pillows soft, and the air conditioner did its job. They were dancing around the idea of fucking or falling asleep when—

knock. knock. knock.

—everything changed.

Stacey, fresh out of the shower, a blue towel upright on her head like a Marge Simpson beehive, glanced from Scott on the bed to the door and back again. He shrugged, reached for the lamp to turn it off. She frowned, rolled her eyes.

"Subtle," she said quietly.

"Unlike whispering," he retorted, pulling his arm back and reaching on the floor for his Slayer T-shirt instead.

She took a step back toward the bathroom, pointing to the front door.

"You want me to answer it? You're already up." He had the medium shirt halfway over his extra-large torso. "Are you serious?"

She was. She retreated another step and jabbed her finger forward again - shorter, sharper. Scott sighed and gave up on the shirt. He swung his legs over the side of the bed, grateful he'd kept his pants on. His socks were crumpled on the floor, and he reached for them.

"Are *you* serious?" Stacey asked. She huffed but made no movement. Scott looked back at her. She bulged her eyes, bobbed her head forward like a bird. He threw up his hands and as they came down, popped himself up with the momentum. The bed wobbled behind him.

knock. knock. knock.

Soft, evenly spaced, unhurried.

"Just a second!" Scott yelled. He felt for his fly, having lost the ability to see it beyond his gut six months into his first year at college. Higher education had ended eighteen months ago, but the freshman fifteen was pushing sixty pounds now. Beer and pizza will redefine a man.

"Why are you yelling?"

"Why are you whispering? They clearly know we're in here."

"They don't know you're an asshole, though. But keep it up."

Scott sighed and started for the door.

"Jesus, Scotty, pull your shirt down. You look like Winnie the Pooh for Christsake."

He stretched the black Tee out and over his belly. It complied but almost immediately began to roll itself back up in regret.

"I wish you'd just throw that fucking thing out."

He shot her an angry glance. "Now? You say that now? And besides, it's Slayer, Stace. Fucking *Slayer.*" This last part, he growled, shaking his head so his jowls shook. "I'll be buried in this shirt."

"What's gonna cover the other ninety-five percent of your body?"

"You're a—"

knock. knock. knock.

She stabbed a finger at the door. Scott shook his head and stepped up to it, one hand tugging the shirt down, the other reaching for the knob.

The man standing in the rain on the other side was very tall and thin. And very old. He was dressed in a loose-fitting suit, a shade of crimson so dark it appeared black everywhere the light from the doorway did not touch. In contrast, his hair was thoroughly white and combed back, with sideburns that reached down past the earlobes. His skin was dark around the eyes but pale the further out from them one looked. The eyes themselves were narrow and deep brown, set above a long, thin nose giving the countenance a natural intensity like that of a bird of prey. Scott found himself at eye level with the stranger's mouth, which was broadly shaped by burgundy lips. The corner of one side glistened for a moment before the tongue darted out and licked whatever had been there away.

"Good evening," the stranger said. His voice was deep and throaty, untouched by age, and carried just a hint of an English accent. His lips curled into a slight smile before he continued speaking. "Sorry to disturb you at such a late hour."

From behind the door, Stacey whispered, "Who is it?"

Scott leaned back and glanced at her. "I *just* opened the door."

"Well, get rid of them."

Scott sighed and turned back to the stranger in the doorway. The old man's smile continued unabated. It was unsettling, a sensation Scott struggled to conceal. "How can we— I help you?"

The stranger leaned to the left to look into the room, saying, "We? Is that a young lady I heard hiding back there?"

Stacey held her breath. Scott tilted to his right, and the man leaned back, his smile spreading. He looked down at Scott's T-shirt as it restarted its slow ascent up his gut. The word "Slayer" was written in deep, dripping red inside a pentagram. Below it were the words:

"'Reign in Blood'..." the stranger read. He met Scott's eyes with his own. "Indeed."

Scott frowned. "Okay, whatever it is, we're not interested." He began to shut the door. The old man held up his right hand, and the door shuddered to a stop as soon as it made contact. Scott began to press harder, then stopped. He stared at the stranger's hand. The knuckles were thick with hair, and all but the index finger adorned with rings of various pagan symbols, including a pentagram on the pinky. The thumbnail was longer than the rest and refined to a point, like that of certain guitar players Scott had admired over the years. He looked down at the other hand, which was holding a very expensive-looking violin case. Like the man himself, it was getting wet.

The stranger turned, looked back to the parking lot one floor below and nodded toward the dark red Cadillac near the motel manager's office. "Is that your vehicle there? The red one?" He turned back, still smiling.

"Tell him no. Jesus Christ, Scotty, just shut the damn door already."

Scott looked at her behind the door. "You know he can hear you, right?"

"What does he want?"

"He asked about our car." Scott turned back to the stranger. "What about it?"

The old man's eyes brightened. "Ah, so I was not mistaken. It is yours."

"I didn't say that."

"You didn't have to, Mr...?"

"Stark," Scott said, unable to tear his eyes away from the stranger's. They were still brown but infused with swirls of burgundy bordering on crimson.

"Like Iron Man," the stranger said pleasantly. He extended his hand. Scott barely noticed. He was transfixed. A pleased grin of his own was spreading across his face.

"Exactly," Scott said slowly.

"John Polidori." The old man's eyes flicked toward his outstretched hand, and the spell was broken. "But you may call me J.W."

As soon as the old man looked away, Scott felt his heart palpitate like it had momentarily stopped and restarted. He shook the stranger's hand almost as an afterthought. It was cold and smooth as though all the lines had been eroded with time. He tried to let go, but the old man held on.

Stacey appeared behind Scott, tugging the towel free from her head. Her hair fell across her face, and as she wiped it away, Polidori turned his eyes on her.

"Mister, we've had a long day. Whatever it is you need, can it wait until—?"

"Morning? I'm afraid it cannot. Most assuredly." Soft rain speckled his shoulders and cheeks. He didn't seem to notice. "Mr. Stark here was about to invite me in from the rain, and I promise you, you won't regret it."

Stacey was about to protest, felt the words form in her mouth, building up on her tongue, but instead, she swallowed them whole. She couldn't look away from Polidori's stare. She realized she could no longer do anything except say:

"Okay..."

*   *   *

"It's gonna be okay," Scott said, holding Stacey's head in his hands. "Look at me, Stacey."

Her entire body was rigid, no longer under her control. Even her chest was still. The regular rise and fall of her breathing had ceased. Drool leaked from the corner of her mouth over Scott's thumb. He didn't notice. His arms strained to move her head down to face him.

"We'll do what you asked. I swear it! Just let her go, goddamn it!" Scott stared into the back seat as he spoke. No reply came. Through the rear windshield, he could see the trooper preparing to exit his cruiser again. "Listen to me: she does this, okay? She's difficult. She likes to push people's buttons. Especially mine. She was just being a bitch. You get used to it. But I swear, she never meant it. We need the money too bad, trust me. You've got nothing to worry about."

Outside, the sun still burned across the horizon. As the trooper shut his car door, the lenses of his aviators were bright orange ovals. He flapped the license and registration absently against his thigh with each slow step.

A hot rush of air burst from Stacey's open mouth, and she gagged. Her body relaxed, and her eyes fell back into position, as if everything was being pulled down by a sudden shift in gravity. She sucked in oxygen, staring at Scott with terrified eyes. She tried to speak, but nothing emerged. She grabbed for her throat, and he held her hands back.

"H-h-he was... he was in my head, Scotty. I saw... things—"

"It's okay."

"No." She knocked his hands away and took his head in her own hands. "I watched you dying, and I couldn't move. And my God, that noise!" Tears swelled in her eyes.

Scott darted his eyes back and forth between her and the trooper, who was halfway to their car. "What noise?"

"The violin. It sounded like... screaming."

"He just wanted to scare you. I'm okay, Stace. See?" He pressed her hand harder against his cheek, then he grabbed his gut and shook it for her. "See? I'm still here. Every bit."

She giggled and sobbed all at once, and the tears spilled out. "I fucking hate you."

"I know," he said. They both laughed. It was the first genuine one in forever.

She looked quickly past his shoulder and wiped her eyes. "How's my face?"

"Ghastly," he said with a grin.

"Rick Ghastly?"

"The one and only."

"Here's your paperwork back," the trooper said beside the window. Before turning, Scott noticed Stacey's choker had fallen on the armrest console. He swiped it and put it in her hand, his eyes flitting to the pair of inflamed red marks on her throat. They exchanged a concerned glance before he completed his turn, and she wrapped it back around her neck.

For a moment, Scott only stared at the documents. Then he snatched them back and forced a smile.

"Everything checked out fine," the trooper said.

Scott nodded, stuffing the license and registration messily into his jeans pocket.

"But you have a non-functioning brake light on the rear driver's side. Are you aware of that?"

"No," Scott said honestly. He looked at Stacey, who was also shaking her head a little too agreeably. "Not at all."

The trooper leaned on the open window frame. At this distance, Scott could smell the man's musk mingled with cologne. It made his dick retreat like a frightened turtle.

"Well, I imagine Big Steve didn't lend it to you kids in that condition, now did he?" They both shook their head. The trooper studied Stacey's face for a second, then said. "Have you been crying, ma'am?"

"Yes."

The trooper's eyes narrowed and fell on Scott, but Stacey wasn't finished: "It's just, we've never been pulled over before. This whole trip has been perfect, right up until now. I know we should have noticed that broken light, and I know we shouldn't have messed up the car. We've just been in such a rush to get to Vegas."

"What's in Vegas?"

"There's only two things people do in Vegas, and we already spent all our money." She laughed at her coyness. Scott was speechless. The trooper held her gaze and sighed. He looked in the back seat again, shook his head slightly, then stood up. "Fuck it. I'm gonna let you off with a warning. But get that fixed at the next exit."

"Will do."

"Promise."

"Don't make me regret it." The trooper stepped back and shielded his eyes as he studied the horizon. He walked back along the side of the car. Scott watched him go in the side mirror, one hand on the ignition, the other about to roll up the window. There were still about thirty minutes of daylight ahead of them. They'd have to stop for the night before long, but with any luck, they'd be in Vegas first thing in the morning. Marriage was the last thing on their minds. But they were less than 500 miles from being a whole lot richer.

"That's it, that's it..." Scott said quietly. "Nothin' to see he—"

At the back of the car, the trooper did a double-take glance at the trunk. Scott held his breath. Stacey tapped him on the shoulder.

"What's he doing?"

Scott didn't know and didn't answer. Stacey persisted and pinched the fat at the back of his arm. "The fuck, Stace?"

They both turned to look out the back window as the trooper bent down to get a better look. A moment later, he stood back up and tapped on the trunk.

"Could you pop the trunk, please?"

"Fuck," Stacey uttered.

knock. knock. knock.

The trooper appeared to reach down and tug on something by the trunk latch.

"The hell is he doing?" Scott asked. He turned and rolled the window all the way down. He leaned out, saying: "Something wrong, officer? I thought we were good to go."

The trooper straightened. "So did I. But you got something sticking out of the back here, and it got my curiosity. So, please pop the trunk and satisfy it."

"The, uh, the switch is busted. The trunk switch."

Stacey was tapping his shoulder again like a woodpecker relaying Morse code. The trooper stepped out to the side.

"Busted, how?"

"Not sure. Hasn't worked since, you know, we put all the clothes in there. Right, Stace?" This was her lie, and he could really use her help keeping it going. He turned to her, but she was no longer in control. Her eyes were back in her head, her body rigid against the seat.

knock. knock. knock.

Scott leaned back out the window, grateful he hadn't eaten in two days. He'd never had the urge to shit his pants more in his life.

"You two really haven't been good to Big Steve's car, have you? Grab the key, Iron Man, and get out here."

*   *   *

Scott heard the old man's words, but they trailed the movement of the lips, like watching an out-of-sync movie. They sounded slightly muffled, the way sound carries through a door. Only there was nothing between Scott and the old man except six feet of space. He had a sense that Stacey was sitting cross-legged beside him on the bed, but whenever he tried to turn to look at her, his head remained locked in place, facing forward. It was only the scent of vanilla and lilac that reassured him she was there.

"Comfortable?" Polidori asked. His eyes passed from Scott to Stacey, held on her for a moment, then settled back on Scott. "Excellent."

Polidori was sitting on a chair he had pulled from the motel room alcove and placed near the foot of the bed. He uncrossed his right leg from the left one and reached down to retrieve the violin case. He laid it carefully across his lap with the kind of practiced, gentle movement a parent handles an infant. He grinned at the pair on the bed as he snapped open the buckle locks at each end.

"It's really quite painless, you see. I require your assistance with a simple task, and in exchange, I will pay you a very consequential sum of money." He lay both hands flat across the top of the case and tapped very softly with his thumbs.

"Who do we have to kill?" Scott asked. He had a goofy grin that he was only partially aware of. He was too busy trying to discern how he had heard his own words before he felt his lips move. It was the opposite problem he had observed with the old man, as though they were moving through time and space at different speeds.

Polidori leaned back in his chair, chuckling. "Kill? Killing is an ugly business. I am in the business of beauty, my friends." His dark eyes lingered on Stacey once again, the swirls of crimson catching the light from the lamp. He looked down at the violin case and spun it around on his lap. "Do you know what a Stradivarius is?"

Scott wanted to shake his head but could not. When he was a teenager, he had experienced bouts of sleep paralysis frequently enough to know that this was not that... but it was damn close. Those experiences had terrified and confused him, and while he was plenty confused right now, he felt no terror, just calm.

Polidori frowned at them. "No? That is a shame. To be honest, I cannot say I am surprised. But, no matter. This, my friends, is a Stradivarius."

The old man lifted the lid of the case open. Scott expected to see jewels or gold coins spill out. 'Stradivarius' certainly had that pretentious European jeweler aura to it, especially when spoken by this tall stranger. But what lay in the case like a body at a wake was simply:

"A violin," Stacey said. They were the first words she had uttered since allowing Polidori into their room. Hearing her voice elevated Scott's sense of calm.

"This is not just any violin," Polidori said proudly. "This is a—"

"Stratocaster," Scott said. Or at least he thought he did. He was closer to believing it when he felt his mouth open and close a moment later. It was only upon seeing Polidori's intense stare lock onto his own that all doubt fell away. He giggled. Stratocaster was a guitar, not a violin.

Polidori's smile retreated. He lay the case on the floor next to his chair and stood up. The six feet between them evaporated, and Scott suddenly felt the old man's cold breath next to his ear. Unable to turn and see him, Scott could only watch as Polidori's hand covered his mouth and pressed him back against the headboard.

"*There is no darkness but ignorance*," the old man whispered. Scott felt his arm raise parallel to his shoulder, the hairs rising as cold air ran along the pale skin of the forearm, followed by an intense, sharp pain at the crease opposite the elbow. A warm and wet sensation spread up and down his arm for a full minute.

And then Polidori was back in the chair, the open violin case across his lap, his lips glistening crimson. When he spoke, his teeth were stained red.

"This particular Stradivarius was constructed in 1721 and once belonged to the granddaughter of a very dear friend. Upon her death in 1917, it passed into my possession, where it has remained to this day."

"That would make you... very old," Stacey said with a soft giggle. Polidori showed her a sympathetic smile. Scott felt very weak and nauseous. He desperately wanted to close his eyes. The longer he stared at Polidori, the more he was certain he was losing his mind. The old man's face was smoother than before, and there were black streaks through his thick hair that Scott could not recall being there when he had first opened the door. Polidori tapped the violin case three times, and Scott noticed the hair on the knuckles had also darkened considerably.

"Indeed," Polidori said. "Even older than I was then."

"You don't look it," Stacey blurted.

Polidori leaned his head back and laughed. "I am in very good company. I knew it the moment I saw you."

Scott felt his tongue dangle out the left side of his mouth. Drool slowly followed.

"I can't feel my legs," Stacey said. She did not sound alarmed by this fact.

"It will pass, my dear. It will all pass. In the morning, you will both be right as rain." Polidori closed the violin case and set it on the floor. "And that is when we will head west to Las Vegas. Together."

"Why?"

The old man walked to Stacey's side of the bed and sat next to her. He gently patted her hands in her lap. "A very foolish man of some importance has agreed to purchase my violin for a vast sum of money. My previous traveling companion was only able to bring me this far before he... ran out of fuel. A shame. He stood to make five percent. But for you, for your trouble, I will give you ten percent."

"Ten percent?" Stacey asked sleepily. "Of what?"

Scott watched from the corner of his eye as Polidori leaned across Stacey's body. The old man looked directly at Scott for a brief moment without pausing, and Scott saw hunger in Polidori's eyes. Polidori whispered in Stacey's ear. Scott heard her gasp, saw Polidori's head lower to her throat, then heard her muffled scream.

*   *   *

Scott withdrew the key from the ignition and stared at it. It would be so easy to stab it back in, twist and flee. They had a near-full tank of gas, and with a head start and a little luck, they could make it to the next town and duck out of sight. After that, their passenger would take care of any trouble. That was their unspoken deal, wasn't it? They needed each other.

He had almost convinced himself it was possible when he heard the trooper knock on the trunk again. He looked in the rearview mirror, then to the sun on the horizon. It was falling, but not fast enough.

"Motherfucker," Scott muttered. He shoved open the door and stumbled out, catching his balance with a hand on the window. He stole a glance back at Stacey. She was still there but not *there*. He was on his own.

"You are one hot mess, son." The trooper had one hand propped above his weapon, the other fingering the head of the flashlight hooked in his belt, watching Scott plod his way along the side of the car. "If you weren't on your way to get married, I'd toss your whole car to find whatever it is you're on."

Scott felt very weak. He leaned his hand on the roof, trying to look casual and failing miserably. "I'm not on anything, I swear."

The trooper removed his sunglasses and pinched the bridge of his nose with a heavy sigh. "Then I hope you clean up nice."

Scott caught his reflection in the backseat window. He was pale despite having spent the last week traveling across the hottest states in the republic. The dark under his eyes gave them a hollowed-out appearance, and his lips were almost corpse blue. His shaggy brown hair hung lifeless along the side of his head. The trooper wasn't wrong.

Scott pushed off the car and made his way around the back. The trooper took a step back, hand never leaving its perch above his gun. Scott finally saw what all the fuss was about. A piece of dark crimson fabric the size of a folded napkin was sticking out of the trunk just below the latch. It might have gone unnoticed were it not resting against the top of the white license plate. He tried to recall who had closed the trunk that morning, then quickly realized it no longer mattered. The trooper was going to force him to open it up, and then things were going to get incredibly, irreversibly strange.

Scott pretended to look through the keyring. His small, meaty fingers fumbled the keys, and they flopped into the gravel at his feet. "Sorry," he said and stooped to pick them up. While down on one knee, he heard the screeching creak of the passenger door open and saw Stacey's right foot step into the gravel.

"Ma'am, stay in the vehicle," the trooper said sharply. "Stay in the vehicle!"

Scott watched the trooper's stance drop lower, the muscular thighs tense up. The gun hand still hovered above the weapon, but it flexed, ready to pull it free. Scott turned his head and saw all of Stacey land in the gravel on her knees. She buckled over, holding her stomach and retching painfully.

"Ma'am, I'm only going to ask you once more. Return to your vehicle, please." The trooper took two steps to the side to get a clearer look at her. Scott snatched the keys out of the dirt and stood up. The trooper spun on him, hand firmly around the handle of the holstered pistol. "Sir, don't move!"

Scott froze, his hands halfway raised, arms against his body like a T-Rex.

knock. knock. knock.

The trooper cocked his head toward the trunk and—

The sound of iron cracking bone was one of the most disgusting things Scott had ever heard. His jaw fell open from the shock of seeing the tire iron shatter the side of the trooper's skull, and in that instant, a bright spray of blood coated Scott's tongue, teeth and face with all the subtlety of a rodeo clown. The trooper stumbled to one knee, the light in one eye already blinking out. His gun hand twitched at the holster as though recalling some sensory memory more than an actual attempt to draw the weapon out. It was horrifying and sad to witness all at once. And mercifully, it was brief, for the trooper had fallen into the perfect position for Stacey to swing a second blow right across the base of the skull. The sound was even more disturbing than the first, and when it was followed instantly by the horrid *clack!* of the upper and lower jaws biting into each other, Scott felt his scrotum retract tight enough to send his balls high into his groin. The trooper uttered a sound that might have been the middle syllable of almost any word, then fell face-first into the gravel.

Scott shook his head and stared at Stacey. She stood over the dead body, panting, tire iron still in both hands, her posture frozen in the end position of a perfect swing-through.

"What the everlasting fuck?!" Scott looked at the two hundred pounds of pussy-soaking swagger and muscle lying motionless before him in the dirt, and screamed. The trooper's blood was already drying on Scott's skin in the Arizona heat, leaving cracks in the creases around his mouth. He buried his head in his hands and screamed again. "We're so fucked! Oh God! Oh sweet smothering Christ!"

"Scotty," Stacey said, her voice calm, disconnected.

"I can taste him in my mouth... Oh, Jesus." He spit, retched, and spit some more. He started to wipe his tongue with his shirt, then realized it was also coated in blood.

"Scotty."

He looked up at her, hot tears in his eyes. "What? Jesus, Stace. You fucking killed him."

The bloody tire iron slipped from her hand into the gravel, already forgotten. "We have to go."

"Go?" He blinked. Tears slid across his cheeks, carving pathways through the maroon. "Go. Right. Right. Fuck. Okay."

He slid behind the wheel and watched her get in on the other side. She leaned over and kissed him on the lips, letting the moment linger. When she sat back, he turned and watched the bottom of the sun dip below the horizon. He turned the key.

*   *   *

They never made it to Vegas that night. Or any night after that.

When the first series of heavy knocks hit the motel room door, Scott was slumped on the floor at the foot of the bed, staring at the blood on his shirt. He raised his head slowly and felt hot liquid course down his neck. Another set of knocks came, louder, more aggressive. It was followed by shouting. Someone was ordering him to open up immediately. That wasn't going to happen. He could barely open his eyes, let alone a door. Everything was slowly going dark.

He turned his head, and another spurt of blood spilled down his chest. Stacey was staring at him, but her eyes were glazed over, her head upside down as it dangled over the end of the bed. Her throat was open wide, like a second grinning mouth. Her bleeding had stopped a while ago. It was pooling in the carpet beside him, reflecting the red and blue lights spinning outside the window. He raised a hand to try and touch her hair.

That was when the door exploded inward.

He never saw the SWAT team charge in. He never heard the order to put his hands in the air. He stared past them, past the noise, to the second-floor balcony on the other side of the motel lot, where a tall, dark-haired man in a crimson suit stared back for a moment before turning to a door and raising his hand to

knock. knock. knock.

Notes on Zombay, NL

Where I come from, the people talk funny. Oh, *we* don't think so, but everyone else does. It's part of our charm. Just like our ability to fly in the face of adversity and keep going. And boy, have we seen our share of adversity. Our capital city burned to the ground in 1892, and exactly 100 years later, our greatest natural resources dried up... in the *ocean*, no less! And in between those disasters, an iceberg sank an unsinkable ship off our coast. But we had nothing to do with that one. Promise.

The following script began life as a joke while on a road trip with my wife about ten years ago. The song *Zombie* by The Cranberries came on the radio, and we kept singing along as "Zom-bay" because, let's be honest, that's how it sounds. Turns out, The Cranberries come from a place where they talk funny, too. Just on the other side of the Atlantic.

As we continued our trek to one of the hundreds of small bay towns in Newfoundland, we concocted a scenario so preposterous, it would be impossible to pull off in real life. But that doesn't mean we Newfoundlanders wouldn't try.

The hard part is never the plan. The hard part is always sticking to it.

ZOMBAY, NL

FADE IN:

EXT. CALAMITY, NEWFOUNDLAND - DAY

VARIOUS SHOTS: *A small town surrounded on three sides by low mountains. The fourth faces the sea. Quiet streets, boats in the harbor, clothes on the line.*

Curiously, the windows are boarded up everywhere.

From our POV through a second-story window, WE SEE a pickup truck slowly move into town along Main Street. It creeps to a halt in front of a convenience store. Three paunchy men (let's call them LARRY, CURLY and MOE) get out, look around cautiously, rifles over their shoulders. The truck idles.

The men rattle the store doors. Locked.

> LARRY
>
> Shit.

> CURLY
>
> Wut?

                    LARRY
          What do you think?

He rattles it again.

                    CURLY
          Locked?

                    LARRY
          Jesus, you're stupid.

Moe, the burliest of the bunch, barrels past them,
grabs the door handle with both hands and gives it
a hard shake.

                    LARRY (cont'd)
          The <u>fuck</u> are you doin'?

Moe shrugs. Larry grabs them and pulls them to the
driver's side of the truck like children, opens the
door.

                    LARRY (cont'd)
          What's this?

                    CURLY
          The door...

Larry knocks his hat off. Curly reaches, Larry
kicks it. Curly reaches again. Larry kicks it so
hard, he has to catch his balance.

                    LARRY
          I will end you.

Larry shuts the door, slowly opens it again. He
motions for the other two to speak.

                    CURLY
          The d--

                    MOE
        Open!

                    CURLY
        --Open!

                    LARRY
        Very good.

He locks the door and shuts it. He tugs on it.

                    LARRY (cont'd)
        And this?

                    MOE
        Locked.

                    LARRY
        Always said you were the
        bright one. Now, when I
        find a door and it does
        this...
            (tugs it)
        ... what are you gonna do?

                    MOE
        Leave it.

Larry smiles and then looks at Curly. He frowns.

                    LARRY
        And you?

Curly is looking at the passenger door.

                    CURLY
        Wish I hadn't locked my
        door.

                    LARRY
        What?

He turns sharply to the passenger door, sees that
the lock is indeed in place. The keys are in the
ignition, a cat keychain smiling mockingly at him.

Larry's face flushes red. He's about to let them
have it when an OLD WOMAN shuffles out from behind
the store. Her left arm hangs limply by her side,
but that's the least of her problems: rotting flesh
droops from her face, and her clothes are tattered
and bloodied. She moans hungrily.

All three turn. It is only then that they see
several more zombies shuffling toward them from the
street.

                    LARRY (cont'd)
          Goddammit! You've gone and
          woken' 'em up, rattling
          that damn door!

Curly aims his gun at the old lady. Her eyes open
wide-

INT. A SMALL OFFICE - DAY

A friendly man, 30's, sits at a nice desk. A small
sign says: MAYOR DENNY SANDERSON. He smiles into
the CAMERA.

                    MAYOR
          We always start with
          Sylvie. Especially when
          they bring their rifles.

                  CAMERAMAN (O.C.)
          Isn't that dangerous?

                    MAYOR
          I'm not sure what you
          mean?

> CAMERAMAN (O.C.)
> It's just she's not
> very... fast...

> MAYOR
> Oh... 'cause of the
> bullets. Yes, well, we
> don't expect her to dodge
> 'em.

> CAMERAMAN (O.C.)
> That's not what--

> MAYOR
> Yes, yes. But she is
> adorable. Like a granny
> or great-aunt. A real Golden
> Girl, that one. And they
> never shoot the grannies.
> No, No. Besides, this
> ain't America. Not a lot
> of guns 'round da bay.

As they speak, WE CUT TO:

EXT. CONVENIENCE STORE - DAY - CONTINUOUS

As Curly aims, Larry knocks the gun away. SYLVIE
stumbles sharply away to the right as though
distracted. She secretly crosses herself, ever the
grateful Catholic.

> LARRY
> Don't waste the ammo. She
> didn't even have any
> teeth.

Curly slings his rifle back up. Larry glances
around at the rest of the zombies and shakes his
head.

                    LARRY (cont'd)
          I really thought this
          place would be it. But
          it's just like all the
          rest: Dead as a dick on
          a dinosaur.

He spits on the ground before using the butt of his
rifle to knock a nearby ZOMBIE to the ground. He
turns and SMASHES the truck window in, never seeing
the zombie hold his throbbing head.

The men pile into their truck, back up, and head
out of town. As the vehicle disappears, the rest
of the ZOMBIES stop shuffling and rush over to help
the fallen one.

INT. MAYOR'S OFFICE

                    CAMERAMAN (O.C.)
          So, people do get hurt.

                    MAYOR
          Oh, that's just Cecil,
          b'y. He's fine. How many's
          that for you now, Cece?

The camera swerves to show CECIL, 50's, grinning
like a fool, half of his teeth are missing. He's
peeling zombie makeup off, holding an ice pack to
his head.

                    CECIL
          Hits to the head?
               (thinks on it)
          Must be eight by now. No,
          no... Nine. Jesus, yes.
          Nine.

                    CAMERAMAN (O.C.)
          Nine... hits to the head?

MAYOR
You'd never say though,
b'y, would ya?

Cecil continues to grin, staring into the camera.

MAYOR (cont'd)
That's Cece, m' son. He's
been beat on the head,
kicked in the shins,
smacked in the nuts - both
of 'em - and not at the
same time, neither, like
some wuss. Punched in the
ass-

CECIL
Each cheek.

MAYOR
Right... What else?
Slapped, God knows how
many times...

CAMERAMAN (O.C.)
Really. People slap the
dead?

MAYOR
Well, sometimes, what are
you gonna do, you got no
gun or, or, or stabby
thing. But, you know, like
I said, that's Cecil,
right. He's old school.
What's that they call it
in the movies?

CECIL
Method.

                         MAYOR
              Method.

He smiles awkwardly for an <u>uncomfortably</u> long time.
Cecil's smiling face slowly enters the frame from
the side.

SMASH CUT TO:

TITLE: ZOMBAY, NL

FADE IN:

EXT. MAIN STREET - DAY - LATER

The mayor leads the CAMERA along the street, waving
to a few people as they go about their business.

                         MAYOR
                You know, for a while
                there, after the plague hit
                and turned everyone into
                R.A.F.E.'s, we didn't know
                what to do.

INT. A TINY KITCHEN - DAY

SYLVIE PIKE, 85, sits at her table sipping tea.
She looks at the camera, her face as wrinkly as a
crumpled paper bag.

                         SYLVIE
                Oh, yes, I came up with
                dat. R.A.F.E.: Recently
                Alive Flesh Eaters. Has a
                nice ring to it. Not like
                the other names being
                tossed 'round.

                         CAMERAMAN (O.C.)
                What do you mean?

                          196

                    SYLVIE
          Well, we had a vote down
          to the hall. Right after
          Bingo. Ya can't skip bingo,
          no sir. And that we didn't.
          Calamity is a civilized
          town. Dead don't change
          that. So afterward, since
          we was all there anyway...
          on accounts of the bingo,
          like I said... we all put
          our suggestions on a piece
          of paper and put 'em in
          the spinner with the balls
          and gave 'em a nice toss.
          And I won! The vote, not
          bingo. Stacy Sheldon won
          bingo. I'm not a fan, let
          me tell you. She's got
          these blotters--

                    CAMERAMAN (O.C.)
          What were some of the
          other suggestions?

Sylvie scowls at being cut off. She shakes it off.

                    SYLVIE
          Oh, nothing any good.
          P.A.R.T.S. was one--

                    CAMERAMAN (O.C.)
          P.A.R.T.S.? What's that?

                    SYLVIE
          People Are Rotting Too
          Slowly, I think. Not that
          I think they are. That's
          just what it stood for.
          Personally, I think the
          dead is doing a fine job
          ... rotting, dat is.

INT. MAYOR'S OFFICE - DAY

The mayor props up a poster board. He stands next
to it like Vanna White as the CAMERA PANS down the
list:

"D.E.A.D. - Dead Enough And Dumb
W.R.A.F. - Well Rested And Famished
P.A.R.T.S. - People Are Rotting Too Slowly
R.A.F.E. - Recently Alive Flesh Eaters
~~Zombie - stupid, not even a word~~
C.B.D.M.N.T - Could Be Dead, Maybe Not Though"

The mayor frowns at the last.

>   MAYOR
>   Bit vague, that one.

INT. A TINY KITCHEN - DAY

Sylvie stirs her tea.

>   SYLVIE
>   And then there was Cecil's
>   pick: Y.I.D.S.: You Is
>   Dead. Sorry.
>   (pause)
>   He's a special boy...

EXT. MAIN STREET - DAY

The mayor arrives at the convenience store just as
the owner, JIM SMITH - a lean, attractive 40's - is
pulling down boards from the windows.

>   MAYOR
>   It was actually Jim's idea
>   that saved the town for
>   us. Ain't that right, Jim?

Behind the glass, Jim waves, not hearing a word.

                    MAYOR (cont'd)
He's got a head on his
shoulders, that one.
Always thinking. And he
didn't want to lose his
business either,
apocalypse or not. Those
are the first thing to
go. People looting and
burning. You see it on the
telly all the time. So he
comes to me at the office
and says: "Denny, I know
how to save Calamity!"
Well, I tell ya, I gave
'em a good listen.

INT. CONVENIENCE STORE - DAY

Jim is tidying some shelves, talking to the camera.

                    JIM
Calamity's been my home my
whole life. My family
started this town way back
in 1802. My great-great
grandfather, Gussy, his
brother Phonse and their
wives came here with little
more than the clothes on
their backs. Blacksmiths,
they was. Smittys they
called 'em back then. Ain't
much call for it these days,
but back in the day, Smittys
were all the rage. Treated
like royalty. No wonder it
went to their heads.

                    CAMERAMAN (O.C.)
          Right...

Jim finishes stocking the shelf.

                    JIM
          Phonse Smith was an
          asshole. No sense
          buttering that up...
          that'd just be a buttered
          asshole. Ain't no better.
          Hell, might be worse,
          come to think of it.

He shakes the image from his mind.

                    JIM (cont'd)
          Phonse hated sharing the
          attention with Gussy.

EXT. CALAMITY - DAY - FLASHBACK - 1802

Twin brothers, GUSSY and PHONSE SMITH, march down
the main street toward each other carrying large
mallets, entourages in tow, as Jim NARRATES what
happens next:

                    JIM (V.O.)
          One day things boiled over
          and it came to blows. You
          ever seen blacksmiths
          fight? It ain't like in
          the movies. You got these
          big hammers smacking into
          each other, making all
          kinds of racket. The whole
          town came down and
          watched. When it was over,
          Calamity was a town
          divided. Phonse took his
          family and headed over
          the mountain to start up

                    200

>   JIM (V.O.)(cont'd)
> New Calamity on the other
> side. Bunch of folks
> followed soon after.
> Place was never the same
> after that. Still better
> than New Calamity, though.

EXT. NEW CALAMITY - DAY - FLASHBACK

WE MOVE QUICKLY through a small town similar to
Calamity. Except for the fires. And PEOPLE running.
And screaming. The living dead are everywhere.

Suddenly the CAMERA topples forward and skids along
the ground. WE SEE a horde of zombies swarm in as a
fallen BEARDED MAN in hip-wader rubber boots yells:

>   BEARDED MAN
> By da Jesus! Get off me ya
> bunch of fuckin' skeets!

INT. MAYOR'S OFFICE - BACK TO SCENE

>   CAMERAMAN(O.C.)
> Guess you couldn't do this
> just anywhere?

>   MAYOR
> Jesus, no. 'Scuse me
> French. There's just the
> one road into Calamity and
> we got them high hills all
> around with lookouts.

>   CAMERAMAN (O.C.)
> What about the beach?

>   MAYOR
> What about it?

>   CAMERAMAN (O.C.)
>   Well, it's another way in,
>   isn't it?

>   MAYOR
>   You haven't been down
>   there yet, have you?
>   Nancy?!!

EXT. CALAMITY BEACH - DAY

The mayor, his assistant NANCY, 60's, and the
CAMERAMAN stand on the sand looking toward the
water. WE ZOOM out to see the beach littered
with propped-up mannequins in zombie makeup and
cardboard standees of zombies. Many of them are
withered and falling apart.

>   CAMERAMAN
>   And people think this is
>   real?

>   MAYOR
>   Oh yes. It's very
>   lifelike. Especially from
>   a boat.

>   CAMERAMAN
>   There's a dog chewing the
>   ass off that one.

On the far side of the beach, there is indeed a dog
tearing the cardboard ass off a zombie.

Nancy throws her coffee, rushes across the beach,
screaming. The dog makes a final tug and runs into
the trees, cardboard ass bouncing along in its jaw.

>   CAMERAMAN (cont'd)
>   Spared no expense.

The mayor forces a smile.

202

INT. PRINT SHOP - DAY

> BOYD
> Goddamn right, they did.

The print shop is buzzing with the sound of large printing equipment. BOYD BAILEY, the artsy 50-ish owner, moves about, checking the progress.

> BOYD (cont'd)
> And with the goddamn
> upkeep of those cutouts,
> I'm losing a fortune every
> week. Who's gonna pay for
> it? No one, that's who.
> They expect me to just
> take the hit, for the good
> of the town, like everyone
> else. But no one else can
> do what I do. I'm an
> artist. A goddamn artist I
> tell you.

Boyd lifts the cover off a massive printer and holds up a large sheet and studies it.

> BOYD (cont'd)
> Son of a <u>bitch</u>! Charlie!

Boyd tosses the paper at the camera before rushing off to yell at his hapless assistant, CHARLIE - 20's, nerdy. The camera tilts down to the sheet on the floor. A glossy bare ass lies there.

> CHARLIE (O.S.)
> You said "an ass".

> BOYD (O.S.)
> With pants, you idiot. Why
> would I want a life-sized
> print out of a naked ass?

Charlie glances awkwardly past him to the camera, not wanting to answer that.

>   BOYD
>   Well?

>   CHARLIE
>   I'll... I'll print some
>   pants. Cover it right up.

Boyd lowers his head. He skulks back, muttering:

>   BOYD
>   Jesus wept...

EXT. A SMALL HOUSE - DAY

WE FOLLOW the mayor and Nancy up a path to the front door. Nancy brings the dog on a leash. The mayor rings the door. FRANK - a stern 70-year-old in just his underwear - opens it quickly, eyes them and says:

>   FRANK
>   (disgustedly)
>   Fuck off!

He slams the door shut. The mayor turns to CAMERA.

>   MAYOR
>   He's really a kind fellow.

The mayor knocks on the door again.

>   MAYOR (cont'd)
>   Father Frank? We need--

The door whips open. *Father* Frank glares at them.

                    FRANK
         What do you need?
         Confession? Fuck off.
         Burial? Baptism? Wedding?
         Fuck off, fuck off, fuck
         off. That about covers it.
         Anything else? No? Fuck
         off then.

The door slams again.

                    NANCY
         He hasn't taken the whole
         apocalypse thing too
         well... as you can see.

                    MAYOR
         More of a rupture than a
         Rapture, I believe is what
         he called it. Plus he
         thinks we had it coming.

                    CAMERAMAN(O.C.)
         You'd never tell...

The mayor and Nancy exchange looks, walk away.

                    CAMERAMAN(O.C.) (cont'd)
         What about the dog?

Before anyone can answer, the door opens and Father
Frank storms out and grabs the leash from Nancy's
hand, yelling:

                    FRANK
         Leave da Jesus dog,
         missus! Christ!

Frank leads the mangy dog back inside and slams the
door. From inside a bark is heard.

FRANK (O.C.)
Did they now? Yeah, well,
fuck you, too!

EXT. BINGO HALL - NIGHT

The parking lot is packed. A sign declares: BINGO
WEEKLY! BIG MONEY! BYOB - BRING YOUR OWN BLOTTERS

INT. BINGO HALL - CONTINUOUS

The mayor stands beside a huge bingo ball spinner,
microphone in hand. At least 30 long tables fill
the place end to end, 12 people to a table.

CECIL
The whole town is here.

Cecil is sitting with his back to the mayor in the
distance. The mayor calls out a number and everyone
checks. Cecil blots two cards. Next to him, Sylvie
shakes her head in frustration. At the table behind
her, STACY SHELDON - an old woman with a short,
poorly dyed hairdo - blots 4 separate cards.

STACY
Oooh! I'm on a hitch!

Sylvie grips her blotter so tightly that ink
dribbles out.

SYLVIE
Bitch is always on a
hitch.

Cecil glances at her, bug-eyed.

CECIL
Lucky I guess.

                    SYLVIE
          Lucky schmucky. Let <u>her</u>
          dodge the bullets next
          time if she's so lucky.
          She cheats, she does.
          Cheats. She's got these
          blotters--

                    CECIL
          You can't cheat at Bingo.

The mayor calls out a number.

                    STACY
          Bingo!

                    FRANK
               (in the back)
          Fuck you!

Sylvie leaps angrily from her chair--

-- just as an alarm bell goes off inside the hall.
Everyone jumps up, alarmed.

                    MAYOR
          Okay, everybody. you know
          what that means. Head home
          and follow your
          instructions just like
          before.

People gather their things and hustle out,
mumbling. Cecil leads the CAMERA out.

                    CECIL
          Must be a boat in da bay.
          First one in a while, too.

EXT. CALAMITY BEACH - NIGHT

A fishing vessel is entering the bay. On the

beach: locals in zombie makeup stumble among the
mannequins. More shuffle in from the road.

> MAYOR
> This is where the magic
> happens.

The boat drifts closer. Suddenly a spotlight
spreads across the beach from the deck.

> MAN'S VOICE
> Ok, boys! Open fire!

A hail of GUNFIRE erupts from the boat.

Everyone jumps into the sand. The standees and
mannequins are shredded with bullets. When the
smoke clears, the light spreads across the beach
once more.

> MAN'S VOICE (cont'd)
> Jesus, bullets don't even
> stop 'em anymore. C'mon,
> let's keep going. This
> place is a write-off.

As the boat sails off, the locals stand, cheering.
The mayor wraps his arm proudly around a standee.

> MAYOR
> Boyd's a goddamn artist
> alright!

The wind catches the standee, rips it. The paper
pants float away, leaving a glossy bare ass facing
the CAMERA.

The mayor blushes, moves in front of it.

> DISSOLVE TO:

EXT. CALAMITY - MORNING

A series of shots: *Quiet streets; wind billowing
the shredded standees on the beach; clothes on the
lines; the sun rising.*

EXT. BINGO HALL - MORNING

The town has gathered. The mayor is at the podium.

> MAYOR
> Hope you all got a good
> night's sleep. Got a bitta
> work ahead of us--

> FRANK (O.C.)
> Day's half gone for
> fucksakes!

> MAYOR
> (wincing)
> Yes, Father... well, for
> some of us--

> STACY
> What about da bingo?

> MAYOR
> What about it?

> STACY
> When are we gonna finish
> last night's game?

All of the townspeople turn in unison to each of
them as they speak. In the back, Sylvie rolls her
eyes.

> MAYOR
> Stacy, I think we can all
> agree that we'll have to
> void it and start a new--

> STACY
> The hell we will, Mayor
> Sanderson. The hell we
> will! I. Was on. A hitch!

> SYLVIE
> You're always on a hitch
> you cheating old bitch!

The turning heads stop sharply, mouths fall agape.

> STACY
> What did you call me, you
> crooked old biddy?

> SYLVIE
> Biddy?? Well if it isn't
> the pot calling the kettle
> black! Just look at that
> Magic-Cut you call a 'do!

Frank's dog barks. The crowd gives a collective
gasp.

> STACY
> Magic-Cut--?! Outside! Now!

EXT. MAIN STREET - MOMENTS LATER

Sylvie and Stacy march toward each other, a crowd
of supporters behind each — a town divided. They
stop in the middle, wrinkly face to wrinkly face.

INT. MAYOR'S OFFICE - DAY - LATER

The mayor sits at his desk, shirt torn, blood
caking his face. He looks, for lack of a better
word, like a zombie.

> CAMERAMAN(O.C.)
> It got so out of hand...

>   MAYOR
>   Yes.

>   CAMERAMAN (O.C.)
>   I didn't think they would
>   survive. They're so, so...
>   old!

The mayor considers it and nods.

>   MAYOR
>   That's bingo for ya.

EXT. MAIN STREET - DAY - MOMENTS EARLIER

The entire town is fighting. Hair pulled, punches thrown, bodies tossed, screams are HEARD. Somewhere, a dog barks.

>   MAYOR (V.O.)
>   Sometimes, to keep the
>   peace, you need a little
>   war from time to time.
>   This is Calamity, after
>   all. We do things a
>   little differently here.
>   Always have. Always will.
>   Dead or no dead. It's the
>   greatest place on earth.
>   Ain't no other town like
>   it anywhere.

EXT. MAIN STREET - DAY - MOMENTS EARLIER

Smoke settles over the town as little fires burn themselves out. The street is littered with bodies, moaning and contorting on the ground. They slowly get to their feet and shuffle home, nursing their wounds.

WE PULL BACK to the top of a hill. A car stops on

the road. A YOUNG MAN gets out and holds his hand
up to a YOUNG WOMAN and CHILD inside the vehicle.
They all look like they've been through hell.

He looks down at the town. Everywhere he looks,
figures shuffle and limp through the smokey
streets. He returns to the car.

                    YOUNG WOMAN
          Well?

                    YOUNG MAN
          Worst one yet.

                    YOUNG WOMAN
          Worse than New Calamity?

                    YOUNG MAN
          It's overrun. Place never
          had a chance.

The woman sighs, looks at the child sleeping. She
unfolds a map, crosses Calamity off with a Sharpie.

                    YOUNG WOMAN
          Where to now?

                    YOUNG MAN
          Anywhere's got to be
          better than here.

The car backs up, turns the other way, drives off.

INT. MAYOR'S OFFICE - DAY

The mayor shakes his head smiles at the camera for
an uncomfortably long silence. Cecil's battered,
toothless face slowly enters the frame...

                                   FADE TO BLACK
                    THE END

Notes on Rainfall

In the introduction to this book, I mentioned that the following story is the oldest one here. When something is with you that long, change is bound to happen, especially as the times change around you.

When I first wrote this story, it was part of a much bigger tale - a vignette if you will. When that story hit a wall, I plucked this small part from it, like a leaf or a flower to be saved, pressed between the pages of a book.

That much bigger story, however, was a drama with no elements of speculative fiction whatsoever. It was a story of grief and loss and coming to terms with imminent death. I liked it, but I didn't love it. Something was missing.

When the pandemic hit and turned the world upside down, I revisited the story with fresh eyes. We were all in this new world together, but the cracks in human nature soon began to show. After struggling for thousands of years to overcome inexplicable prejudice, we managed to create new ones in record time. Kindness became a commodity, as hard to find sometimes as toilet paper.

I like kindness. I like kind people even more. When you find them, you never want to let them go. So I trapped them here, pressed inside the pages of this book.

I don't mind sharing. Just be sure to close it when you're done.

RAINFALL

1.

HE NEVER ASKED ABOUT THE SCARS, AND SHE WAS THANKFUL FOR THAT.

She sat at a picnic table outside the gas bar and watched him pull a six-pack of Budweiser from the cooler inside and bring it to the cash. The pretty girl at the register smiled shyly as she rang his purchases through, bagged them, and returned his change. He nodded politely on his way out, letting the girl down easy with a smile of his own.

Heartbreaker. She watched him cross the lot toward her, tossing her greying hair out of her eyes. The sky behind her was bleeding magenta, only a wisp of clouds above the horizon. The breeze had picked up, but the humidity had leveled off, not dropped. She was out of the city. She was free.

A tall piece of grass tickled her ankle, and she reached beneath the table to scratch. She had visited places like this as a child – places where families could stop along the highway and let the kids out for some air and a snack. There was a time after her parents were gone, and the world spun in another direction, that she thought she would never experience it again. She ran a finger along the boards of the table, smiling as the red paint chipped free and fell into her palm. Souvenirs.

"Now *that* I could never do," he said, laying the bag on the table. She sat up.

"What's that?"

"Look under these things. Too many spider webs." He shivered. She was reminded of just how young he was. Nineteen, he had said. That was pushing it by two for sure.

"Two legs good, eight legs bad?"

"Something like that." He flashed his boyish grin, letting his eyes stay on hers longer than usual. She didn't mind. She liked him smiling at her. There was no judgment in it.

"What's in the bag?" She hoped he would sit. The sunset lingered. It had been so long since she had enjoyed one. Longer still since she had shared it with someone else.

He opened the brown paper bag and lifted out a pair of foil-wrapped hot dogs. He passed her one and laid his own on the table. He reached back in and pulled out a can of Coke for her and a Bud for himself. She eyed the cola before accepting it.

"Not gonna offer me a beer?" she asked. She rolled the can between her hands. The moisture cooled her palms. In the distance, the crickets started their evening serenade.

"I just…" He sat and started over. "I didn't want you to think I was trying to get you drunk or anything. That's all."

He took a bite of his food to cover his embarrassment. He was either the slyest fox on the highway or genuinely sincere. She hadn't made up her mind.

"I won't think that if you won't," she said, unwrapping her hot dog.

He stopped chewing, then swallowed the rest whole. He reached inside the bag.

"Okay. Would you like a beer, madam?"

She grinned and held out her hand. "Hot dogs, beer, and a side of chivalry. What more could a lady ask for?"

He nodded past her shoulder. "How about that sunset?"

"Absolutely," she sighed, turning her head to see it. He glanced down, his eyes drifting across her neck and shoulders. She never saw him do it, but she felt it, and she did not object. The rains had left her scarred, disfigured and ashamed. Strangers shunned her, grateful to have been spared her fate. But even before the Scourge had come, it had been forever since she felt seen as more than an object to be used for detached sexual gratification. As day eased into night, she watched the earth move and was too humbled to say anything, and he watched her and smiled.

She turned back around and popped open her beer. It felt cool on the way down, raising the fine hairs on her arms. The breeze brushed them back. "Thank you."

"Sure. You looked like you could use something to eat." He sipped his beer and took another bite of his hot dog. "Besides, this is the last place for chow for a while. Now or never, know what I'm saying?"

She did. She took a long swig and gazed across the parking lot at his car. A rare, mint-condition '74 Trans-Am. His words, trying not to boast and nearly succeeding. It had been the first instance when she felt she could trust him. That had been four hours ago.

It *was* a nice car, though something of a relic. Neither of them had been born when it had rolled off the assembly line, and if he continued to care for it as he had so far, it would undoubtedly outlive them both. He cherished it. That much was obvious. It was charming in a post-high-school-first-wheels kind of way. He took the car seriously, but not himself. That alone probably separated him from the vehicle's previous succession of owners. *A genuine antique*, he had called it, caressing the leather steering wheel. She had suppressed a laugh and now regretted it. She knew about antiques. She had left a bookshelf full of them behind.

"You have a jacket to throw on? It's gonna get chilly soon."

She shook her head. As the darkness crept in, the colder air came with it. He stood, removed his jean jacket, and walked around the table. He laid it across her shoulders and sat beside her, facing the opposite direction. She pulled the jacket tight and leaned against him. She felt his arm tense up, then relax.

"You weren't planning a long trip, were you?"

"No," she said. "Not long at all."

"Didn't think so. You packed light. One bag and that book I've never heard of."

"That's a shame."

"What is?"

"That you've never read Steinbeck." She lifted her legs out so she was facing the same way as him. "You'll see a whole other side of America you never knew existed."

"I've got my ride for that," he said, more innocence than ignorance. It was easy to forgive.

"That's not exactly what I meant."

"I know. I'm just not a fan of old books."

"Just old cars," she said lightly.

"Time doesn't age cars. The road does. Mine's still in her teens."

That makes two of you, she thought. And by his definition, *she* was an antique, but she forgave him that, too.

2.

His name was Michael, last name unknown. He had picked her up less than three hundred miles south of the Canadian border. Of the thousands of vehicles that had passed her since Los Angeles, fewer than a dozen had stopped. All but two of those had sped away once they saw her skin.

The first to stay had been a young Pakistani couple with a seven-month-old son who shared the backseat of an Escort with her as far as the outskirts of San Francisco. The couple bore scars similar to her own. The boy had been spared. They never discussed it. The deep red lesions running along each of their faces spoke for everyone. At some point since the rains had *turned*, they had been caught in a downpour. Surface scars were the first symptom. Deep inside, another slowly developed. Incurable, indiscriminate, unstoppable. Millions had already died. Millions more would follow. Something in the Earth's atmosphere had shifted three years ago. The Scourge was here to stay, but the world below carried on. Everything was filtered now, new chemicals to fight the old. Water was safe again except when it fell from the sky.

She had taken a Greyhound from San Francisco to the Oregon border. Out of cash, she continued on foot for three days before another car took her in. An elderly hippie couple driving their Volkswagon van across the country to visit their daughter in Philadelphia. They were not sick, but their daughter was. Before they left home, they sold almost everything they owned. A tiny U-Haul trailer hitched to the rear carried all that remained. They had no intention of going back. She was welcome to travel with them as long as she liked, but she had a one-way ticket of her own, headed north. They parted ways at a rest stop diner just outside of Washington State. The man said he would mention her in his prayers. It left a bittersweet taste in her mouth. Drizzle began to fall a short time later.

From there to here, Michael had been her companion. He had not said much before the gas station, just a few vague questions about her trip and where she was from. He went to great lengths to ensure the air conditioning was just right and asked once too often if she was comfortable. She was. She didn't think anything could be better than the front seat.

And then he bought her dinner.

It may have only been hot dogs and beer, but few things had ever tasted so pleasing. She ate slowly, concerned that she was keeping him from getting back on the road, but he never rushed her. He seemed to understand how badly she needed to take her time and savor the taste, the moment.

After the meal was done, they packed the remaining four beers in the trunk and headed for the border. He had told her early on that he was heading to Canada, but wanted to take the "leisure route" and crossover into British Columbia sometime "down the line". She pegged him for a surfer – waves in the summer, snow in the winter – living off his college fund for a year or two before making up his mind about school. She admired his confidence that the world would wait for him. She had been there once, charging headlong into the unknown, but she had faltered. In her heart, she wanted to tell him to not stay away too long, but she knew it would fall on deaf ears. A wandering soul cannot be contained. There is only the journey to and the journey back.

An hour out from the border, she noticed his eyes grow heavy. He pushed on.

"What's the hurry, cowboy?" she asked. He shook his head and seemed to wake a bit. "You want to pull over?"

"No." He checked his mirrors. They were alone in their lane. No other cars had come up behind or in front of them for ten minutes.

"Okay. You just seem tired."

He made a face, but his eyes betrayed him. "I'm fine." She knew it was a lie and he knew she knew it. She let it go and looked out the window.

Ten minutes later he came clean: "I don't have enough cash for two rooms. I thought maybe I could get you to your destination and then crash somewhere on my own."

"Crash is exactly what you're about to do. Let's find a motel. I'll sleep on the floor."

"*Bullshit.* You'll take the bed, or I keep going."

It came out of him so quickly there was no way for it not to sound ridiculous. She burst out laughing. He looked at her, confused, then laughed too. She wiped her eyes with the sleeve of his jacket. It smelled of Polo and weed.

"Sorry," she said. "I didn't mean to laugh."

"It *was* funny," he admitted. "Just, you know, I like your company and..."

A warmth spread through her belly into her chest. "I like your company, too."

He looked at her, grinning. "Cool." And whether that was how he intended it or not, that was exactly how he sounded. Cool.

3.

With less than sixty miles to go, they pulled off at the nearest motel to settle in for the night. Bed, chair or floor it didn't matter. The promise of a hot shower was too much to shake off once planted in her head. She felt dirty and she could still feel Tancredi's blood and scent all over her body even though she had washed it away a hundred times in the days since she'd run. A thousand more would not be enough.

He signed them into the registry of the Ranger Motel and paid in cash while she waited inside the car. He winked on the way out of the manager's office and she rolled her eyes playfully. He retrieved the beer, her small bag, and dog-eared copy of *Of Mice and Men* from the trunk and she followed him down the track to the door of room 107. He put the key in the slot and started to turn the knob when she stopped him with a hand on his shoulder. He turned to face her, his pale blue eyes a touch fearful.

"Are you really a gentleman or is it just talk?"

"The floor is mine. Scout's honor." He held up his left hand, palm out, fingers together.

"You were never a Boy Scout."

"Sure I w—"

She lowered his hand and raised his right one in the same pose. "But I trust you anyway."

He frowned, embarrassed, and opened the door.

4.

She did trust him, but she locked the bathroom door while she showered. The water felt better than she imagined it would, and she let it wash over her until her fingertips wrinkled. Afterward, she stood behind the lime green curtain, watching the moisture draw lines down her body and fall away to the porcelain floor. The water slowed and changed course along her multitude of scars. Not all of them were from the Scourge. Some were man-made, far more recent and raw. She had not hidden them, and she had seen Michael's eyes linger from time to time. But he never asked.

Heartbreaker, she thought again. She stepped from the shower, fumbled her towel from the hook on the back of the door, and dried off. Her wounds stood out violently in the harsh glare of the single overhead bulb. Steam fogged the mirror, obscuring her reflection. Small mercies.

She smothered herself in the oversized robe that shared the back of the door and wiped a small circle clean on the mirror with her towel. She leaned on the sink and looked closely at the recent cut on her forehead. It was healing slowly and would leave a permanent scar, though she was uncertain what that meant to her anymore. For now, she would still have to carry Tancredi's final mark with her wherever she went. In time, like the monster himself, it would be a memory.

There was a soft knock on the door. "You okay in there?" It was Michael.

She opened the door and stepped into the main room. There was a small bed along one wall and a dresser in the far corner by the window. No television, no chair, no table. Not exactly the Honeymoon Suite.

He backed up, let her pass. She sat on the end of the bed and pulled her feet up underneath her robe. He sat on the floor and faced her, a pillow against his back.

"I took one of the pillows," he said, adjusting it for comfort. "You don't mind, do you?"

"Stupid question." She lay back on the bed. The ceiling was marred with water damage. It saddened her to look at it. "How come you never asked me my name?"

He rested his head against the wall and pulled his knees up. "You never offered it, I figured you had your reasons."

"I don't. Would you like to know it?"

He thought about it and shook his head. Realizing she couldn't see him, he responded, "No."

She rolled on her side. By lamplight, he was even more attractive. His shaggy blonde hair fell in a heap of curls over his forehead, almost to his eyes. His face was long and chiseled, with just enough scruff to make him the man in the shadows he was years from being in the light. His lips were full, slightly feminine. There was a time in her life when she had found that irresistible. But that was when she still had the power to choose men and not the other way around.

"No? Why not?"

He looked sheepishly at the floor. "You'll think I'm being stupid."

"Maybe," she said. "But who cares? It's just you and me and the ghosts that haunt this place."

He looked up. "Fine. I was just thinking, while you were in there, that this has been the best part of my trip. And if I know your name, I just know I'm gonna want to tell someone about it, and I don't. I just want this to be our story." He stopped and checked to see if she was laughing. She wasn't.

"I don't think that's stupid at all." She rolled onto her back again. "I don't think that's stupid at *all*."

Silence filled the space between them. A soft tap dance of rain began on the roof. She closed her eyes and listened.

"I used to love the rain," Michael confessed from across the room. "Seems so long ago now. Before it became something else."

"Me too."

"Sorry, I didn't mean—"

"It's okay." She held a disfigured hand up to her face, looked at the unblemished shadow it made on the wall. "Rain is always gonna fall. It won't be the last beautiful thing to leave a scar."

He lay flat on the floor, arms folded behind his head. The rain grew heavy, pounding away at the roof and windows. "When I was a boy, maybe six or seven, I used to lie in our backyard and let it hit me with everything it had. My parents thought I was nuts, of course, and my mother used to scream at me about having to wash the mud out of my clothes, but... but you know, I think she just missed doing it herself. That's all it was. She wanted to be out there with me every time."

"That's what happens when you grow up." She kept her eyes closed. Her voice was little more than a whisper. "You have to leave some parts of yourself behind. Sometimes it's the best part."

Michael nodded. He turned toward the bed. "This place you're headed to, you ever been there before?"

"No."

"Somebody waiting for you there?"

"No. Maybe. I don't know."

"But you hope so."

Just the rain. And then: "I'm afraid to hope."

The silence found them again and stayed a while longer. It grew late and they were less inclined to chase it away. In time, he broke it: "I'm glad you made me stop the car."

She did not know if he meant when he first picked her up or when they pulled into the motel, but her answer was for both: "So am I."

Sleep came easy, and it wrapped its arms around him first. She listened to his steady breathing between the showers outside and fell under the spell of both. She dozed off on top of the sheets, robe wrapped loosely around her naked body. She had not intended to leave herself so vulnerable and exposed, but sleep overpowered her and took her away.

Tancredi found her in her dreams.

5.

She awoke with a fright, gasping for air. She clawed at her throat, desperate to tear Tancredi's hands away. He held her firm, pressed her into the bed. She could feel his breath on her face, sickly sweet and hot from a cigar. She gagged, his grip tight around her neck. She was helpless, afraid to open her eyes.

But she did. It felt like pulling against glue. She swung her arms wildly, striking only air. She sat up, alone on the bed. The monster only existed in her dreams. Scorned lover, pimp and devil. In life, he had been all of these things to her.

But Tancredi was dead. She had killed him.

It was still dark in the motel room. The rain replaced with the early wake-up call of birds. She looked at the bedside clock. Just after five in the morning.

She slid off the bed and tip-toed to the bathroom. At the door, she looked at Michael. He was lying on his side, his back to her. She returned to the bed and removed the top sheet. She laid it over him.

She dressed quietly in the bathroom. The same pale blue dress and sandals she had been wearing for three days. She brushed her teeth, packed her few belongings in her bag, and closed the bathroom door behind her.

The first rays of sunshine were creeping across the floor. Her heart encouraged her to linger. It would not be hard. She could just curl up beside him and sleep her worries away. But no. She was close now. She could walk the rest of the way. What lay beyond that, she did not know, but there was a promise of dignity there she would not find on her own. It called to her even as she knelt beside him and brushed his hair from his eyes. He stirred but did not wake.

She leaned in, kissed him softly on the forehead, then laid her book on the bedside table. A moment later, she stood by the front door, her hand on the knob.

"*'Don't think twice, it's alright',*" he sang to her. His voice was still thick with sleep, but he could carry a tune. She smiled and turned around.

He was leaning on his elbow, watching her through squinted eyes. He yawned, stretched his back, and expelled a mild groan. "Bob Dylan," he told her.

"I know. I love that song."

"Me too. I used to think it was heartbreaking."

"But now?"

He grinned. The morning light moved across his face, and she could see the boy in him once more. "Seeing you stand there, knowing what you want, ready to move on, I don't know… It just seemed appropriate and not sad at all."

She walked back, cupped his face with her hands, and kissed him deeply on the forehead again. It took him by surprise, but he did not try to return the kiss. A gentleman to the end.

"Thank you," she said.

"Stay," he whispered.

"I can't."

"I know. But you know I had to ask."

"I know." She lifted her hands away from his face.

"Be safe," he said. She had no answer to that. A lie would hurt too much. She stood and went to the door, tears in her eyes. He hefted himself off the floor, grabbed his jean jacket and held it out to her. She shook her head.

"I can't," she said.

He covered her shoulders with it anyway. "You will," he told her. "I want to be there. In the end. Now part of me can."

She pressed her cheek into the collar and inhaled the scent of his cologne. "You will be."

She opened the door and stepped outside. He urged her on with a nod. She glanced down the highway.

Don't think twice, it's alright...

And though she never looked back, she knew he watched her until she faded from view. And that was enough.

Notes on Gadget

The first seed planted for what eventually became the short novella that follows was the song *Fix You* by the band Coldplay. I often walk at night to work through writer's block, and when I do, there is always music with me. One night in early June 2005, I was listening to this song and in my mind's eye, I saw a music video play out telling the story of a young girl and her puppy who grow up together. The dog is always there for her through the trials and tribulations of her young life - lying with her when she is sad, playing with her when she is happy, cuddling her when she is sick. And then, when the song reaches that beautiful crescendo, we see her as an adult running frantically to get home because something has happened to the dog, and she needs to be there for it no matter what.

Imagine my disappointment with the actual video for that song when it was released a few months later. But I digress.

It was just a nugget of an idea. I wasn't ready to write about it at that time. That happens a lot.

Ten years later, while on a similar walk, a scene played out in my head: an old man breaking down as he explains to a loved one that he is dying. I stopped in my tracks and wrote the entire monologue on my phone. None of these things made it into the novella, but I knew now exactly what the story would be.

Or so I thought.

Turns out, Gadget had his own story to tell. I was just along for the ride. And now you are, too.

GADGET

1.

THE OLD MAN WAS DYING.

John sat looking out on the dry front yard and the long stretch of highway beyond. The morning had been quiet, calm. An untouched slice of buttered toast rested on his lap. Despite having little appetite before dropping it in the toaster, he had given in to the ritual. Now he glanced at it and moved it to the small bistro table next to him. His thoughts were elsewhere, asking the same question over and over: *Did he load the shotgun before laying it on the table?*

The question hovered above his head like a blackfly, buzzing, going nowhere. He turned and peered through the dark screen door to the birch table in the kitchen at the end of the hall. There it sat, round double barrels staring back. He coughed painfully, spat, and looked down at the liquid already drying in the arid late summer air. Dark pink. It had been like that for a while now, long before he'd had the good sense to see a doctor about it. Too long. The prick doctor had made that clear. Might have had a chance if only he'd had it checked sooner.

If only.

Fuck you.

The sound of distant tires on dirt shifted his attention. A slow-building plume of beige dust was chasing a small dark car along the main road a half mile to the east. Another lost traveler on their way to the city to the north. Seeking directions from the directionless. He hadn't been expecting company today, and he was in less of a mood to accept it than usual.

Again his mind wandered back to the question.

Yes, he thought, *loaded it and set it down*. He remembered how his hand had shaken. Not with the quiver of age or weakness. No. Something else had caused him to tremble. Fear.

The car was almost upon him now, making the wide turn onto his gravel drive. There was no wind on this side of the large house, and the tail of dust settled quickly. By the time the vehicle stopped, there was almost no sign of its journey, just the destination.

If only life were like that, he mused.

He spat again, not bothering to look at it this time. As the car rolled to a stop twenty feet from his porch steps, he noted that it wasn't a lost traveler at all. He knew this car, and he knew its owner. A lifetime ago, he had known her intimately. A pair of marriages behind them both, and they still had not been together for more than just that one hot August night of their youth. He thought on it less frequently as the years became decades and the lines on their faces grew ever deeper. He could no longer recall the 16-year-old cheerleader who had lain beneath him under the stars, her round eyes rolling back as they came together, her gentle moan keeping in sync with each muscle squeezing around him inside her. That memory had long since been replaced with the 68-year-old woman stepping from her car in the dry autumn heat.

Still beautiful, he thought. The work of a mature, experienced artist. He felt a stirring in his seat. He crossed his legs, forgoing the formality of standing to greet her. Such ceremony would be wasted between them anyway.

She let the door close and walked to the front of the car. She wore a pale green summer dress that clung to her small frame in a way that a younger woman would find self-conscious, accented with a red scarf draped loosely around her slight shoulders. Her long strawberry-blonde hair was tied back in a ponytail and hidden beneath a green baseball hat. She kicked gently at the dirt with her Blundstones as she leaned against the hood, placing one leg casually across the other.

"Mary," John said, leaving any hint of a question behind his lips. If she was here on a weekday in the early afternoon, there was purpose behind it, and he knew she would get to it before long. Such was her way.

"Afternoon, Jonathon," Mary said pleasantly. Her voice had taken on a husky affectation as age and experience crept in. He liked the way his name sounded in her mouth. She was the only one who called him by his full name, and he had never corrected her. To everyone else, he was John, or Jack if they were a close friend, of which fewer remained than he had thumbs. But to her, he had always been Jonathon.

"Just thought I'd stop by and see how you were doing." She squinted at him as she said it. He glanced at the cloudless sky. A grin highlighted his face.

"No you didn't," he said gently.

She looked at the dirt as sadness crept to the edges of her lips. She slid the toe of her boot across the line she had made earlier, forming something between an "x" and a cross.

She shrugged. "How are you? Honestly."

He thought of the shotgun staring at them from the kitchen table, the same table he had crafted himself from a tree in the yard, the same table he had eaten a thousand meals from, the same table he had once swept clear with a passionate arm to lay his second wife across and make love to under the October moonlight spying through the window.

He shook his head clear, met her eyes with his own. "Still here," he said.

"Still an asshole," she replied. "Guess there's no getting rid of that."

He chuckled. "Old dogs."

She smiled, but it was forced, and faded quickly. She glanced back at the dirt. A wave of anger coursed through her. A single sweep of her boot erased the cross from the earth. Anger gave way to sadness. She chewed her bottom lip. "Can I come up there?"

He blinked at the shift in her tone. Her voice was so soft and low that he almost missed the question. "You know you don't need an invitation, Mary." And then, because he suddenly felt it inexplicably necessary, he added: "Ever."

Mary pushed off the hood and climbed the four short steps to the porch landing. There was a single empty chair across from John's and she sat in it. She pulled the green hat off and laid it on the table between them, running her other hand through her hair as she did so. The heat would be oppressive by three o'clock.

"Can I get you a beer?"

"No," she said, "but a glass of water would be lovely."

"Sure." John stood, felt the tingle of blood flush back into his legs. How long had he been sitting there with a gun to his back? A *loaded* gun, he corrected himself. A man with his days numbered was in no position to lose track of time. *Fuck it. Not like I can get it back now.*

He made his way to the kitchen, glancing back to the screen door as he reached the table. He could see one of Mary's boots tapping the base of the chair as her leg swung gently over the other, but that was all. He grabbed the shotgun and leaned it barrel-up in the crevice between the side of the refrigerator and the wall. He stared at it, down the barrel to the burnished wood stock. The dark impression of his hand had found a home there over time. It beckoned.

The faint sound of Mary humming a vaguely familiar tune reached him. A moment later, he reappeared on the porch and placed a tall glass of ice water on the table beside her, along with a cold beer for himself.

"Thank you," she said with a smile. She took a sip and placed it back, wiping the moisture on her hand across her forehead. A few beads glistened between her freckles, and John felt a stirring inside once again as he sat back down.

"What was that song just now?"

"I'm sorry?" Her brow furrowed. John noticed the moisture there had already evaporated.

"That tune you were humming."

"Was I? Funny." She shrugged. "Gone now, whatever it was."

John twisted open the beer and took a long swig. The familiar cascade of notes was already fading from his memory as well. He enjoyed a second swallow, closed his eyes, and savored the silence. There had always been a peaceful calm with Mary, a sensation he had not felt regularly since his second wife, Michelle, had passed on three years prior. Mary's visits were rare but welcome, and her departure always left a pocket of emptiness in the air around him.

"I've been thinking about you," she stated. John's eyes remained closed, but he lowered his face from the sky.

"Have you?"

"Yes. More than usual, I guess." She started to reach for the glass, then drew her hands together in her lap instead. "I'm sorry I haven't been by to visit as often."

He looked at her. "Not like we were ever regulars, Mare."

"I know. But maybe we could have been."

Her words trailed off. She seemed uncharacteristically remorseful. "You didn't come all the way out here to talk to a dying man about regret."

She exhaled. "No." She reached for the water again, successful this time. It tasted dusty, the heat already stealing much of its coldness. "I came to offer you something. Something that would... I don't know...?"

"Make you feel better?"

Her mouth closed around the rest of her words in surprise. "What? No. If anything, I want to make *you* feel better."

John finished his beer and set it on the table. He began to pick at the label with a dirty fingernail. "Will that make it easier for you?"

"Make what easier?"

"My dying."

"You really are an asshole, Jonathon." She spat it at him before she could stop herself. She only half-regretted letting it happen.

He tore the label free and rolled it between his thumb and forefinger like a joint. "Never claimed to be anything but." He considered the rolled-up paper for a moment before finally poking it unceremoniously down into the bottle. "Don't change the fact, does it? I'm dying, Mary. Maybe not today or tomorrow, but it'll be along for me soon enough. Might roll on up my driveway just like you did today and leave just the same with me as passenger. Or it might come in the night while I sleep and fade back into the dark like it was never there."

She chewed her bottom lip, staring at him, her breath coming and going in shorter bursts from her nostrils. He watched the label slip into foam at the bottom of the bottle like a drowning man.

"Point is, whatever you or anyone else needs to do or say to make it easier, that's between you and God. I'd rather be left out of it." He sat back in his chair, wondering if he'd been too harsh, but in no hurry to amend it.

Mary took another sip of water before continuing. She knew John had been slipping. *And* that he had been refusing treatment. Whether it was 68 years of stubbornness or a bitter acceptance of the inevitable, she did not know. Most likely a combination of the two. He had always been a lone wolf. Even in marriage, he seemed better suited to time by himself. But recently, she had witnessed the moat he kept around himself rise into a wall. His heart had hardened behind it like the tumor festering within his lungs.

"A couple of years ago, I started volunteering a few days a week down at the no-kill shelter," Mary said. "Taking care of strays and abandoned pets."

John turned his head slowly. "No-kill? What's that mean?"

"Just what it says: no-kill. They house, and feed, and care for the animals until they find new homes or until they pass naturally."

"Sounds unnecessarily expensive," John said with a grunt.

Mary leaned forward. "Like I said, I volunteer. We all do. It's how it keeps going. That and donations from folks around town. Government contributes a little, not a lot. Not enough."

"I ain't got no money, Mary. I certainly ain't got any for some animals no one wanted in the first place."

She appeared stung by his words. "I didn't come here looking for money, Jonathon. And most of these animals will die with us. We do what we can for them. Many are in bad shape when we get them. Some we have to pass on to the vet to euthanize to ease their suffering, but that's rare. More important than money is our ability to find them new homes. It gives them a new life, and it frees up what limited resources we have to better care for the seniors."

John shifted in his seat. He noticed with some relief that her glass of water was almost gone. It wasn't in her nature to ask for another, and in this heat it was likely to hasten her departure.

"You talk about them like they're people," John said. "They're just animals."

"Before someone helped you walk or taught you to speak, so were you. It doesn't make them less worthy of our love."

"You said you came here to offer me something. I'm not hearing it."

Mary held his gaze for a long moment. "Those animals we can't find homes for, they die alone. Not physically, but inside. Inside, they are alone. I don't want the same to happen to you."

She sighed and put her hat back on before getting to her feet. The sun had moved in the sky, and she cast him in a long shadow. John looked up but could not see her eyes.

"If you think on it when I'm gone, drop down to the shelter. I'm there almost every day. The paperwork only takes a minute." She reached down and lifted the glass to her lips. When she was done, she set it in front of him and turned to leave, saying: "Thanks for the water, Jonathon. Remember what we talked about."

"What paperwork?" He asked as she stepped from the porch to the dirt drive. She opened the car door and slid behind the wheel. "What paperwork?"

A moment later, she was gone.

2.

"Wolf's in the henhouse, Jack." It was his brother Billy. But Billy had been dead these past twelve years.

John opened his eyes. It was dark, with only a sliver of moonlight slicing through the gap in the curtains. It cut across the bed, dust swirling within. The room was silent and lingering at the precipice of uncomfortably warm. He waited a moment before pulling away the thin bed sheet. The quiet was unnatural.

He swung his legs out, sat up. His withered bare skin glistened pale in the low light, covered in sweat. His brother's words faded away into the dark, almost forgotten. The dream certainly was. They hadn't had hens since they were boys.

The stillness was interrupted by a soft breeze that billowed the curtain inward. The sliver became a wave that covered the entire foot of the bed. John stood and leaned on the window sill, peering out. Other than the gentle wind, the night was a void. Barren, black, silent.

The clock on the bedside table read 4:36 a.m. He sighed. Sleep would not return for another eighteen hours. Something had woken him, then left him just as quickly. Perhaps he should be thankful. Time was growing shorter by the moment. His lungs felt heavy, full of death.

Twenty minutes later, he settled into his chair on the porch with a mug of coffee. The sun would be rising over the eastern road in less than an hour. After watching it, he would get dressed, head around back to the garage, and fix the brake line on the 741. The bike had languished for almost a year. It deserved better than to suffer with him.

The horizon bloomed – carnation pink followed by the long, slow saturation to blood orange. By the time the sun fully emerged from its slumber, the porch was empty.

*   *   *

The blood was still where he had left it.

He stood in the garage doorway, staring at the dark brown stain on the concrete floor. It stood out against splotches of motor oil and errant dollops of paint. It stood out against the dark, soiled impressions of a thousand footsteps. It stood out against the memory of another life. It had been the first time he knew something had gone horribly, irrevocably wrong inside him. And now, here it remained on the outside, staring back at him like the pupil of a judging eye.

"I'm still here too, you bastard," he said, resisting the urge to spit. He stepped inside and reached for a rag from the ancient oak counter along one wall. The bottle of *Spray-9* was a little more difficult to locate, but once in hand, he knelt on the cool floor, poised to strike.

He couldn't do it. Wiping it away would not feel like a victory. It would not erase the memory or fix what had broken inside. He stood back up and looked at the Indian motorcycle in the middle of the garage for a long time.

He finished at sunset, emerging from the garage with a half-finished beer in one grease-black hand. He mounted the steps to the porch. He paused on the second to last one, eyes drifting to the tire treads on the dirt drive. It already felt like a week had passed since Mary's visit. He expected it would be much longer before she returned. He had been coarse with her and unwelcoming.

He sat in his chair and slowly finished the beer. It had long ago warmed over and the taste of yeast was heavy in his mouth. Still, he drank. This was the end of his first full day of work in a dog's age, and nothing capped it better than a beer, warm or not. Behind the house, the sun was gone. The day was bleeding into night. Out front, the veil of twilight had already fallen, the moon conspicuously absent.

He studied his hands. The work had flared his arthritis, leaving the fingers twisted and swollen. The lines of his palms were stark against the ebony grease, like words on a chalkboard. It would be a bitch to get off, but he could use a good bath anyway. It had been a few days since the last one. The stench of his sweat hung about him in the air. He found it oddly comforting, a reminder that he still had work within him and more to do. The 741 was finished, at least. Had the day not faded, he might have taken it out, let it feel the wind across its chrome and steel. But his sight was a far cry from its youthful heyday, and he had no interest in being found mangled in a tree or crumpled in a ditch.

Once again, his thoughts went to the shotgun in the kitchen. He pushed them away this time. He went upstairs, ran a bath, and eased into the tub. The water welcomed him, opening his pores, pulling the pain from his joints as easy as the dirt from his fingers. When he was done, he strode naked and dripping to his bedroom. He stood at the open window, the warm air pleasant against his wrinkled flesh. His eyesight may have receded, but his hearing was as sharp as ever. He closed his eyes and listened: leaves settling in the trees, the rustle of wind in the tall grass, a semi throttling down far off on the highway, the opening notes of evening birdsong.

He dozed.

*   *   *

He awoke in the dark, covered in sweat. He had thrown the sheet off in his sleep, and the curtains were motionless before the open window. He stood and pulled them apart. The sky was a blank dark canvas, but the yard was partially illuminated by orange light from the garage window.

He was certain he had turned it off when he had left.

Wolf's in the henhouse, Jack.

He dressed quickly in old jeans, deciding to forgo socks and a shirt. The clock on the bedside table read 2:47 a.m. Still time for sleep before sunrise.

He paused in the kitchen, eyes fixed on the shotgun wedged between the wall and the fridge. He grabbed it, popped open the barrel. The shells glinted silver in the dim florescent light above the stove. He hesitated a moment, the weight of the weapon straining his aching hands, and wondered if it might be better to get the pistol from the sideboard in the den. It had six rounds, but it hadn't been fired in over a decade. He was just as likely to put a hole through his foot as he was to stop an intruder. If it fired at all. He snapped the stock back in place and headed out.

The dirt was coarse under his feet, but he barely noticed. It was ten yards to the garage once he was around the corner of the house. Adrenaline made short work of the distance. He stood outside the bay door, exhaling a slow breath. For the first time since awakening, he rationalized that the garage light being on had to be his own doing. He must be mistaken in thinking he had shut it off. Why would anyone expose themselves like that if they had broken in to steal his bike?

Because the lack of moonlight would make fumbling around in the dark garage difficult. And a 1941 Indian 741 was worth the risk.

John knelt and quietly inserted the key in the lock. He turned the key, twisted the handle, and hauled up the wide sliding door. It rattled back along the rails, chain clattering. The noise was enormous in the still air. As the door slammed into place just below the ceiling, John gripped the barrel of the shotgun and held it out from his chest.

The 741 was just as he had left it. It gleamed in the spill of cool light from above the counter, its low, long frame casting a shadow toward the door, ready to escape. The leather seat attached by a single thick spring beckoned him to sit astride and hit the road. The machine was ready.

The man was not.

He looked away, his eyes adjusting to the dark. Nothing appeared to be disturbed or out of place. No one was lurking in the shadows. Aside from the bike, he was alone.

The shotgun suddenly felt very heavy in his arms. He lowered it and let it swing by his right leg. A glint of light caught his eye from the far edge of the counter. He walked over and saw only a pile of grease-smeared rags. He brushed them to the side.

The light through the window reflected at him from the tiny lenses of a pair of goggles. Landon's goggles. His dead son.

John gently held them up. The tinted lenses sat in copper rims bound with a brown leather strap. He had crafted them himself when his hands were more nimble, his mind more focused. He felt the rough stitching, the well-worn leather. The last remnant of his first riding jacket. He could have bought something more suited to the purpose, but the leather had allowed him to pass down part of his past to his son. His finger stopped on the first hole. It was stretched and frayed, unlike the others. Landon had never grown beyond it.

Twenty-four years had passed since he stored the goggles in a shoebox, along with several other memories. For the last twelve years, that shoebox had been sitting on a forgotten shelf in the attic. And yet, here they were in his hand. The only cogent explanation cloaked him in shame and regret. He had no memory of doing so, but at some point in the years since, the bottle had driven him into the attic and then led him out here. The realization made him nauseous.

John started to put them in his pocket, then hesitated. The shoebox held many things. If there was a silver lining to his blackouts, it was that the rest of the contents in the box remained trapped within. He laid the goggles back in the corner of the counter and replaced the rags over them.

After a moment, he shut off the light and went inside the house. Sleep found him soon after, but it was a barren wasteland until dawn.

3.

The no-kill shelter was a nondescript single-level building at the neglected end of a strip mall parking lot. On one side sat a long-abandoned taxi stand, while the other hosted the tiny office building of the town's last remaining tax accountant. If there was a less inviting location to house the county's lost and abandoned animals, John had yet to see it.

He sat in his idling pickup, hand on the ignition, hesitant. Switching it off was committing to going in. And going in had its own series of expectations.

The paperwork only takes a minute.

Damn you, Mary.

He glanced around the parking lot. A handful of vehicles sat clustered together three rows ahead, presumably the staff. Volunteers, he corrected himself. He grunted.

Fuck it.

He shut the ignition off and waited for the engine's ancient prattle to wind down. When it ceased, he stepped out and made his way to the front door. The main window was tinted, reflecting more of himself than he cared to see. Whatever lay beyond the glass remained a mystery. Not for the first time, he considered just how much this place had going against it. The sign above the door had been painted by an unsteady hand, with strong indications of being hung before it had dried. *FUR-GET ME NOT* it read. The words were surrounded by hastily drawn paw prints. One inexplicably had five toes.

"Jesus wept."

With a sigh, he opened the door and walked in.

The smell hit him straight away. He'd had dogs as a boy, and they almost always ended up smelling the same – old and damp, like a pissed-on blanket. He grimaced, letting a precious breath of air in before closing the door behind him. It was bright inside. Too bright. Somehow, it bolstered the stench. He squinted, looked around. He was at the corner of a wide open room, separated from the doorway by a low makeshift fence. Each wall housed a series of cages stacked three rows high on unpainted wooden platforms. In the central open area, no less than a dozen mutts ran in tight circles, sniffing each other's asses as though they were trading secrets. Atop the tallest cages, looking down from up high, was one of every imaginable breed of cat. They paid no more attention to the old man in the doorway than they did to the clock on the wall. *Fair enough*, John thought. *Don't care for your kind either.*

"Jonathon?"

He turned at the sound of Mary's voice. She stood in the archway of a curtained-off section behind the counter. It was the only side of the room not overrun with animals. He welcomed the sight of her warm smile.

"I didn't think you'd come," she said. The honesty in her words delivered an unintentional sting. She stepped around the counter, letting the curtain fall back behind her.

"That makes two of us," he told her. "Still not sure why I did. To be honest."

She placed a hand on his arm. "It's only been a minute. You'll figure it out."

"Does it always smell this bad?"

"You stop noticing after a while. The animals are bathed regularly. Well, the dogs, anyway. Cats are likely to leave you with a scar if you try to put them in a tub. But the smell remains. You get used to it." She let his arm go with a gentle pat and walked to the middle of the fence where a small latch gate had gone unnoticed until now. She paused, looking at his drawn features. "They don't take it home with them. I promise."

He forced a half-smile and followed her through the gate. All twelve mutts spun to face them, collectively pausing in startled surprise. It lasted less than a second, then the dogs were upon them. John held out his right arm to hold back the slobber of a greying German shepherd. The motion presented an opening for three of the smallest dogs to jockey for position against his legs. They hopped excitedly at his knees, desperate for so much as a glance down. Their barks were high pitched, brittle - a sound more likely to irritate than to endear. The shepherd had managed to wrap both front paws around John's wrist and was nuzzling affectionately at his out-sized knuckles. He saw that one paw had no nails, but before he could ask Mary about it, a large setter propped its paws on the back of his shoulders and began licking behind his left ear. John took an uncomfortable step to the right as Mary ushered the setter down. The shepherd relented, and Mary directed the entire pack to the back of the room.

John leaned on the fence. "Are they always so aggressive?"

Mary reached in her apron pocket and hand-fed each of them treats. "Actually, no." The dogs sat watching him, tongues dangling to one side or the other. Despite their lot in life, they seemed content. They had no masters, but they had each other. "Must be your warm personality."

John said nothing. He pushed off and walked slowly to the far wall, glancing into the open cages. The cats monitored him suspiciously like prison guards eyeing fresh meat. He gave them no mind. All the kennels had a blanket, and many had chew toys in varying states of destruction. The smell was much stronger here, and he was about to move away when he noticed a cage at the very end with a closed door. As he approached, he felt a dozen sets of eyes follow him and something unspoken in the air. It was only later that he would realize what it was: providence.

"Jonathon," Mary said hesitantly. He looked at her, and she shook her head. Confused, he glanced through the kennel doorway. At first, he thought it was empty - just a crumpled white blanket at the back where the shadows were heaviest. He reached up and gripped the wire screen of the door. The blanket stirred. He leaned closer, eyes adjusting to the darkness. Slowly, like a sail releasing in the breeze, a tattered white ear rose and twitched. It was followed by the turn of a small head. From the shadows, a single brown eye connected with John's own.

John swallowed. Dry and scratchy. He had been holding his breath without realizing it. He cleared his throat. "What's the story with this one?"

"That's Gadget," Mary said. "But, Jonathon..." her voice trailed off. He turned. All the dogs were sitting silently in a semicircle around her. He hadn't even noticed the room grow quiet.

"Gadget." He looked in the cage again. The small white dog slowly got to its feet. Once upright, it turned and looked at the old man, head low, eyes up. The raised ear struggled to stay upright while the other – what little remained of it – stayed lopped to the side. It was half the size of the working one, and the tattered end looked uneven. The hind legs trembled, threatened to buckle. The front legs turned outward like a clown, and the nails were long and unkempt. They clicked on the hard kennel floor as the mutt emerged into the light. John saw that the white fur was actually cream in color, except through the crown of the head, where a large black patch stood out like a poorly fitted toupee.

Gadget was undoubtedly the ugliest dog John had ever laid eyes on. Something in the way the mutt considered him told John that the feeling was mutual.

"Why is his cage locked?"

"It's not. It swings shut all the time, but he can nudge it open if he wants. He just never seems to want to." Mary handed out the last of her treats and shoved both hands in the pockets of her apron. She watched John reach his fingers further through the screen of the kennel door. Gadget stood motionless, studying the work-worn hand.

"Sally had a brother, died a few years back, not long after she passed on. He did a long stretch up in the state pen in his twenties for grand theft auto. Stupid kid shit. Anyway, years later he'd swing through town and

248

stay with us from time to time. On the outside, aside from a few shitty Bic-ink tattoos, you'd never say he'd done time. But I tell you, he couldn't get comfortable in a room with an open door." John turned to her, his hand still on the screen. "After a while in a locked room, you stop trying to force it open. Eventually, you stop checking it at all. After that... it's all you know. All you trust. It's safer behind that door."

He felt a soft wetness on his index finger and turned around. Gadget took a half step back, his loose tongue pulling away slowly. It hung there limp, unable to wind back inside, like a broken yo-yo. The eyes watched the old man cautiously. The single good ear twitched.

"You sizing me up, boy?" John whispered.

Mary moved beside him. "Unlikely. He's half-blind in one eye. The other one's ghosted over with a cataract. He lost most of that ear to frostbite a few years back, along with two toes on his hind left paw. His—"

"Teeth are gone," John interrupted.

Mary nodded. "Mostly, yeah. The few that are left are ground down from gnawing at God knows what over the years. Or rotted away to the gums."

"You couldn't fix that when you saved the ear?" He was surprised to hear a twist of anger in his voice like lemon dripping in a wound.

Mary sighed and said, "Like I told you, money is scarce. Sometimes that means tough choices have to be made of what to fix—"

"And what to forget." John nodded, but his frown grew. His lungs felt heavy in the dank air. He had the urge to cough and spit. He held back. "He's on his last legs."

"Yes." Mary touched his arm, but he held firm to the screen. Gadget shuffled forward again and pressed his nose against the crooked knuckle of John's ring finger. "We don't even know how old he is. He had an owner at some point, we know that. Given the degree of mange and sores he had when we found him, the best we can figure is that he was on his own for a few years. He has a fear of people in general, which is why he wasn't widely seen around. Otherwise, we would have picked him up sooner. He's been with us three years already."

"Three years?" John shook his head. "Always like this?"

"Yeah. We take him out for little walks each day. In here, he'll just sit on the floor, but outside, he perks up a little, long enough to make it around the building on a leash. He won't mingle with the pack, but the cats have taken to him. Sometimes we find one in there with him, curled up in his tail. But he doesn't take to strangers and that hasn't done him any favors."

"When did it ever?" John said. "For anyone?"

Gadget licked the knuckle softly, like a brook over a stone. Mary watched, fascinated at first, and then uneasy. A dog on death's door was more work than companion. Even for a young and able person. And John was neither.

John moved his fingers down and away. Gadget remained in place this time. When John reached under the dog's chin and scratched, Gadget tilted it slightly for a better angle.

"You said the paperwork would only take a minute?"

"No," Mary said sharply. He met her eyes. They were dark and unblinking.

"No what?"

"No, you can't adopt him. Did you not listen to what I said? He's—"

"Dying. Yeah, I got that. So what?" He waved his free arm past her to the pack watching them intently. "They all will eventually."

She stepped away, shaking her head. He pulled his hand out of the kennel. Gadget watched him walk out of sight through the closed door.

"A few days ago, you thought this place was wasting time and money. You thought they should all be put out of their misery." She walked around the counter and crouched down to sort through a drawer. "Now you want to take a broken down dog home— for what, Jonathon? To make a point—?"

"I don't even know what point I'd be making, Mary."

"Hell, ten minutes ago, you didn't even know why you came in here—"

"And you said I'd figure it out."

She stood up, a piece of paper in her hand. "You're an asshole."

"You think I'm going to drop dead and abandon him."

"No," she said, eyes narrowing. "I've known you a long time, Jonathon. All my life, really. I'm not afraid you'll abandon him. I'm afraid he'll be with you and still die alone."

He held her stare for a moment. A cold stone sank along the edge of his stomach, the weight of it dragging his eyes down and away from hers. He nodded and let out a long breath. A moment later, she was alone in the shelter once more.

At the far end of the room, the door to Gadget's kennel gently pushed open a quarter of an inch.

4.

He awoke well before dawn with a sense that someone was in the room. The air was still and silent, the kind of quiet that floods the void when all else has fled. With some effort, he opened his eyes and glanced around. Shapes and shadows, all familiar. The curtains hung limp before the open window.

He sat up, suddenly racked with cold sweat, shivering. The curtains remained still, the humid air undisturbed. He drew the blanket around him, swinging his legs over the side. Not wanting to move further, he peered out into the night. The moonlight was pale, the start of a new cycle. Yet even in the dim visibility, he could see a slight distortion in the tall grass. A subtle path of broken strands ran from the edge of the dirt yard near the garage all the way to the creek by the highway. Something had come and gone.

He wiped sleep from his eyes, barely registering that the arthritic ache was completely gone from his hands. The heaviness in his chest that he often felt in the morning was already squeezing the oxygen from his body, leaving him lightheaded. He coughed, feeling the rattle of phlegm dislodge inside. It made its way up his throat. The taste of copper was horrid in his mouth and he leaned out the window and spit. The dark wad fell away into the dirt.

To the dust returned, he thought humorlessly. He wiped his chin with the sheet and shuffled to the bathroom. He pissed in the dark. It came in painful bursts. He grimaced. When he finished, he leaned on the sink and coughed again. What came up was mostly blood this time. He stared at it, and somehow that was better than seeing his reflection in the mirror above. Better than seeing the fear. He rinsed the blood away. The fear lingered.

Sleep returned a short time later, carrying terrible dreams.

5.

He was studying the buckled grass out back when Mary arrived just before nine in the morning. He stood ten feet into the field, his back to the house, hands on hips the way that old men do when drawing on a lifetime of experience to give cause to effect. Her footsteps on the gravel scattered his thoughts. He turned.

She wore dark jeans and a long black buttoned shirt. The material was airy, easily moved by the breeze. The auburn in her hair caught the morning light at an angle that restored twenty years, if only for a moment. As though aware, she paused and waited for him to make his way out of the grass to see her. He was halfway there before he noticed the pet carrier in her right hand. He stopped.

"What's this?" John asked. "Change your mind?"

She lowered the carrier to the ground and straightened, wringing the strain from her hand. "No. But he changed it for me."

John glanced at the small portable kennel. Just beyond the door, he could see the cream fur around the dark nose. Gadget's eyes were closed, but his good ear was up and listening.

Mary saw that John was about to say something, and she kicked at the dirt, cutting him off. "Don't ask me about it. I'm here— we're here. That's what you wanted."

He squinted but kept silent. He looked down and considered how unprepared for company he was. He wore jean shorts and a faded grey T-shirt with the last remnants of Lynyrd Skynyrd's faded logo across the front. It was almost as old and worn out as the tattered sandals on his feet. Those relics were held together in various spots with duct tape and the enduring power of hope.

"Offer me a coffee, Jonathon, and we'll see if he wants to stay."

He led her to the front porch, and she laid the kennel at the far end, away from the little table and chairs. John continued inside and put the kettle on. Mary opened the kennel door and sat at the table, watching. By the time John returned ten minutes later with two cups of coffee, Gadget had yet to emerge.

John eased into his chair, watching the carrier. "*He* changed your mind, huh? Maybe I changed his." He sipped his coffee. It was black and bitter, but he needed the caffeine. The night had not been kind.

Mary held her hand over her mug, feeling the steam. "We'll give it a few more minutes. Till the coffee is gone, at least." And then, because she saw a flicker of disappointment cloud his eyes, she added: "This is normal."

"There's nothing normal about that mutt," John said with a sad grin.

"He's just old." Mary sipped her coffee. "And at the end of an unkind road."

He drank his coffee, feeling her eyes on him. For a time, she was silent, enjoying the cloudless morning and the quiet that being this far outside the town brought. When she spoke again, her cup was almost empty.

"You look tired, Jonathon. More than usual, I mean. I know the cancer is part of it, but—"

"I haven't been sleeping," he said, hearing the exhaustion in his voice. "Started the past week or so. Waking up in the middle of the night, restless, sweating. Bad dreams."

"Have you been drinking?"

He looked at her sharply - perhaps *too* sharply - and almost immediately softened. "No."

She didn't follow it up. He had been a hard drinker at times, mostly in the bleak gap between marriages and after his second wife died. But in the last two years, he had barely touched anything stronger than beer, and even that was rare. Still, she had cause to ask. He was a mean, surly drunk, and the blackouts that often followed left him deeply depressed and craving another go-round with the bottle to pull him out of it. Hair of the dog that bit you, and he bit often and hard. One bar in town had banned him after too many dust-ups with the regulars, and others would have surely followed. He had struggled to change his path, but small towns rarely forget the road the path turns from.

"I'll be honest with you, Jonathon: I don't know that you're up to caring for a dog that has special needs."

"Mary—"

"Let me finish. I'm not saying any of this because I want to. This was my idea, remember? But you're sick, maybe sicker than you're letting on or willing to admit. And that scares me. It scares me because you're my friend, and in my own way, I love you. But it also scares me because I'm afraid having a dog like Gadget won't make you feel better - it'll make you worse. I don't want to be responsible for that. For either of you."

John opened his mouth to respond when the sound of clicking on the porch made them both turn. The little mutt was halfway to them from the kennel. His steps were unhurried and uneven, and his long nails made a broken rhythm across the boards. John noticed that Gadget's back end drifted slightly to one side, and his hips seemed strained by the effort of keeping up. And yet the dog persisted, not stopping until he reached the table. He lowered his hind legs into a sideways sit, tail wrapped around them, positioned evenly between Mary and John. He looked at them both as best he could with his limited vision.

"Well, hello," Mary said quietly. Gadget licked absently at his nose. He gazed from her to John, who remained silent and unsure.

"Moment of truth, I guess," John quipped at the mutt. The good ear twitched, and the tip of the tail patted the boards. Then the dog eased up, took a final glance at Mary, and walked between John's legs. He settled under the chair and lay down, resting his head on his front paws.

Mary finished the last of her coffee, leaned forward and ran her hands through her hair. "I'll get the paperwork."

She retrieved it from the front seat of her car, and while John read through it, she returned to the vehicle and unloaded a large bag of Purina and a long blue leash. She leaned the food against the porch steps and laid the leash on the table. She removed a small bottle of pills from her shirt pocket and set it next to the leash. John picked it up.

"What's this for?"

"Pain. He has hip dysplasia. That's why his back half is lower than the front when he walks. Measuring an animal's pain is difficult. They can't tell you. And he doesn't need these every day. But if you see him panting without reason or struggling to pick himself up, give him one."

"Sure," John said, squinting at the label. He set the bottle back down. "What about the curve in his spine, the way it bends to the side?"

She shook her head, saying, "No, that's permanent. We think he suffered head trauma at some point. It can sometimes heal itself, but usually, if it's going to happen, it happens sooner than later. With Gadget, it never did." Mary handed him a pen, and he scribbled his initials on the page. She took it. "I'll be back in a week or so to visit. He should be well settled by then. If you want to change your mind, that would be the best time to do it. Before he becomes too attached."

"I won't," John said. He stood up to see her off. She studied his eyes for a moment, then leaned in and kissed his cheek.

"I hate this shirt," she said, tugging at the bottom. She walked down the steps to the car, turned back. There was a fierceness in her face he had not seen before. "You promise me something, Jonathon. On your word. When it's time – and you'll know when it is – you call me. I'll be here."

He did not know if she was speaking of the dog or him, but he suspected it might have been both. Rather than question it further, he held her gaze as best he could and nodded slowly. "On my word, Mary."

* * *

After her car had departed, John sat watching the horizon. Gadget remained under the chair, eyes closed, ears down, enjoying the fresh air. John saw no point in disturbing the little mutt. Neither of them had anywhere to be. No schedule, no plans. And having experienced the stench of the shelter firsthand, he imagined this dalliance in the summer sun was something of a reprieve.

What next, old man?

The truth was, he did not know what came next. "Guess that's up to you," he muttered quietly. Gadget's good ear twitched, but the dog remained still.

A few minutes before sunset, the dog woke and painfully got to his feet. He shook the cobwebs away and slowly emerged from under the chair. He gave a quick, one-eyed glance at the old man before puttering to the edge of the steps and sitting down. He squinted at the orange sky.

John straightened in his seat. If the dog was going to signal a desire to leave, now would be the moment. But he didn't think leaving was on the animal's mind. John leaned forward, watching the back of Gadget's head. The working ear was turned out toward the horizon, listening. The evening was silent, serene.

"No more cage, little fella."

Gadget turned his profile to see him. John smiled, then creakily stood up. His joints popped and his back ached, but he barely noticed. His body had more urgent matters to tend to.

"I don't know about you, but I'm pretty damn hungry."

Gadget looked at the oversized sack of Purina leaning against the porch, then back to John. John sighed, nodded. "Right."

The bag was heavy. As he carried it into the house, he considered writing a letter to the Purina company suggesting they refrain from making bags of food any larger than the dog breed for which they are intended. He knew he'd never put pen to paper, but there was deep satisfaction in working the finer points of his consummate and curt argument out in his mind. Once he had laid the sack on the floor of the pantry, he gave it a soft kick for good measure.

The sound of clicking nails on the floor approached the kitchen. Gadget stood in the archway and watched as John retrieved a small bowl from the cupboard over the sink and returned to the pantry. He pulled his keys from his pocket and used the serrated edge of the house key to tear a hole in the bag. The smell thickened the air in the small space.

"How do you eat this shit?"

Gadget cocked his head to the side. John jabbed the bowl into the bag and pulled it out, full of small brown-green pellets. It looked like rabbit shit and smelled almost as bad. He leaned his head back and looked at the mutt. Gadget took a step into the kitchen and paused. John held up the bowl of food. "If you have to eat it, I have to smell it. No one wins."

He threw it back in the bag, bowl and all.

*　　　　　　*　　　　　　*

The steak was tender and rare, and coupled with a side of mashed potatoes, it proved more than enough to fill them both. After John had finished the dishes, he retrieved the remainder of Gadget's supplies from the porch and put them away. He wondered where the dog would settle to sleep and considered laying a few blankets on the floor at the foot of the bed. He was okay with the mutt sharing the bed (after all, he would barely take up any space), but if Gadget had to pee as often and suddenly as John did between sunset and sunrise, neither would be getting much rest. He'd see how the first night fared before extending that invitation. Blankets it was.

John was pleasantly surprised to see that the dog had no issue communicating when he *did* have to go to the bathroom. Coming down from setting up the makeshift bed, he discovered Gadget sitting patiently by the screen door. John opened it and wandered into the night air as the mutt trotted carefully down the steps and disappeared around the far corner of the house. A few minutes later, Gadget returned and laggardly made his ascent back to the porch. He sat at John's feet, looking up, lopsided tongue dangling like a broken zipper.

John leaned on the porch post, gazing at the stars. Another cloudless night. If this was to be his last August on planet Earth, he couldn't have asked for a better one. The bitterness of winter was still a solid four months in the future. And the future was of diminishing consequence with each passing day.

He looked down at the dog. Gadget's eyes were heavy with the weight of the day's events. They were both ready for bed.

6.

They settled into a routine over the following week. Up with the sun, breakfast on the porch – bacon and eggs for John, leftovers from the night before for Gadget – followed by several hours working the small vegetable garden at the back of the house until noon. As John pulled weeds and ran the hose, Gadget oscillated between rolling in the grass and sleeping in the shade of the pumpkin leaves. If there was an extra spring in the little mutt's step, John never noticed it. But there was an unmistakable gleaming in the dog's good eye.

Each day after lunch, they sat on the porch steps listening to the world pass by - sometimes on the steady hum of highway traffic beyond the horizon, sometimes in the drone of a jet cruising countless miles overhead, and every so often in the laughter of children fading into the afternoon breeze somewhere between the far side of the house and a neighbor's home John would never visit.

Evening suppers became increasingly challenging as John avoided revisiting the Purina, but he managed, and Gadget never complained. In fact, it compelled John to cook decent meals, something he hadn't the inclination for since his diagnosis. At night, they lay with the window open, and sleep pulled them under to the songs of crickets and whispers of wind. The bad dreams and restlessness retreated to memory. The tall grass, like the shotgun in the kitchen, went undisturbed.

For a time.

On the first day of the second week, John awoke before dawn to the sound of heavy rain. It pounded the roof with persistent percussion. When he got out of bed, he saw that a puddle had formed at the base of the window, and the curtains had become too damp to sway in the breeze. Gadget stepped off his blankets and assessed the puddle for a moment before deciding he could help best by drinking from it. It tasted like autumn.

"Fill your boots," John said. He stepped around the dog and retrieved a towel from the bathroom. He ushered Gadget to the side, then lay the towel across the puddle. It darkened quickly. John reached up to close the window and was startled by the crash of an enormous thunderclap overhead. After it rolled off into the distance, he heard a mournful cry at his feet. Gadget was shivering, ears pressed against his little head.

"Just thunder, buddy. Nothing to worry about." He brought the window down firmly. The rain splattered against it. "See—"

A blinding flash of light illuminated the heavy clouds overhead. But it was what the light revealed that choked off his words: a dark shape at the end of the field, motionless in the storm. John blinked, and the sky went dark again, everything beyond the window distorted by thick rivulets of rain. He pressed his face to the glass, the frightened dog momentarily forgotten. But the night held its secrets in shadow.

The thunder came again, closer this time. A frantic series of clicks and scrapes ran across the hardwood. John turned just in time to see Gadget's tail tuck out the door. He started after him, feeling the unpleasant squish of the wet towel fill every crevice between his toes. He uttered a curse and yanked his foot away as though he had stepped on a nail. Lightning split the sky once again. Outside, the shape was gone, but there was a fresh path of trodden grass leading toward the house.

John hurried out of the room and down the stairs. Thunder rolled directly above as he reached the hallway. Dressed in what may well have been his most tattered pair of underwear and nothing else, John threw open the front door and stumbled into the downpour. His sun-baked body was drenched before he reached the bottom step. Undeterred, he wiped hair and rain from his eyes and rushed to the back. The wet towel may have been problematic inside, but now he trod barefoot across all manner of rocks with the carefree abandon of a child on a sandy beach. The sky lit up once more as he reached the edge of the tall grass. If anything was about to emerge, the light refused to reveal it. The dark returned. He paused, breath held in his wounded lungs. The rain pounded his flesh, coursed down his face. Through it all, he waited for the shadow in the field to come forward. But nothing materialized.

"Fucker," he rasped. He paced across the threshold of the field. "What do you want?"

Only the thunder answered. It moved off to the east, and the lightning trailed farther behind. The rain abated. John peered into the grass. The wind swirled within, twisting it into a myriad of forms, none familiar. Certainly nothing like what he had seen in the glow of the lightning.

Just what did you think you saw, old man?

He coughed, hawked bloody mucous into the mud by his feet. "Nothing."

He made his way back to the porch. The screen door was whipping against the siding. The inner door was wide open. His first thought was that Gadget had run out and maybe tried to bury himself beneath the porch steps. The little fella had appeared scared enough to try. The dog seemed smarter than that, though. Running into the storm was the exclusive folly of decaying old men.

He shut the screen door and latched it. The square flap at the bottom that he had cut out for Gadget to come and go fluttered in and out. He stared out at the distant clouds, expecting more lightning, but none came. He shut the main door and flicked on the overhead light. Water dripped off his withered body, rapidly forming a puddle around his feet, not unlike the one he'd tried so hard to avoid stepping in upstairs. What had he been thinking rushing out in the dark, naked except for a pair of old skivvies barely capable of keeping his shriveled cock and balls from slapping between his thighs? What would Mary think if she came through the door just now and saw him standing there in the cold light, every crease and crack exposed, every blemish and scar revealed like landmarks on the map of his past?

She'd be scared. Not of him, but *for* him. And for the dog.

His mind snapped back to the dog. He ran his hands through his hair and wiped the water across his chest as he walked from the hall into the kitchen. It was dark and empty, just as he had left it. The pantry door was shut. The fridge emitted a soft buzz. The analog clock ticked quietly into the future as it had always done. Business as usual.

Except for the pet carrier in the corner under the table. It was where he had left it, the door open. But it was no longer empty. He knelt and crawled beneath the tabletop, still dripping. When he was eye to eye with the kennel, he slid onto his side, and peered in.

Gadget gazed from the shadows, shivering, panting heavily. John could not tell if it was from fear or pain, but he imagined one had led to the other, and now both were coursing through the mutt in equal measure.

"Hey," John said gently. "It's okay, boy. No more cage, remember?"

Gadget licked his nose, and John thought the panting eased slightly. He reached in slowly. Gadget retreated. John paused. He lowered his hand onto the blanket, palm up, open.

"No rush." John sighed and rested his head on his other arm. He shut his eyes and waited. He was asleep when Gadget finally moved again, just enough to lay a paw in John's hand. Then Gadget slept too.

7.

The path through the tall grass was unmistakable in the morning sun. John stared at it from the bedroom window for several minutes before heading to the yard. The grass at the edge was not disturbed. Whatever had cut its way forward through the field had stopped less than six feet from the threshold before retreating. John, wearing considerably more clothing than the night before, glanced around for the garden rake. He spotted it leaning against the wall by the vegetable garden. Gadget appeared from the side of the house.

"Morning," John said, walking back to the field with the tool. Gadget followed. "Thoughts?"

Gadget had plenty, none of which he could communicate. Instead, he stopped three feet from the field and stared anxiously at the tall grass. John used the handle of the rake to part the strands. A low growl rose in Gadget's chest as John stepped into the field.

"Something wrong, buddy? I'll be right back."

Gadget barked. Short and high-pitched. The growling continued unabated. John faced him.

"Whatever it was in there, it doesn't seem to come around before dark."

Gadget was unconvinced. He stared past the old man and barked again - louder, more forceful. His legs quivered as he edged forward and back no more than an inch at a time. Finally, he lowered his front legs and scratched at the soft earth.

"Stop that," John said. "Gadget!" There was no anger in his voice. He found the mutt's antics more amusing than frustrating. When Gadget refused to let up, John swatted a hand in the air toward the dog and turned back to the field. He pushed the grass aside and took two full strides. The grass fell back into place behind him, and he disappeared from view. Gadget lay down, head on his front paws, and whimpered.

The grass ahead was heavily trampled. Some strands were pulling themselves back up toward the welcoming sun, but many more had been buckled over. Most dangled into the dirt or were severed completely and now lay scattered. Something had definitely moved quickly toward the house. Something heavy.

John proceeded forward. The field swallowed him up. With the sun so low in the sky, shadows cast on all sides. He waved the rake handle back and forth like a divining rod. Ineffective in a fight, but it might give the appearance of a threat to anything wandering around waiting to pounce.

The deeper he advanced, the more likely than not it seemed it was an animal that had been coming around at night and not some imaginary bike thief. The shape glimpsed in the flash of lightning had only been illuminated for a second. Not nearly enough time to identify it, but more than enough to cast doubt on whether he had seen anything at all. Were it not for the beaten path, he would have chalked it up as a trick of the shadows or just startled nerves.

He continued for another twenty yards. The darkness thinned ahead. He glanced over his shoulder to check if Gadget had followed him and was disappointed to see the little dog had not mustered the courage. He suddenly stepped in something soft and thick. A warm, wet sensation spread up from the ground over his left sandal. John looked down, expecting to see his foot slipping into fresh mud. He stepped back in surprise, tripped, and fell on his ass. A bolt of hot pain shot up his spine, but it barely registered.

His eyes fixated on the blood.

It was thick and brown on his skin, already beginning to dry in some places. His sandal was black with it. John lifted his leg to the side. A brown and grey mass of fur the size of a football lay in the path. There was a long, thick tail at the far end. There was no head on the opposite side. The side he had stepped in.

John scrambled to his feet, using the rake as leverage. Once up, he was relieved to see – or rather, *not see* – the head anywhere nearby. He poked the body gently with the prongs. The bloody impression of his sandal print had darkened the mud next to it, and rainwater was trickling in. The animal's remains appeared relatively intact other than the obvious. He stepped closer and saw long claws at the end of tiny hand-like paws. He'd encountered enough raccoons in his day to know one when he saw it, head or no head. They were a pest and a menace, especially in urban areas, but out here in the rural spaces, they were just another part of the ecosystem. John bore little opinion of them. Still, this one had a cruelty visited on it that no creature deserved. It had been killed for sport, not food.

He couldn't leave it to rot in the sun. Gadget might have been afraid to follow him into the grass, but if he got wind of the corpse, instinct was bound to take over and draw him in. That was a mess that John had even less interest in cleaning up. He headed back to get a garbage bag.

Mary was waiting for him. She was kneeling on the ground rubbing Gadget's belly, her denim dress short enough to reveal the firm, tanned legs of a woman half her age. Gadget rolled onto his front when John emerged and Mary glanced up, pulling her hand away.

"Morning, Mary."

"Same to you." She stood up, and John envied how easy and fluid her movements were. "He's put on weight."

John looked at the little dog at his feet. Had Gadget put on weight? John couldn't tell, but he supposed it was possible, maybe even likely. By any measure, it wasn't unhealthy.

"How often have you been feeding him?"

"We eat together," John replied. The ambiguity was intentional. She could infer from it what she wanted. The dog could use a little extra padding.

Mary's eyes fell to the rake in his hand. The metal tips were wet and red. "Is that..."

"Blood. Yeah." John wiped the prongs in the short grass of the yard. "Dead raccoon. I was just about to deal with it."

"Dead, how?"

"Dead is dead. Does it matter?" He started for the house. Gadget slowly followed. Mary glanced into the tall grass, then followed as well.

"It might," she said. "Natural causes are one thing, but a predator is another. In case you hadn't noticed, Gadget isn't even the size of an adult raccoon."

"We're working on that," John quipped. He leaned the rake against the wall and smiled at her. Mary was not amused. He continued around to the front of the house. The storm had broken the heat a little, and a cool breeze had taken hold of the morning air. It was refreshing.

John left them on the porch as he went inside. He shot a disgusted glance at the Purina inside the pantry and pulled the chain cord on the bare bulb overhead, thinking he really should just dump the bag down into the cellar. There was a nearly empty box of garbage bags on the second shelf, but when his hand came out of it, it held clear plastic.

"Well, piss on that," John muttered. He pushed things around on the shelves, but there were no other bags. He couldn't dispose of a dead animal in a transparent bag, especially one without a head. He jammed the bag back in the box and headed upstairs to the bedroom.

After Michelle died, he had decided against throwing her clothing away or donating it to charity. The idea held a certain morbidness to it that he was uncomfortable with. Who would want to wear a dead woman's clothes? And worse yet, he did not want to encounter someone entering the grocery store or exiting the gas station wearing them either. So, instead, he had hung everything on three heavy-duty hangers, pulled garbage bags up and over them, and hung them in the back of the closet behind his winter coats. Out of sight, out of mind.

Until now.

John opened the closet door and slid his limited wardrobe toward him. The hanging black bags behind were exactly as he had left them. He reached for the closest one. His hand stopped an inch from the knot. What lay beneath he had not set eyes on for two years. That was the point of putting them back here. He did not want to see them then, and he did not want to see them now. He had accepted Michelle's death, sudden as it was, and he had moved on. But closing the door to a room or a closet was not closure. Closet doors have no lock for a reason. They are meant to be returned to - to be reopened - often. And now, because of a stupid fucking headless raccoon, here he was before it was time.

It occurred to him then with stark clarity that it *was* time. Because for all the days behind him, the days ahead were growing scarce. Life's most precious non-renewable resource.

"Fuck it." A refrain he heard himself saying more and more lately. He undid the knot quickly and slid the black bag free of the swaying bundle of summer dresses, scarves and nightshirts. The potent odor of mothballs filled the closet. There were two of them at the bottom of the bag, and he left them in there. A dead raccoon was going to need all the deodorant it could get, simmering in the long, hot days of August. John gave the hanging clothes a final glance, then shoved his own along the rail in front of it and shut the door.

On the porch, Mary continued to pet Gadget's tiny head. She tempered her concern over the dog's increased weight. He was more mobile than she had ever seen him, and it was only a pound or two at most. It was a fair trade-off.

"What *is* he feeding you?"

"Nothing he can't handle. Now stop fretting, Mary." John let the screen door swing back into place. He walked past her to the steps. She touched him on the arm.

"I won't keep you long, Jonathon. I just stopped by like I promised to see how he – both of you – are doing."

John turned without moving his arm. Her touch was gentle, and he found himself wanting her to linger. He smiled at her. *To tell you the truth, Mary, he hid shivering under the table as I ran naked in the rain like a lunatic, chasing ghosts. Then we slept on the floor like a pair of vagabonds. To say nothing of the raccoon doing a spot-on Marie Antoinette impression out in the field...*

"We're doing fine." It wasn't a lie, just a simplification. There was no easy way to articulate exactly how he was feeling since Gadget had moved in. Except for the previous night, he was sleeping better, and to the benefit of both, he was preparing proper meals. He had more energy, too. If Mary was expecting validation for bringing them together, she wouldn't be getting it from him. But not out of some petty need to withhold it. John just felt it was too early to say either way.

She let his arm go. "Good," she said simply.

"I'll be right back. Keep him here, will you?"

Mary nodded and sat on the steps. She tapped her leg, and Gadget huddled next to her. She hooked her forefinger into his collar, rubbing under his ear with the rest.

John left the rake behind this time and quickly found the raccoon where he had left it. The blood had congealed around the wound, forming a dark crust. He opened the black bag and rolled the corpse into it. He hefted it, tied the open end shut, and laid it back on the ground. He kicked soil over the shoe-print, cursing under his breath for not bringing the rake. His sandals were ruined, something that the frayed duct tape holding them together suggested had long ago been decided.

That left one more thing to do.

He pushed his way into the tall grass to the left, eyes to the ground. With any luck, whatever had severed the head from the raccoon's body had seen fit to take it when they fled. That sense of hope was taking root in his stomach as he moved in an arc around the path to the right side but dissipated when he saw a splatter of dark red droplets across the lower half of the grass by his feet. He stretched his left leg out and parted the stalks with his foot.

John never realized a raccoon had black eyes until he saw two tiny onyx orbs staring up at him from the ground. In the low light of the field, the lifeless gaze was unnervingly grim and sad. The final image they had witnessed was lost somewhere deep in those inky pools, like light pulled over the event horizon of a black hole.

Dead is dead.

The cool breeze reached out to him from the pathway, chilling the sweat on his brow. He needed to make quick work of the disposal. He considered getting the rake but knew that he was not likely to return to finish the job once he was free of the tall grass. It was now or never.

He crouched, feeling his knees pop. He ignored the pain, reached out with one hand, and grabbed the nearest ear. Compared to the body, the head was remarkably light. The hair was coarse and thick, and the inside of the ear felt oily against his thumb. He held it facing away as he stood up, knees popping once more.

John tugged the bag open and laid the head inside. He knotted the opening closed again, then tied it once more for good measure. He hurried out of the grass and dropped it inside the wooden garbage bin at the side of the house. He stared at it for a second before lowering the cover and latching it tight. A few days from now, the sanitation truck would be by to collect it with the rest of the trash, and that would be the end of it. A bleak coda to a gruesome death. The raccoon deserved better, but burying it would do nothing further to put it from his mind.

After he washed his hands and tossed his sandals in the waste bucket, he joined Mary and Gadget on the steps. The dog was asleep, head rested on her thigh.

"You going to report it to the wildlife folks?" Mary asked quietly.

"No," John replied. "Last thing I need is some bureaucrat hanging around lecturing me on what I should or should not do when dead animals show up on my property. Or how to protect against predators."

"So it was a predator?"

John shrugged. "Coyote, maybe. Not much else around here it could have been." That was true, though coyotes were not sport hunters. It wasn't normal for a predator to attack and leave the prey behind unless it was a pure aggression kill caused by something like rabies. Coyotes were also about as large as a mid-size dog. Not the type of creature that would leave a trail of damage in its wake.

Mary nodded and ran a hand over the black patch of hair on Gadget's head. Gadget pressed against her more closely but did not wake.

"I know what you're thinking, Mary. But don't worry. He's fine. He'll be fine."

"I think the cats miss him," she said.

"The cats or you?"

She chuckled. "A little of both, I guess. Silly, I know."

"You're always welcome to visit. He's clearly happy to see you."

"Him or you?" she said.

"Cheeky," John said with a chuckle. The cool morning breeze returned, and a shiver ran through them both. Mary sighed and eased Gadget off her leg. She stood up.

"I should head out. The cats will want to know he's doing well."

After she had gone, John and Gadget ate lunch in the kitchen. John had little appetite after the morning's events, so Gadget had seconds. John tried to fill the remainder of the day with random odd jobs around the house, but his mind kept returning to the raccoon. It wasn't the blood or the brutality that lingered. It was the eyes and the black emptiness within. And the thought came to him once again: Dead is dead.

The death of Landon had left John bitter at God. If there was supposed to be purpose in all things, there was a distinct lack of it in ripping the life of a child from the world. It left only frayed memories, as fragile as the mind they inhabited and susceptible to the erosion of time. And yet, he had kept the faith. Death, John reasoned, was part of life, and memory was the ward of those left behind. He found purpose in keeping that part of Landon alive, and the bitterness waned. When Sally, the boy's mother, adrift in internal darkness and despair, took her own life two years later, his bitterness flared, turned to rage, and his mind turned to the bottle. He had been made steward of two departed lives, and the memories brought only pain. There was no solace in prayer. Only the bottle. Meeting Michelle brought him back from the brink, and throughout their ten-year marriage, she pulled him farther and farther from that precipice. They built a passionate and loving second life, free of excess and expectations. A simple life. Michelle did not want children, and John, having loved and lost one already, had sealed off that chamber of his heart. They were happy and at peace. The sun rose and set over their home each day, and as they watched it together, John found the solace he needed to move on. God was not in the past. God was in the moment.

When death came for Michelle, it took the last of John's faith with her. The aneurysm was swift and cruel and without hope. It was somehow both merciless and merciful in its precision. The young progressive priest who had buried her tried to explain that the paradox of God was exactly that: merciful *and* merciless and that only God could understand God. Those who tried, were doomed to fail. Acceptance, blind and unwavering, was the only road to peace. John knew differently. He knew God had nothing to do with Michelle's death or Landon's or Sally's. God was dead. And dead is dead.

When he closed his eyes that night, the memory of those now gone filled his thoughts, and the realization that when death came for him, all they had once been would be lost in the void as well.

8.

He awoke to the sound of clicking. It started in the distance, his body swimming toward it. As he got closer, the surrounding darkness lightened. Black eased to grey like heated charcoal in a barbeque. The clicking paused, then started again, faster, more urgent. He opened his eyes, saw that he was lying on his side, and quickly realized his left arm was asleep beneath him. He slid it out with a groan and let it dangle over the edge. Pins and needles shot from his fingers to his shoulder. He winced.

The clicking paused as he moved, but now it approached. Something coarse and wet slid along his fingers. He opened his eyes. Gadget stopped licking him and sat panting softly. The dog's good ear twitched forward in anticipation. The good eye stared directly into John's, unblinking as though it might miss something vital in the split second it would take to do so.

John sighed. He had no desire to get up and even less strength to try. Time was a sea with no current, his body adrift. His head, heavy with sleep, sank like a stone to a pillow of sand at the bottom.

He heard the dog whine softly. More clicks followed as the mutt shifted its weight, then sat back down. Gadget licked John's forefinger again.

"Knock it off," John croaked. When Gadget persisted, John rolled over. His tingling arm flopped over and rested on his side. Gadget whined again - a pathetic, lonely sound only dogs can make. John was unmoved.

Gadget tilted his head, thinking. He trotted around to the other side of the bed and stared at the old man's face. John forced one eye open. The dog shuffled excitedly – *click, click, click* – as the mangled tail swayed like a conductor's baton leading the march.

"I said: knock it off!"

Gadget froze and lowered his head. The good ear folded over.

A full minute of peace followed. John dozed.

The sea of darkness grew cold. Shivers coursed through his body. His legs and arms drew in tight, instinctively conserving heat. It was no use. He swam for the surface.

John sat up. The last corner of the sheet slipped off the foot of the bed to the floor. He lunged for it, caught it by the tag and held it tight. Gadget's nails scraped across the hardwood. John leaned further and saw the little mutt backpedalling frantically, one edge of the blanket held firmly in its mouth. Despite his frustration, John relaxed his grip. The battle wasn't worth the toll it might take on the old dog's few remaining teeth.

A look as close to perplexed as a dog could muster spread across Gadget's face. He opened his jaw, and the blanket fell to the floor. John swung out of bed and stomped to the door. He pointed to the stairs beyond.

"Go!"

Gadget tilted his head, first left, then right.

"I know you hear me, and I know you understand what 'go' means." John jabbed his finger back out the doorway. "Go."

Gadget did. He paused at the top of the steps and gave John a final forlorn glance before carefully hopping down. John closed the door. He swiped the blanket off the floor, grimaced at the drool stain. He tucked that end into the foot of the bed and lay down, pulling the remainder up and over his body. Eight hours of sleep felt like eight minutes.

He shut his eyes.

*   *   *

He did not know which occurred first – the incessant barking or his brother Billy's voice in his head, telling him the wolf was in the henhouse again – but the result was immediate: he tore the blanket from the bed and threw it across the room. He slid out and opened the window. The field was as he had left it, the grass slowly reclaiming the path. The dog was nowhere near it. The barking came again - sharp, high-pitched. He looked to the left. Gadget was pacing in a circle in front of the garage. At the end of each rotation, the dog paused and barked toward the sliding bay door before tracing his circular steps once more.

"The hell is wrong with that mutt?" John pulled his head in and dressed quickly in yesterday's clothes. The faded jeans had seen better days, but the red button-down flannel shirt was relatively new and still clean. That was good. He had no intention of opening the closet.

The sunlight was a spike to his eyes. He stomped around the side of the house.

John expected the dog to cease its racket once it saw him, but the barking and pacing increased. John stood watching, hands on his hips, exacerbated. The commotion had loosened a wad of phlegm in his chest, and he coughed heavily, forcing it out. He spat it into the dry earth and wiped spittle from his chin. It glistened red on his finger. He smeared it on the tail of his shirt.

He stepped in front of the dog, his arms out toward the large bay door. He shrugged. "What? What is so goddamn interesting about this now?"

Gadget barked in response. John had no idea if a dog's bark aged the way a human voice did, but the noises coming from the little mutt sounded old and hoarse. Gadget trotted forward and barked directly at the door.

John threw his arms up, then dropped them in frustration. "I'm going to open this door, and you are going to be more disappointed than you have ever been in your life!" John crouched down and squinted into Gadget's good eye. "Last chance."

Gadget's tongue flopped out the side of his snout. He turned his head back toward the house, then looked at the garage door and barked once more.

"Fine!" John shouted. He dug into his pocket and fished out the key. As he stabbed it into the lock and turned the handle, Gadget spun around in a circle, then sat and watched anxiously. The door went up.

The interior was exactly as John had left it. The Indian 741 stood gleaming in the fresh sunlight streaming through the doorway, the chrome polished to a mirror finish. Tools hung from the walls, spare parts and other detritus of John's labor lay in a pile in the far corner. The bloodstain still stared back at him from the middle of the cold concrete floor, but its power was reduced in the shadow of the bike. The unnatural mix of engine oil, rust and cleaning chemicals wafted in the heat.

"See. Told you."

Gadget gripped the cuff of John's pant leg in his mouth and tugged toward the open doorway. John resisted. The desire to crawl back in bed was even more persuasive. The cancer was taking further hold. There would be a time when the spread escalated, when his heart and other organs would fall like dominoes to its cruel will. He would not let it get that far. Death had come for his family, one by one, but when it came for him, it would find him already gone.

The dog was unrelenting, though. As with the blanket, too much pull could injure the mutt, so John gave in. Gadget let go, and together, they entered the garage.

"Now what?" John asked.

Gadget approached the stain. His ears fell forward, and he glanced up at the old man. "Nothing to worry about." John forced a smile, fully aware he was placating an animal. The dog lifted a hind leg and dribbled a few complimentary drops dead center. John chuckled. "Agreed. Piss on that."

Gadget moved on to the motorcycle, firing several short, acute barks at the machine. John rubbed his eyes, pondering what was happening. The mutt had no way of knowing the bike existed, yet had insisted on getting in the garage to see it. Before John could consider why, Gadget hopped up on his hind legs and placed his front paws against the bike's exhaust. The effort was considerable. John squatted beside the dog and ran a gentle hand along Gadget's twisted back.

"If you want to go for a drive, we can take the truck," John said, pointing toward the ugly rusty vehicle in the yard beyond the open bay door. Gadget turned his good eye to the old man. He was panting, tongue drooping and swaying. John ruffled the black patch of hair at the top of Gadget's head. "You don't want to take the truck, do you?"

Gadget responded with a bark. He turned back to the bike and whined.

"I don't have a bucket seat or saddlebag for you, buddy. It's not safe." Another whine followed. Safety was a human concept. Experience had taught John that a person, seeing an animal in imminent danger, will hesitate more often than not, to avoid visiting that danger upon themselves. A dog on the other hand, would never hesitate to protect a human life, even at the expense of their own life. Danger from the bike would never have even crossed the dog's mind.

He wondered how long it had been since Gadget had felt the joy of wind on his face. They could take the truck, and he could stick his little head out the window, but it would be short-lived before his little legs and crippled spine gave out. Hell, they might not even get out of the driveway before that occurred. No, the dog was right. And didn't John want to take one last ride himself? Wasn't that the whole point of fixing it up? Not to sell it. No. He knew he was never going to sell the bike. He hadn't put all that effort, all that polishing and tweaking, into something that some stranger would never appreciate the way that he did. How long had it been since *he* had felt the joy of wind on his face?

Too long.

The bike was ready.

And so was the man.

"Fuck it," John said, and Gadget barked the same. The mutt's tail found a second gear and wagged back and forth. John stood up, retrieved his brown leather riding jacket off the wall, and pulled it on. It was surprisingly big. He knew he had lost weight *(that makes one of us, buddy)* but not how much. The heavy coat slouched across his slender shoulders, weighted with memory as much as with material. He hesitated, second-guessing what he was about to do.

Just go back inside, John. Lie down, close your eyes. Sleep safe.

Gadget barked excitedly at the site of him in the jacket. It chased the doubt out into the light, where it was rendered innocuous. He zipped the coat up, pulled his helmet off the shelf, and hooked his hand through the open visor. Gadget barked, pacing. *Wag-wag-wag. Click-click-click.*

A glimmer of the day reflected from the corner of the countertop. The goggles. *Landon's* goggles. Hadn't he buried them beneath the pile of rags a week earlier? Out of sight, out of mind. But the rags were no longer on top, and the goggles were now very much in view. He reached out to cover them again, then pulled his arm back. He spun slowly around and looked down at Gadget. This time, it was John's turn to tilt his head in thought.

He lifted the little mutt off the floor and sat him on the counter. Gadget stared but made no effort to get down. John held the goggles in his palm. Unlike the jacket, they still appeared the same size they had always been. *The jacket didn't change - you did, old man*, he reminded himself.

But Landon had not.

John slipped the goggles over Gadget's head and adjusted the strap so they fit snugly. The dog scratched at the leather, and John thought Gadget meant to tug the goggles off, but then the dog stopped and looked at the old man with its one good eye. It was comically enlarged behind the glass. John smiled and pulled both of the dog's ears up and over the strap.

"There," he said satisfactorily. "Good to go."

Gadget barked.

*　　　　　*　　　　　*

The feel of the 741 between his legs on the open road was not what he remembered. It was better.

John kept the bike in low gear out of the yard and onto the dirt road, but once he hit the highway, he slowly throttled to an adventurous cruising speed. The pavement welcomed them, spreading out in a long, unbroken path to the east. Shimmers of heat rose in the distance, always just beyond reach, urging them on. The wind pushed back playfully as they pressed forward, and for a fleeting moment, John felt like riding until they simply ran out of gas.

The oversized jacket proved the perfect pouch for the little mutt. Gadget sat on the front edge of the seat, wrapped comfortably up to his chin inside of the coat, back pressed safely against John's belly. The goggles kept the wind out of his eyes, but unlike John, he got to experience the full feeling of the open road on his face. Gadget's tongue - always a wild card - dangled to the side, tasting the air. His lips flapped, revealing a broad, goofy smile that could only express a fraction of the joy he was feeling.

Twenty minutes into their journey, they approached the county limits. It was all farmland out here. Acres and acres of corn fields and vegetable crops. In the spring, the rich, pungent stink of fresh manure was inescapable for fifty miles in every direction, but in the late autumn, the air was pleasantly sweet. They flew past a row of wheat silos and apple-red barns on the left, and John raised a hand to wave at a burly man in a ridiculously quaint straw hat steering a tractor on the right. The farmer slowly waved back, confused by what he was seeing. John laughed and switched gears once more. The road ahead appeared to go on forever.

The bike eased over 70mph without hesitation. Despite its age, it was a formidable beast when let loose. John had always been a handy mechanic, and his skill with this bike in particular was clear. The Indian hummed like it had just rolled off the assembly line. The temptation to push it harder was overwhelming.

John looked down at Gadget. "Well, buddy, what say you?"

The little dog tilted his head up and licked his nose. In for a penny, in for a pound.

John looked back to the road and gunned it. The bike revved eagerly, thrusting forward. The speedometer needle inched over 80mph, and the fields on either side of the blacktop whipped by in blurs of green and yellow. Years peeled away from the pair of old dogs as the pleasure of their youth raced toward them from the road ahead. Despite the tumor festering inside, despite all that he had loved and lost, John had never felt more alive. How far and how fast would that feeling take him?

He never had a chance to find out. The short burst of a siren came upon them suddenly from behind. John glanced at his side mirror. It filled with the unwelcome reflection of a police cruiser. Red and blue light pulsed impatiently, and the siren burped again. John eased the throttle back and brought the bike to a careful stop on the gravel shoulder. He kicked the stand out, lifted his helmet off and propped it on the handlebars. He heared a car door close behind him, and the crunch of heavy boots on gravel approached.

John patted Gadget on the head. "Let me do the talking." Gadget replied with a sad whimper.

A deputy came up beside the bike, stepping back onto the pavement. He was young, no more than thirty, and surprisingly tall. His left hand casually rested on his holster, and his right pulled a pair of well-polished aviators from his face, revealing the greenest eyes John had ever seen. The young man's cheeks and nose were peppered with pronounced freckles, drawn out by the long summer sun, and below his standard issue deputy's hat, red hair curled out on each side. John stole a glance at the name tag above the left shirt pocket: Deputy Molloy.

The deputy folded the aviators with one hand and held them. He looked from the old man to the ugly little dog inside the man's coat. He pointed the aviators toward the mutt, saying: "Well, ain't that a sight."

John arched an eyebrow and gave a slight shrug but remained silent.

Deputy Molloy sighed and kicked a tiny rock at his feet. "Any idea how fast you were going back there, sir?"

John grinned. "I imagine the answer is 'too fast' one way or the other." Gadget lowered his head as though he were embarrassed for them both.

The deputy finally pocketed the glasses and drew a black citation pad from the back of his belt. "License and registration, please."

John slid his wallet out from his back pocket, rifled through the clutter inside, and withdrew the requested documents. Deputy Molloy took them.

"You know you can't have a rider on this thing without a proper seat or saddle, right?"

"Yessir."

"You live in town?"

"Just outside. We were about to turn back and head home, actually."

The deputy turned the registration and license over in his hand and uttered a soft grunt. "I'd like to see a sudden 180-degree turn at 86 miles per hour someday, except cleaning the two of you off the pavement hardly seems worth it."

Gadget barked and let his tongue hang loose, panting. John pressed him close. "I do the talking, remember?"

Deputy Molloy gave them a curious look over the top of his pad before turning his attention to the documents. "'Jonathon Milgard'. And the dog's name?"

The question caught John off guard, and he stifled a cough. It lingered unpleasantly in his chest. "Gadget," he managed.

Deputy Molloy considered it. "Gadget. How long you had him?"

"Not long. He's a rescue."

"No doubt. Looks like he's been through the wringer."

John coughed again, loosening the phlegm enough to spit it out. It was dark red. He looked at the deputy squarely. "We have that in common."

The deputy nodded slowly, looking up from the spittle. His green eyes cooled almost to hazel. He passed the documents back. "Milgard.

You know, I knew a kid by that name. I remember because he died when we were in kindergarten. Hit and run, I think. We had a special assembly at school and everything. Funny the things you remember, but I can't recall his first name—"

"Landon," John said softly.

Deputy Molloy looked up from his citation pad. "Landon... that's right. A relative of—"

"My son," John looked down at Gadget. The little dog licked his fingers gently.

"Son," the deputy repeated. His cheeks flushed red. "Well, that was ignorant of me."

John returned his wallet to his pocket and shook his head. "Don't worry about it. It's kind of you to remember him, just the same."

The deputy was momentarily silent, then flipped the pad closed. "It's a beautiful day, and that's a hell of a bike, Mr. Milgard. It'd make me a lot happier knowing you won't let it get over fifty on your way back. Fair?"

Gadget barked. John nodded. "Fair. Thank you, deputy."

Deputy Molloy put his aviators back on and scanned the horizon. "Gonna be a fall like no other if this keeps up. You take care now, Mr. Milgard."

John waited for the deputy to return to his vehicle and shut off the lights before starting the Indian back up. Deputy Molloy watched as John guided the bike back onto the blacktop and carefully turned it around. They exchanged a wave as John drove by, and a short time later, John saw the cruiser pull back onto the highway and disappear over the horizon.

The road home was long.

9.

Though the ride had been cut short, John felt drained as he guided the Indian into the garage and killed the engine. Maybe his initial thinking about the bike had been correct – perhaps he wasn't ready, or maybe he was too old to be racing around on all that horsepower. Maybe it *was* time to sell it. He lowered the kickstand and eased himself off the seat. His fingers ran along the chrome of the handlebars before settling on the rubber at the end. He gripped it tight. *Piss on that*, he thought bitterly.

John tugged the helmet off, slung it on the handlebars. He unzipped his jacket and sat Gadget on the seat facing him. The little dog panted heavily, and John wondered if the vibration of the ride had triggered pain in his back. He unbuckled the goggles and slid them off. They left an impression on the fur that would take a while to fade. It made John think of the trampled grass behind the house.

"Let's get you some of that medicine," John said. Gadget stood on all fours, and John helped him to the floor. The dog trotted slowly out of the garage and disappeared around the side. John walked to the end of the counter to put the goggles back beneath the rags but stopped halfway. He looked outside - past the driveway, past the dirt road, all the way to the highway beyond.

He hung the goggles around the other handlebar and headed toward the house.

John tucked the tiny pill inside a teaspoon of peanut butter and watched carefully as Gadget devoured the whole lot in a matter of seconds. John rewarded the mutt with a second helping. The smell of peanuts made John's stomach rumble, and he realized he had not eaten today himself. He patted Gadget on the head, then gently tapped the dog's butt with the empty spoon.

"Go on now, and let me make supper."

John opened the fridge as the click of Gadget's steps faded into the next room. There wasn't much inside the main section or the freezer above. A couple of Swanson TV dinners, a frozen piece of salmon so old he couldn't even recall having bought it, a bag of frozen vegetables proclaiming in large print to be the perfect blend for stir fry, which John felt was a dubious oversell at best. The rest was an eclectic mix of condiments and forgotten leftovers. A trip to the pantry did not fare much better. The bag of Purina was now the dominant species inside, sitting comfortably on the floor below mostly barren shelves. John cursed under his breath.

He found Gadget asleep on the couch, curled into a ball in the lingering warmth of the recently worn leather jacket. It seemed neither would be accompanying John into town. He watched to see if Gadget's breathing was steady and unlabored before grabbing the truck keys off the rack by the front door. As he climbed inside the vehicle, the screen door clicked shut behind him.

*　　　　　　*　　　　　　*

Aside from the weekly farmers market every Wednesday night in the town hall square, *Food Palace* was the only place in town to buy groceries. The parking lot was dotted with vehicles as John swung the pick-up into a space close to the door and shut off the engine. He hated shopping for most things, but groceries were a particular nuisance because nothing was ever the same price twice. He also hated the crowds. The few cars around him suggested a mercifully quiet night.

A large drop of water hit the windshield as he opened the door. He shut it again and waited. Several more drops splattered in succession. He got out, looked at the darkening sky. A drop pelted his cheek immediately, like someone had been lying in wait to spit in his face. John wiped it away and hurried inside.

The interior was offensively bright. The rows of overhead florescent lights and the multi-colored advertising signage posted everywhere were an assault on the senses. A pretty, blue-haired cashier in her late teens smiled at him as he entered, and he gave a quick nod. Her name eluded him. He was pretty sure she had changed the spelling of it anyway, an act of defiance in line with the hair dye and excessive eye shadow. He realized he'd been staring at her the whole time, trying to remember her name, and now her smile fell away into an insecure grimace. Her eyes slipped under a veil of indigo bangs, but not before flickering with irritation: *Crusty old fuck.*

John grabbed a bag of potatoes and made his way to the meat coolers at the back. He added a pair of rib eye steaks to his collection and looked around for a cart or basket.

"Watcha lookin' for, John?" He spun at the sound of his name. Craig Sooley, the store's butcher, stood less than ten feet away, dropping sealed styrofoam trays of meat haphazardly into a cooler. His white work coat was splattered with a mix of old and new reddish stains, not unlike the first stage of a Bob Ross canvas. Sooley finished loading the bin and dragged his oversized hands across the front of the coat, leaving fresh streaks.

"Cart," John muttered, holding up the steaks. "Or basket."

Sooley put his hands on his considerable hips and said, "Didn't see the ones up front?"

John had never been a fan of Craig Sooley. The heavy-set bald bastard walked around the store most days like his smock was a surgeon's coat, bellowing at whatever random kid was tasked with stacking displays or mopping floors. He was a bully and an asshole who asked vaguely rhetorical questions just so he could watch you squirm to find a response. John was already deeply regretting making the trip into town.

"Is that what those were for?" John asked, grinning humorlessly. Craig Sooley's smile drifted away. That warmed John's heart.

"I'm sure you'll find one around here somewhere," Sooley said. He held John's gaze a moment longer before finally retreating to his lair through a set of swinging black rubber doors.

John did find a basket a minute later, abandoned on the floor in the cereal aisle. He plucked out the box of Rice Crispies and dropped his finds into it before tossing the cereal on a random shelf. He hurried through the rest of the store, gathering cans of soup, sandwich meat, and several boxed pizzas that assured him they were better than delivery. John had experienced the local pizzeria, *Hal's*, on many occasions and figured the bar was set low enough to trip over even by accident.

He stopped in the last aisle, where they kept the toilet paper on one side and pet food on the other. There was a slender rack of pet accessories and toys at the very end. He scanned it and settled on a bright orange plush ball with large sock-puppet eyes. It squeaked as he picked it up and then again as he dropped it into the basket.

By the time he arrived at the checkout, he had forgotten all about the blue-haired goth waiting for him there. She was sitting on a short stool, blowing gum bubbles behind the counter and stood up as he approached. When she saw that it was him, she hiccuped and inadvertently swallowed her gum. She grimaced, but for an entirely different reason this time.

"One... sec..." she said, holding up a hand to him, palm out. She turned and bent over, coughing.

"Take your time," John said. He loaded his groceries onto the counter, ending with the squeeze toy. The front doors suddenly slid open as a short blonde woman hurried in, holding her jean jacket over her head. The effort had not been terribly effective. Both the jacket and her red dress were soaked. John barely noticed. He watched the heavy rain behind her, his frown deepening. The sky had turned headstone grey and bloated with clouds. Sunset was still an hour away, but it would only be a formality. Night had already fallen.

"Ahh, sweet!" The cashier's voice drew him back. He turned to face her, instinctively reaching behind for his wallet. She was holding up the plush ball and gave it a squeeze. The sound forced a girlish giggle out of her. John glanced at her name tag: Dayzee.

Jesus wept.

"What's his name?" Dayzee asked, their earlier awkward interaction swept under the rug. "Or hers? I just always assume all dogs are boys. Just like all cats are girls. Weird, huh?"

John gave up trying to keep track of her questions and just nodded.

"So which is it?" She blew a bubble at him. It snapped back against her blue-black lips and clung there messily. Why a pretty young girl was in such a rush to look like a corpse was beyond him. John brought his wallet around.

"Boy," John said.

"Sweet," she said, chewing. She lay the toy on top of the rest of the bagged groceries. "Big or small? Or somewhere in between?"

John kept his eyes on his wallet but not really seeing it. He flicked through the contents for the second time that day. His fingers passed over his license and registration, moved on to ancient receipts, and finally settled on a folded twenty-dollar bill.

"Um... small. He's a small dog. A mutt." He looked at her and managed a smile. It was easier than before. She seemed genuinely interested.

"And his name? Did I already ask you that?"

"Yes," John replied. "But that's okay. I didn't answer." He paused again. Her eyes never left him, but they quickly began to dim. He realized if he withheld the answer, he might witness her cry. "Gadget."

"Gadget," she repeated slowly, like it sounded foreign to her. It was an odd name for a dog, but John had heard stranger ones. And this girl had butchered her own name, so it couldn't have been that odd to her. Unless it was the lack of a 'z' in the middle that threw her off.

"It suits him," John assured her. "He's really old. Looks like he's made of mismatched parts."

"Like a Frankenstein?" Another bubble popped. She licked it away. "You got a picture in there?"

John stopped fingering his wallet and pulled out the twenty. "No. Haven't had him that long." That was half true. John didn't even own a camera. Michelle had owned a cheap point-and-shoot at one time, but it was in the attic with the rest of her things. Except for her wardrobe, John reminded himself. As with the goggles, a few tactile memories were still tucked away just out of sight.

"You should take some. Pictures, I mean. I'd love to see him. And if he's old, well, you know... when they're gone, that's all you—"

Thunder clapped overhead, cutting her off. She jumped and squealed, and another piece of gum found its way down her throat. It was becoming something of an occupational hazard for her. John shot a glance out the doorway. The rain was so heavy it obscured the vehicles in the parking lot. When he looked back, Craig Sooley was looming next to him, staring outside.

"This is twister weather," Sooley said ominously. "See if it ain't."

The big man leaned on the front of the counter, his hands caked with dried blood. He didn't seem to notice. Or didn't care. John figured the latter.

"Pass me one of them Snickers, Dayz."

Dayzee gave a subtle eye roll toward John before reaching into a box of Snickers at the end of the counter and tossing one in front of the butcher, like a bone to a surly dog. John had misjudged this girl. He was starting to like her.

Sooley pawed the bar and peeled it open. It lasted two bites. "Put it on my tab," he said and chuckled to himself. He wiped melted chocolate on his coat amidst the blood. "Twister. Mark my words."

As Sooley headed back to the rear of the store, John handed the cash to Dayzee. She took it absently, grabbed the wrinkled Snickers wrapper off the counter, and tossed it angrily in the trash below her register.

"Asshole," she muttered. She rang in the cash and handed a few quarters and dimes to John. He shook his head and retrieved his bag of groceries. "You just made my day."

She blushed and pocketed the coins. The color brought her face to life.

"Next time, throw him some Tic Tacs," John said on his way through the door. Her laughter followed him out into the dark.

Water dripped off him as he drove home. The paper bag of groceries clung to life-support, drenched and tattered on the seat next to him.

Outside, the wipers worked double time to sweep the downpour aside. The heavy drops pounded the roof like machine gun fire from the heavens. It was full dark now, and the road was a blur.

The thunder continued to roll closer, and John pressed the gas. There had been no lightning, but it would be along soon enough. He cursed at himself for leaving Gadget behind. The mutt would have awoken to the storm and found itself all alone in the dark house. The pet carrier was still under the table, and he expected to find the frightened little dog huddled inside when he got home. The truck swerved against his control, and he eased his foot away from the pedal. Until he arrived, he was at the mercy of the rain.

The wind had picked up considerably while he was in the store. Despite Craig Sooley's confident prediction, John doubted the butcher's forecast would prove true. There hadn't been a tornado touch down in the county in thirteen years. Three people had lost their lives that day, and a dozen homes, four businesses, and a water tower had been reduced to rubble. A photographer with the local paper had snapped a shot of the twister at the exact moment it tore through a gas station, spinning a smaller tornado of fire within. The photo had been long-listed for *Life Magazine*'s Picture of the Year and the photographer did the national morning talk show circuit for a week before the world moved on to more urgent matters and let John's little mid-western burg slide back into obscurity.

And since that day: nothing. Craig Sooley couldn't predict the winner in a one-man race. He was talking out of his ass. As usual.

The pickup turned onto the dirt road that led to the driveway. Rain had made quick work of the loose earth, whipping up giant puddles of mud. The truck bounced chaotically, and large swatches of brown goop splattered across the windshield every ten feet. In the distance, John's house came and went out of view as the wipers struggled to keep up.

The light over the garage was on.

John rolled to a stop in front of the building a minute later. The bay door was up. The driver's side headlight partially reflected off the back of the Indian inside, but the majority spilled across the side of the building. John shut off the vehicle and stepped out.

The wind tore at his clothes and hair, pelting his face with sharp strands of tall grass from the field like unleashed archers. The rain was receding, but it only made the humidity more pronounced. There was a loud bang from the house. The screen door whipped back and forth against the wall as it desperately clung to the top hinge. The bottom hinge was torn free of the door frame and clapped open and shut on the door.

John's throat tightened. His heart raced. The house revealed only darkness.

John ran up the porch steps and through the open doorway, the groceries long forgotten. Once inside, he shut the inner door. The sound of the storm faded enough to gather his thoughts. He flicked on the hall light and entered the living room. The leather jacket was still on the couch, but Gadget was no longer asleep on it. At the first sound of thunder, the little mutt had undoubtedly rushed for the safety of his kennel under the table.

But he wasn't there either. John was on all fours in the kitchen when the clatter of the screen door slapping the inner door reached him, and the dreaded thought of the mostly blind and cripple little dog wandering in the storm stole the strength from his legs. He collapsed in a heap, stretching an arm underneath his face just in time to prevent his cheek from crashing into the hard floor. He lay there, winded, cursing.

Mary's voice washed through his thoughts: *I'm not afraid you'll abandon him. I'm afraid he'll be with you and still die alone.*

But he had abandoned him, if only for an hour.

Get up, old man.

He did. Strength returned to his legs in a hot rush of blood. He crawled out from under the table and got to his feet. He steadied and drew a deep breath. If the dog wasn't in the kennel, there were still plenty of other spaces where he could have hidden in the house.

"Gadget!" John yelled. Silence. "Here boy! Come on now!"

Not waiting for an answer, John went upstairs, calling the dog's name in each room. There was no sign of the mutt anywhere. He hurried back to the kitchen. Still empty.

He focused. He had looked everywhere except the cellar. The entrance was next to the pantry, but the slide lock was in place. There was a second entrance outside on the far side of the house that had not been utilized in over a decade. A heavy-duty lock kept it securely sealed off from the rest of the world. Gadget was not in the house or under it. John went back outside.

The screen door was gone. In the end, the top hinge had given up the fight and let the door go. It lay on the ground a dozen feet from the bottom of the porch. The hinge hung loose against the door frame by a single crippled screw.

The rain surged. It poured down his face, into his eyes and mouth. Mixed with his sweat, it tasted unclean. He spit it out and rushed across the front of the house to the truck. He was an arm's length from the passenger door when something caught the corner of his eye. Before fully registering what he was seeing, his feet skidded in the mud, and he lost his balance. He fell hard on his side, wet earth flying up around him. His left foot struck the front bumper, and a bolt of pain flared from his ankle to his hip. He bit hard, his teeth making an awful *clack* in his head. He rolled onto his back, grabbed for his foot. The pain was excruciating.

The sky suddenly lit up with lightning. John thought he saw a distant spiral arc horizontally below the clouds before bending toward the earth. His breath caught in his lungs. He sat up and swung his legs around so he was facing the field beyond the backyard. The house lights extinguished with an audible *pop!* followed immediately by the one over the garage door as the electricity succumbed to the storm. In the instant before darkness engulfed him, John saw what had caught his attention in the first place, and despite the oppressive heat, a chill ran through his entire body.

A wolf stood watching him from the edge of the tall grass. It was almost four feet at the shoulders, sheets of rain flying off its coal-black fur in the wind. The ears were drawn down, the head lowered, eyes staring straight ahead. The paws were disproportionately large for the legs, which, like the thick neck, displayed a pronounced musculature John had never seen in any other wild animal. Even at this distance, John could tell the creature outweighed him and could be upon him in seconds.

Something dangled limply from the massive jaws. Fear gave way to dread.

John wiped his face, squinted. The wolf dropped its prey, its amber eyes never wavering. The small dead animal flopped to the ground, half in a puddle. Brown mud splattered over the light-colored fur, and John's heart sank as the motionless body slid into the dark water. The wolf's mouth hung open, tongue gliding over lethal teeth. The short triangular ears angled back against the skull, and the squarish black nose rose as though the entire snout was being bridled by some unseen hand in the darkness. It was the most terrifying thing John had ever witnessed.

A deafening crack like the splitting open of an ancient tomb rumbled overhead. The wolf took a quick step in retreat, long tail brushing the ground. This was John's one chance to escape. The garage was closest to his left, but if he couldn't get the door down in time, he'd be trapped inside with certain death. To his right was the house, and even if the wolf was on his heels, he might make it to the shotgun, fully loaded for a purpose so far removed from what he currently faced it would have been laughable were he not so scared. But first, he had to get up.

His legs refused. He sat in the mud, thighs like jelly, impotent with fear. The wolf edged forward. This was the moment it had been waiting for. Night after night. High enough on the scent of the old man's sickness to come down from the northern forest to pluck him from the earth and disappear again, the way some unseen driver had once done with John's son. Was this God's great stroke of mercy or more of His immeasurable cruelty?

Only God can understand God.

Piss on that. Get up, old man!

John got to his knees. A cough erupted in his damp chest, the familiar copper taste of blood filling his mouth. He spit it into the mud. Twenty feet across the yard, the wolf advanced another step. When the thunder returned, the massive canine did not retreat. Its confidence was growing. The old man was frail and lame. The scent of blood was in the air.

John knew the ankle would not take the weight, but he stood nonetheless. He leaned heavily on the good foot and grabbed onto the side of the truck for balance. Everything was slippery to the touch. His grip faltered. The wolf bolted forward.

10.

Thunder filled the air.

But below the thunder, there was suddenly something else. Something familiar. The rumble faded, and the new sound grew louder, moving from the garage to the front of the truck. John threw a headlock around the side mirror with his left arm and held on.

Gadget stood on quivering legs a yard ahead. Swift, harsh bursts exploded from the little dog's throat in a fearless salvo. The wolf skidded to a startled stop. It scrambled to all fours, clumps of mud dripping from its underbelly as it paced back and forth, confused. Its leering mouth looked massive enough to swallow Gadget whole.

The little dog faltered, slipped, and quickly stood back up. Ten feet away, the wolf snarled, jaw trembling. It darted to the right, and Gadget countered, blocking the way.

John pushed free of the truck, ran for the porch. Adrenaline numbed the ankle as far as the front steps, and he dragged himself up and into the house. He could still hear Gadget barking as he reached the kitchen and pulled the shotgun out of its hiding spot. He hobbled back out into the rain.

On the third step down, he went over on his ankle and crashed into the ground face-first. The shotgun went off next to his head, spraying the earth six feet ahead with buckshot. He cursed, got up, and popped the barrels open. One shot remained. He stumbled to the corner of the house and raised his gun squarely at the wolf.

Gadget's legs gave out. The wolf's eyes narrowed, flicked from the dog to the old man, and back again. The snarl spread into a savage grin.

John squeezed the trigger.

Nothing.

Lightning cast down through the clouds like a lifeline thrown just out of reach. In the afterglow, John saw that everything a mile beyond the highway was gone, hidden behind an enormous spinning veil of wind, rain, and debris. Sooley had been right. The final insult.

The wolf leaped forward in a single thrust. It clamped its jaws across Gadget's back and tossed the little mutt across the driveway. Gadget crashed on his side next to the garbage bin and lay motionless among the weeds.

John flipped the shotgun around, and swung the stock at the wolf's charging head. He missed, and the slippery weapon flew from his hands. The momentum threw him off balance, but he miraculously remained upright. He ran for the outer porch. His hand clutched the first post at the exact instant the wolf's jaw clamped around the calve of his good leg. He screamed. The beast hauled him back. His palm shredded open as it tore free of the wood. His chin smacked into the earth, smashing his jaws together.

The wolf's teeth plunged deep into his soft flesh. He could feel hot liquid gushing down his leg. Blood. His blood. The wolf dragged him, the pressure tearing muscle from bone. He clawed at the ground, desperate to catch hold of a rock, a bush, anything. His fingers scraped across a long stone, but the force was too great, and it ripped from the earth and out of his hand. He kicked with his free leg. Searing pain shot through his shin as his previously fucked ankle made solid contact with the wolf's head. The creature did not relent. It thrashed its head to the side, flipping John over onto his back. He landed on a jagged rock below his shoulder blades. The air gusted out of him. His lungs shut down.

The wolf let go, triumphant. John lay there, back arched awkwardly, hands clenching his throat, gasping for breath. The pounding in his head echoed his pulse, but it was lost under the roar of the approaching tornado, the air around him sucked away in a vacuum. The wolf's massive head leered above, its monstrous paws crushing his chest. Blood and spittle dripped on his face and neck. His vision began spiraling shut.

For the last three months, John had planned his death to be instant – one moment full of light, lungs full of oxygen, his mind at peace, the next moment nothing. No awareness, no sensation, no distant beacon or flashing memories. No pain. Merciful, as it had been for Michelle. He had endlessly pondered it, eroded it, numbed himself to it. But he had never *truly* understood or faced it until now. The dead raccoon had shown him death was a black void, and staring into it he had his Nietzche moment, his great and terrible abyss. It scared him. And in truth, he had always been terrified – terrified of losing all he was, and all he had been charged with carrying on for those gone before him. In refusing to fight for his own life, he had betrayed them. Now it was too late, and the weight of what he was sacrificing to the void crushed him and filled him with regret.

The wolf's yellow-brown eyes met his as it closed its jaw around his throat. Black pupils deep inside an amber pool. The last of John's being dived into it. He opened his mouth to scream.

Oxygen seared into his lungs. He gasped. It burned, but he drew in another breath. And another.

And then his hands were flailing forward, launching punch after punch at the side of the wolf's head. The beast's jaws snapped at his arms, catching the left and biting down. John screamed as blood poured along his forearm. The pressure was immense, bones about to shatter. His right hand scraped the ground and found the long, thin rock he had pulled loose. He smashed it into the wolf's eye.

The wolf yelped, released John's arm, and slid off him to the side, dazed. It shook its head and stumbled. John clutched his arm into his chest to stem the bleeding. He scrambled back, but only about a foot before the wolf turned. The left eye was shut, leaking dark blood along the jaw like warpaint, but the right burned with rage. John gripped the rock tight.

A faint, high-pitched, broken howl filled the air. The wolf turned toward the house, listening. John froze. Beyond the rooftop, he could see the boiling clouds rotating ever closer. A sound halfway between a moan and a whine gurgled in the giant canine's throat. The broken howl came again. The wolf lowered its back, arched its head upward and howled back, driven by an ancient instinct more powerful than bloodlust. It rose into the night, a beautiful and terrifying siren carrying anguish and loneliness within its notes. When Gadget limped out from around the side of the house and gave a final guttural cry of his own, John realized they were singing the same song.

The wolf retreated, snorted and dragged its claws through the soft earth. Gadget held his ground. John lay still, afraid any sudden movement would trigger another attack. But none came. The wolf looked past the little mutt, then turned and ran toward the main road. Gadget collapsed.

There was no time to consider what had happened. The scream of the wind grew deafening. John scrambled to his feet, limped over and scooped the tiny dog into his arms. The ground trembled as he rushed to the house. Hot air pelted him with branches and small debris. He shouldered the door open and dragged his lame foot through the hall into the living room. He lay Gadget in the leather riding jacket, returned to the inner porch, and shut the door.

He buckled over and sucked in a breath, getting the first real look at the damage. One pant leg was torn away below the knee. He was oozing blood. The house shook.

No time. Get moving.

John lifted the jacket by the sleeves like a swing and held the dog to his chest. He slid the lock open on the cellar door. Stale air released into the room as the old house surrendered its dying breaths. The cellar was pitch black beyond the first three steps. John descended into the dark.

11.

The old dog was dying.

John sat on the dirt floor, back against the wall nearest the stairs. Gadget lay in the warmth of the jacket next to him. The dog's breathing was labored, hitching in and out in wet bursts.

"The fuck have I done?" John whispered.

Outside, the night raged on. The foundation above the cellar shuddered. Dust that had gathered for a decade sifted from the ceiling and walls, thickening the air with a grey haze. On the way down, John had discovered a small oil lantern hung on a post at the base of the stairs. He rested it on the floor by his feet and kept the wick low. The dim light spread in a hazy circle, never fully reaching the other walls. Even at this level, the fuel wouldn't last an hour, but he hoped the storm would blow out before the flame.

Gadget rolled onto his belly and sat up with considerable effort. Water dribbled from the creases of his mouth. Yellow gunk ran from the inside corner of each eye and hardened below like candle wax. A sequence of red punctures riddled his back. The bleeding had stopped, and scabs had formed in the fur. John's wounds had also started to scab over. The bites on his leg were ragged at the edges, and the skin deeply bruised. His arm was slick with blood, the extent of the damage hidden beneath crimson. Pain came and went in throbbing waves.

John gazed into Gadget's good eye. "I'm sorry, buddy," John said softly. He petted the dog's dark fur atop its head, then scratched under Gadget's chin. The dog nuzzled into John's fingers, then reached forward and licked the outer edge of the wound on John's arm.

"I'm okay," John said. He drew his arm back, and Gadget lay back down, panting. The pills for the pain were upstairs, and the First Aid Kit was in the garage. John's busted ankle was a purple swollen mass, no longer capable of supporting his weight. He hated seeing the little mutt suffer, but even if he dragged himself up the stairs on his hands and knees, there was no guarantee he'd make it back.

A window shattered somewhere above them, and the door at the top of the stairs rattled in the frame. Gadget curled into a tight ball. A long, terrible moan followed. John punched the hard floor, frustrated. He had brought them down here for safety, but instead he had trapped them in a tomb.

"I'm sorry," was all he could manage.

The house shivered again, shaking free more dust. John uttered a dry cough and propped himself against an unattached wood stove, long forgotten and left to rust in the corner. From this perspective, he could see more of the room. On the opposite wall, a metal shelving unit hid in the shadows, holding several cardboard boxes. One of them was marked *Evian* in faded pink ink. A Sharpie had been used to slash a line through the word, and above it, "castaways" was written in Michelle's familiar cursive. John hopped across the short distance and grasped the cool metal frame.

The box was mostly empty. A cobweb spanned the top, drooping in the middle with the weight of mummified insect husks. Whatever had spun it was thankfully long gone. John swept it aside and reached into the box. He felt a small wrench and a handful of rough nails along the bottom. He rooted in the corners and, in the third one, his hand brushed against plastic. He poked his finger forward, felt the plastic indent, then pop back out. A bottle. He grabbed it and turned to the light.

The cap was still sealed in place. The label was bleached white, coated in grime. He rubbed it across his shirt and saw water inside. He doubted water aged as well as wine, especially in cheap plastic, but was grateful just to have it. He limped back to the wall and slid down next to Gadget. The dog strained his head around to see.

John twisted the cap off, smelled inside. It was odorless. He took a quick swig, then filled the cap and offered it to the mutt. Gadget's erratic tongue lapped it up. John refilled the cap and gave the dog some more.

He took another taste himself before drizzling some over his mangled forearm. He wiped the blood away. The bones and tendons beneath the skin were crushed, but he was able to wiggle his fingers. The punctures were fewer and less pronounced than he expected. He gingerly prodded one with a finger. He felt pressure but no pain. It was numb.

John replaced the cap and sat the bottle down next to him. Gadget lay his head on his paws and released a heavy sigh. The panting leveled off, but each breath sounded heavy and wet. John leaned his head back. The pain was manageable. It was already fading. He needed a minute to think, to rest, just one or two, then he'd crawl upstairs. Eight steps. He could handle that, then slide back down if need be. He had to try. He had to...

John awoke with a start. The air was still, the dust settled. He couldn't tell if he'd dozed for five minutes or an hour, but the lantern still burned, if barely. In the gloom, his leg didn't look as bad as before. Neither did his arm. Most of the blood appeared to have been cleaned away. That was when he realized he could no longer hear Gadget's labored breathing.

The dog lay near the wood stove, facing the wall. John crawled over and placed his hand on the mutt's back. It rose slowly on a drawn-out breath and fell again. A few seconds later, it repeated. John gently wrapped his hands around Gadget's belly and turned him. The dog whined.

"Okay. No more moving. Promise."

Gadget licked his lips. His tongue was dry. John turned to the stairs and struggled to his feet.

He had barely taken a step when he felt the bottom of his pant leg tugged back. He pulled it forward, but Gadget held on. John glanced down at him.

"Let go, buddy. I'm gonna go get your medicine. I'll be right back."

Gadget tugged again. In the pale light, his cataract had a ghostly sheen that hid whatever thoughts were going on behind it. But John knew just the same. Mary had said that he would.

John slid down the wall and sat facing the mutt. As soon as he did, his body felt weightless, and his strength evaporated. Gadget released the cuff and crawled in between the old man's legs. John rubbed the dog's snout and nodded. He leaned forward, nose to nose. Gadget licked John's face.

"Okay, buddy. Okay."

John wiped away tears and lay on his side. Gadget snuggled under his arm and lay down. John could feel the little dog's heart beating hard in his chest. He ran his fingers down Gadget's neck and back, and the panting eased.

"It's okay. I'm here. I got you. You hear that? Quieter now. The storm's moved on. It's moving on."

The heartbeat slowed. Gadget moaned quietly. Little plumes of dust swirled with each breath. John watched them get smaller and smaller, like ghosts drifting into the ether. He drew the mutt's little broken body closer to his chest. Warmth passed between them. His lungs ached sharply, then cooled.

The lantern flickered twice and went out.

John leaned his head close to Gadget's good ear. "Tomorrow, we'll take the bike out again. Feel the wind on our faces. You feel it? Yeah, I agree, let's take her up to eighty. Deputies be damned. Just you and me and the open road." He stroked the little dog's head. Both ears fell forward and ceased twitching. A moment later, only one heart beat in the darkness.

12.

Mary found them at first light. John was sitting against the wall as she hurried down the stairs, calling his name. Gadget lay motionless on his lap, wrapped in the leather jacket. She froze on the last step. John told her he was okay. His bloodshot eyes told her otherwise. She sat with him for a while. Then, when he was ready to let go, she carried Gadget upstairs.

13.

He told Mary about the wolf the following day. She listened quietly.

When he described the attack, she didn't question it. He knew it sounded crazy. How could it not? He had no scars to show her. He tried not to think about it.

The tornado had carved a zigzag track from the eastern highway across his field to the main road to the north. The garage had been directly in its path and shown no quarter. Only the concrete floor with its dark stain remained. The Indian motorcycle was found crumpled over a mile away by a farmer whose crops had been otherwise untouched. Deputy Molloy had delivered the news. He said it was a real shame but suggested the insurance claim on such an antique would no doubt soften the blow. John thanked him but said nothing further. He had already decided to give the money to the animal shelter.

The next day, he dug a hole in the earth where the yard met the tall grass. It was slow work, but he insisted on doing it alone. The swelling in his ankle had receded to a faint bruise, and he worked the spade without any pain. When John finished, Mary brought Gadget's body to him, still swaddled in the riding jacket. John lay it in the grave and covered it over, using his hands to move the soil. He placed several large rocks across the top. Instead of prayer, Mary read from a Wordsworth poem about dogs:

> *We grieved for thee, and wished thy end were past;*
> *And willingly have laid thee here at last:*
> *For thou hadst lived till everything that cheers*
> *In thee had yielded to the weight of years;*
> *Extreme old age had wasted thee away,*
> *And left thee but a glimmering of the day...*

They made love that night, and afterward, they shed their grief with their tears. Sleep came easy and without dreams. John awoke before dawn and sat on the edge of the bed. The curtain fluttered in the warm air, reaching for him. He stood and looked out into the night. The storm had removed any sign of the trail through the tall grass. Only the wind moved through it now. From far in the distance, he thought he heard a soft howl. John leaned on the windowsill and listened. It sounded lonely.

His chest felt heavy, and not wanting to wake up Mary, he went to the bathroom to clear his lungs. It felt like fire tearing through him, each cough loosening more and more. He spit.

It was clear.

He stared at it for a long time, then rinsed it away. He crept back to bed and lay next to Mary, watching the curtain come and go in the breeze.

He tried not to think about it.

About the Author

P.D. Hogan was born in St. John's, Newfoundland. He started writing at a very young age and hasn't found a way to stop. In 2011, he published his first novel, the YA fantasy *Believe*, after which he turned his attention to screenwriting. His feature-length screenplay, *Fall Not Into Darkness*, won a Creative World Award in 2019 and in 2021, his follow-up, *1892*, finished in the top 10% of more than 8100 entries in the Academy of Motion Picture Arts & Sciences *Nicholl Fellowship in Screenwriting*. He currently lives in Mount Pearl, Newfoundland with his wife and their 2 cats. *Ghosts in the Ruins* is his first collection of short fiction.

www.ingramcontent.com/pod-product-compliance
Lightning Source LLC
Chambersburg PA
CBHW010258100726
47904CB00011B/2645